W9-BYB-184

More praise for *Willing Spirits*

"*Willing Spirits* is like a string of pearls—one familiar, fragile moment linked to another and another to form the rope of women's lives twined together. Beautifully written, full of wit and wisdom and heart—read this one with your mother, your daughter, or your best friend."
—**Jodi Picoult**

"Women are still from Venus and men from Mars in Schieber's strong debut, a paean to the healing power and enduring strength of female friendship."
—*Publishers Weekly*

"What a warm, oh-so-human account of love and women's friendship! These are women I know, and I'm recommending the book to all my female friends and students."
—**Rosemary Daniell, author of *Sleeping with Soldiers***

Praise for *A Sinner's Guide to Confession*

"An absorbing read in its breezy study of friendship, family, and couple relationships...In a fast-paced revelation of complicated real life, each friend's secret becomes an admission leading to 'confession.' A real page-turner." —**Helen Barolini, author of *Umbertina***

"Phyllis Schieber gets into the hearts and minds of her wonderfully rich and well-rounded characters in a story that touches the readers' hearts and minds. Smart fiction that makes you think...what could be better?"
—**M.J. Rose, author of *The Reincarnationist***

Willing Spirits

Phyllis Schieber

BERKLEY BOOKS, NEW YORK

THE BERKLEY PUBLISHING GROUP
Published by the Penguin Group
Penguin Group (USA) Inc.
375 Hudson Street, New York, New York 10014, USA
Penguin Group (Canada), 90 Eglinton Avenue East, Suite 700, Toronto, Ontario M4P 2Y3, Canada
(a division of Pearson Penguin Canada Inc.)
Penguin Books Ltd., 80 Strand, London WC2R 0RL, England
Penguin Group Ireland, 25 St. Stephen's Green, Dublin 2, Ireland (a division of Penguin Books Ltd.)
Penguin Group (Australia), 250 Camberwell Road, Camberwell, Victoria 3124, Australia
(a division of Pearson Australia Group Pty. Ltd.)
Penguin Books India Pvt. Ltd., 11 Community Centre, Panchsheel Park, New Delhi—110 017, India
Penguin Group (NZ), 67 Apollo Drive, Rosedale, North Shore 0632, New Zealand
(a division of Pearson New Zealand Ltd.)
Penguin Books (South Africa) (Pty.) Ltd., 24 Sturdee Avenue, Rosebank, Johannesburg 2196,
South Africa

Penguin Books Ltd., Registered Offices: 80 Strand, London WC2R 0RL, England

Copyright © 1998 by Phyllis Schieber.
"Readers Guide" copyright © 2009 by Penguin Group (USA) Inc.
Cover design by Lesley Worrell.
Cover photo © Veer.
Text design by Tiffany Estreicher.

PRINTING HISTORY
William Morrow hardcover edition / October 1998
Berkley trade paperback edition / March 2009

Library of Congress Cataloging-in-Publication Data

Schieber, Phyllis.
    Willing spirits / Phyllis Schieber. — Berkley trade pbk. ed.
       p. cm.
    ISBN 978-0-425-22585-1 (trade pbk.)
    1. Female friendship—Fiction.   2. Women teachers—Fiction.   3. Adultery—Fiction.
4. Psychological fiction.   I. Title.
PS3569.C48515W55 2008
813'.54—dc22
                                                                            2008032633

PRINTED IN THE UNITED STATES OF AMERICA

10   9   8   7   6   5   4   3   2   1

In memory of
Bette Miller and Polly Miller
My sister, my girl, my friends

ACKNOWLEDGMENTS

I began and finished the first draft of this book in a writing seminar at The New School. During the years I was part of that group, my mentor, Hayes B. Jacobs, never faltered in his unwavering support and enthusiasm for my work. I owe him much.

Much thanks goes to Harvey Klinger, my agent. His reliable judgment, steady good humor, and consistent accessibility have eased my way and reaffirmed my faith in the impossible. I am also indebted to his assistant, Dave Dunton, for always knowing who I am when I phone and for treating me with such genuine courtesy.

I want to thank everyone at William Morrow, especially Claire Wachtel, my editor, who helped shape this book. Thanks also to her assistant, Jessica Baumgardner, for her cheerful diplomacy.

I am grateful to my mother, Henia Schieber, for her devotion and for teaching me early on that little else can take the place of a good book. The spirit of my father, Kurt Schieber, continues to sustain me, and I hold his memory very dear. I would be remiss if I did not thank Anna and Mitchell Yager. They have always treated me as one of their own.

Every day, I give thanks for Isaac. Through him, I understand passion. Because of him, I am never able to lose my sense of perspective for very long. I thank Howard Yager for being part of this joy. And because I have faith in the value of a shared history, I am grateful to him for sharing mine.

Mostly, however, I am indebted to my friends, the women who embrace me with their open hearts. They nourish me with their love and goodwill. I have been blessed to be surrounded by women who indulge my moods, allow my eccentricities, listen to my complaints, and applaud my triumphs. I cannot imagine how I would thrive without any one of them. They never disappoint me.

Chapter One

Jane never knew her mother to tell a lie that would make it seem that life could be anything other than hard or sad, or terribly lonely. The only lies she ever told were really for herself, never for Jane. So Jane fashioned her own lies and used them in much the same way a child stuffs a fisted hand into her mouth to comfort herself until the morning arrives.

As her mother, Dorothy, lay dying of cancer, she assigned the pain a number and a color. "How bad is it, Mother?" Jane had asked. "It's a ten," her mother almost always said. "And it's red. Blood red." Each time she asked, Jane hoped the answer would be different. But not once did her mother ever say, "It's a five, and a pale shade of blue." And Jane still could not forgive her for not wanting to protect her own child.

On the Tuesday afternoon that she arrived home from work and saw Arnold's car in the driveway, Jane's elaborate system of denial took over. Even though in all the years they had been married Arnold had never missed a racquetball game, Jane ignored the approaching danger. Just that morning he had complained of a "damned scratchy throat" and accepted the salted water she had brought for him to gargle with. "You're a good wife," he had said. Arnold could no longer differentiate between the truth and a lie. It was all one and the same for him. Jane had smiled anyway, more out of habit than anything else.

Later, after it was all over, Jane would go over all the signs she had chosen to ignore. The music coming from the upstairs bedroom. The corkscrew near the stove. The stack of unopened mail. Instead of fitting all the pieces together, she glanced through the bills and advertisements. There was a letter from her cousin Francine, in Wisconsin. Jane went into the front hall for the letter opener. Then she heard the laughter. For a moment, she assured herself that Caroline must be home. But Caroline was away at college and couldn't be upstairs. And Jane never really believed it could be Caroline.

As Jane climbed the stairs to their bedroom, she wondered what prophetic hand of fate had intervened to stop her from calling out Arnold's name the minute she turned the key in the door. It might have prevented her from seeing Arnold's muscled rear end flexed with the effort of satisfying the blonde who was probably less than half Jane's own age. The girl moaned and clutched at the sheets Jane had changed just that morning. The girl's eyes were tightly shut. But Jane's eyes were wide open. They saw her husband's indifference to anything but his own pleasure. They saw the girl's willingness to pretend that sleeping with a married man in his own home didn't matter. Jane leaned against the doorjamb and politely waited for them to finish. The girl let out a series of high-pitched *oh!*s and then seemed as surprised as Jane always was when Arnold slumped against her in silent completion.

"He isn't dead," Jane said, "but it is sort of like making love in a tomb. Don't you think?"

The girl screamed. Arnold tried to position himself as if to hide her. Jane believed he would have attempted to convince her that the girl wasn't there if she, poor thing, hadn't started to vomit all over the bed.

"I feel sick," the girl said.

"I know the feeling," Jane said.

The girl couldn't have been much older than Caroline. Jane actually felt sorry for her.

"Arnold," Jane said, "I think your guest might need a towel. I'll just wait downstairs."

"Jane," Arnold said. "I want to explain."

"And I want you to," Jane said. "I really do. However, right now, there's an ill young woman in my bed, and I'd like you to take care of things. All right?"

Arnold nodded, suddenly meek and compliant.

"All right," he said. "I'll take care of it."

Once and for all, she might not be able to find an excuse to stay with Arnold. Jane walked down the stairs. She kept her back straight, and her head high. But she had to hold on to the banister to steady herself.

Jane heard the front door close, waited for the sound of hurried footsteps to disappear, and then looked up as Arnold entered the room. He looked remarkably neat for someone who had been naked just moments before. Not a hair was out of place. The buttons on his white shirt were closed, except for the top two, which he always left open when he wasn't wearing a tie. Jane wondered why he hadn't bothered to put his tie back on. Perhaps he felt this was not a formal enough occasion. Even his khaki trousers still held a firm pleat. In fact, his oxblood loafers looked as if he had just stopped for a shine. She folded the letter she had been reading and slipped it back into the envelope.

"Francine says to say hello."

"Stop it, Jane. This isn't funny."

"Oh, but it is, Arnold. I mean, if this had happened to someone else, you'd think it was hysterical. I know you would."

Arnold ran his fingers through his full head of perfectly graying black hair. He had grown more handsome over the years, and it had served him well.

"Was your game canceled today?" Jane said.

"Yes," Arnold said.

Jane just knew that he wouldn't have missed his game—even for a twenty-year-old blonde.

"A student of yours?" Jane said.

"Yes. Well, a former student."

"She must be Caroline's age."

"No," he said. He blushed deeply. "She's older. Twenty-five."

"I see." Jane folded her hands. "The faculty meeting was canceled," she said. "That's why I was home early."

"First Tuesday of every month," he said.

"That's right."

She couldn't believe he had actually remembered that bit of information. It didn't seem that he had ever heard anything she ever said. That's when it started to hurt. The pain caught her off guard. She weighed it as if someone else were feeling it, but she still could not be her mother. Even now, in the midst of this indignity and anguish, Jane's response was measured.

"It's a five and a pale shade of blue," Jane said. "It's not too bad."

"Don't do this," Arnold said. He poured himself a glass of mineral water. "You're not your mother. You don't have cancer, and you're not dying."

Jane slowly forced herself off the stool. She was a small woman and practically had to jump. The stools were too high for her. She had wanted the shorter stools, but he had liked a different set better. "I won't be comfortable," she had told Arnold. It was only a matter of an inch and a half, but it was an important inch and a half. "Yes, you will be," he had said because, clearly, Jane's discomfort was not as important as the aesthetics of the breakfast nook.

She pulled at her skirt. It had hiked up when she jumped. Arnold's eyes wandered to her legs. They were fine legs for a woman of her height and age—five-one and forty-four as of last Friday. Arnold reached out a hand to touch her arm. The events of the afternoon had excited him. Being found with another woman. This glimpse of his wife's black panty hose. He had won Jane over before.

"You're right," Jane said. "I'm not my mother. If I was, I would've said, 'It's a ten. And it's red. Blood red.'"

Her voice had become edged with rage. Even with that warning he did nothing to protect himself against the fist that came crashing into his jaw. He saw it coming. Jane knew he did. It was just like those cartoons in which the tormentor suddenly gets his due. He watches as the object of destruction comes whistling through the sky, but doesn't have the sense or the dexterity to step out of its path. And then it's too late.

"Jane!" he said. He put up his arm to shield himself from a second blow and tenderly touched his jaw with his free hand. "What are you doing?"

"That was for the stools," she said. "Now *this* is for the girl."

He blocked her with his arm, and they struggled briefly. She managed to drag her nails along his smooth cheek and leave a gash that made her wonder at her own fury. He shouted her name again and again until it seemed to her that he was calling out to someone else, someone she was supposed to recognize.

"Damn it, Jane, I'm bleeding," Arnold said. He ran to the sink and splashed his face with cold water. "I swear it never happened before. Listen to me. Please, Jane."

Jane picked up her briefcase and turned to leave the room.

"I want you out of this house by tonight," Jane said, "or I have every intention of killing you."

Arnold pressed his hand against his cheek and shook his head.

"How could you do this to me?" he said.

Jane didn't answer. Her breath came in hard, short gasps as she strained to regulate her breathing. She didn't want him to know that the pain had been a ten all along. And it was red, blood red.

Jane stripped the sheets from the bed and threw them on the floor. Arnold had artfully covered the soiled spot with a towel. She lay down on the bare mattress. The room smelled of vomit and good perfume. She listened for Arnold. There was silence. For a moment, she panicked. Then she remembered how it had felt to see him on top of another woman. It had felt like nothing. It had felt like swallowing air to make yourself burp. She had often watched the boys in her third-grade class practice this exercise. Jane tried to take in large gulps of air, but it only made her feel bloated and uncomfortable, as if she were pregnant. Only Gwen had understood about being pregnant. Only Gwen would understand about Arnold.

Nineteen years earlier, Jane had sat in a sweltering auditorium and listened to various administrative staff rephrase their already tired back-to-school speeches from the year before. Next to Jane had sat a woman more beautiful than anyone Jane had ever seen. Gwen's long, bare legs were crossed and locked at the ankle. Her black hair was pulled into a ponytail. Her blue eyes had flickered, but just barely, as a hugely pregnant Jane had taken the seat next to her. The heat in the unair-conditioned auditorium had been unbearable. Sweat poured from Jane's forehead. Jane would have sworn that Gwen had not even registered her presence as she sat beside her, panting in discomfort. Suddenly, Jane had felt a spray of cologne and then cool air on her hot neck. "I've been there twice myself," Gwen had said. She had folded the printed program for the morning and used it as a fan, which she moved continuously alongside Jane's flushed face. Gwen had then spoken in a firm whisper that Jane found mesmerizing. "The best thing about being pregnant is not getting your period. My mother used to call it her *friend*. Now I ask you, who welcomes a friend who visits once a month, rips your guts out, and stays too long?" Jane had laughed out loud, causing heads to whip around. Gwen had continued fanning her and glared at the others as if *they* were creating a disturbance. That had been their beginning.

Now Jane waited for her to answer the phone.

"Hello?" she said.

"Gwen? Are you busy?"

"I'm grading papers. Are you all right? You sound funny."

They both still taught, but they were in different schools now. Jane was lucky enough to have remained local, but Gwen had been transferred to a school in Manhattan.

"Funny?" Jane said. "Yes. Well. I guess I feel funny."

Jane could hear Gwen rustling papers. It pleased her to know that her next words might create a fixed moment in time. It was likely that Gwen would always remember what she was doing when Jane told her the news about Arnold.

"I found Arnold in bed with a woman," Jane said. "Well, not really a woman. More like an older girl. I threw him out of the house."

"What did you do with the girl?" Gwen said. "Did you keep her?"

"No," Jane said. "I let her go."

"What did you do to him?" Gwen said.

"I punched him. I also scratched his face."

"Did you hurt him?"

"I think so," Jane said.

"And what about you?" Gwen said. "Did he hurt you?"

Jane couldn't speak. Her throat closed. She parted her lips and the tears ran into her mouth. She nodded into the phone.

"I'll be right over," Gwen said. "Don't touch anything."

Jane felt as if she were a victim at a crime scene. Gwen would come over and dust for fingerprints. They would cordon off the bedroom and get to the bottom of things. Gwen was efficient. Her husband had left her to raise an infant, a toddler, and herself more than twenty years ago. She would know what to do. She would be able to determine why Jane had needed to find Arnold in bed with another woman to finally end their marriage.

Gwen had once confided that her mother had suffered from spells. Several times a month, she took to her bed and lay quietly in the dark. More often than not, when the spells occurred, Gwen was summoned by her mother's maid, Regina. "Your mama wants you to brush her hair," Regina would say. She would hand Gwen the wooden brush with the boar's bristles. They bought all their brushes from the Fuller Brush man. "They'll outlast us all if you take good care of 'em," he promised. Of course it wasn't so, but it was nice to hear. Gwen remembered how Regina would soak the brushes in diluted ammonia. Gwen had loved to watch the hairs come loose and float to the top of the milky water. She laughed at the memory of how she would follow Regina to the porch and wait as she set the brushes out to dry on a worn towel reserved just for such purposes. The hot sun drew out the smell of the ammonia. She always inhaled deeply and pretended she was faint and needed the salts the way her mama did. "Such a long time ago," she said to Jane. "Another lifetime."

But Gwen's confession really had to do with her dread of the ritual hair brushing. She lowered her voice as she explained how she would kneel beside her mother's still body and brush her permed hair. Soon Gwen's arm ached, and her eyes smarted with unshed tears. But she brushed on until her mother's raspy snores signaled freedom. Jane had been heartbroken for the little girl, who must have felt that the minutes were hours. Even then, in the first telling so many years before, Jane had almost mistaken the confession for her own.

Jane knew that Gwen portioned out her disclosures with careful regard. By way of explanation, she once told Jane, "It's only because I feel it would be too much for others. What I really think, that is. It would be too much." But Jane had never been afraid to insist that Gwen reveal everything. All there was to be told with no holding back.

She knew that Gwen still held back, but less than before. And even though Jane believed that nothing Gwen told her would ever be too much, it was often a risk. Gwen's insights could sometimes cut as deeply as her confessions. Knowing this, Jane braced herself and invited Gwen to offer.

"I'm listening," Jane said. "Tell me."

Gwen set her cup down on the counter and pulled a stool alongside Jane. Gwen unfolded Jane's clasped hands and held them tightly.

"It's about time," Gwen said. "It's been about time for years."

Jane nodded. Her head slumped forward onto her chest. Gwen pulled her hands away and circled Jane in her arms, pulling her head against her shoulder. They stayed that way—Jane's brown curls spread over Gwen's shoulder like some exotic ivy. And the skin of Gwen's pale, white cheek pressed against her friend's head as if to anchor her.

"You don't have to do anything you don't want to do," Gwen finally said. She stopped patting, but kept her arms around Jane. "You can do whatever you want. It doesn't matter what anyone thinks, and you don't have to do anything today."

"What about Caroline?" Jane said. "Will she be all right?"

"She'll be all right if you're all right."

Jane paced around the kitchen.

"I told him I'd kill him if he didn't get out. I meant it."

"I'm sure you did."

"What if he comes back and kills me?"

"He won't."

"But he'll come back. Won't he?"

"I'm sure he will."

"What will I do when he does?"

Gwen sighed deeply. "I know you're scared. But what if this hadn't happened?" She stood and grabbed Jane's arm. "As long as I've known you, Jane, you've been unhappy."

"That long?"

"That long."

"Do you know what he said when I told him to get out?" Jane said. Her voice was a whisper. "Do you know what he said?"

Gwen shook her head.

"He said, 'How could you do this to me?'" Jane pressed her fingers against her mouth and groaned. "That's what he said. How could he say that to me?"

"I don't know," Gwen said. "No. That's not true. I do know. He said it because he believes it. Because if he didn't believe his own words, he would have to acknowledge all the mistakes he's made. All the pain he's been responsible for. If it's *your* fault, he's exonerated. And the plain, simple truth of it all, Jane, is that he's a self-centered bastard."

"Why am I so sad then?" Jane said.

"It doesn't matter," Gwen said.

"Then what does?"

"Did you know that the Japanese call a fountain pen a ten-thousand-year brush, and they call a porch a moon-watching platform? *That* matters."

"Why?" Jane said. "Why does it matter?"

"Because it means we have the power to change things. You know, to transform the ordinary into the extraordinary. Something like that."

"I don't get it," Jane said.

"Jane, don't think so much," Gwen said.

"But what else is there?"

"*Everything* else. There's everything else."

"But I don't know how," Jane said.

"You do too know how. You've just forgotten. We're born knowing how."

Gwen was still holding Jane's arm as if she were a recalcitrant child. Jane wriggled out of her grasp. Then she threw her head back and screamed. When she was finished, she began to hiccough.

"I feel sick," she said, and shuddered. "That's what the girl said. The one Arnold was screwing. She said, 'I feel sick.'" Jane shook her head in amazement. "The funny thing is that I feel sorry for *her*."

"I know," Gwen said.

"I lied to Arnold today. I told him it didn't hurt. I wanted him to think I didn't care."

"Do you care?"

"I don't know. I know a porch is a porch, and a fountain pen is a fountain pen," Jane said. The words came out in a wail.

"Then you have a lot to look forward to," Gwen said.

"How could he do this to me?" Jane said. "In my own house? How could he?"

Gwen said nothing at first, then she reached for Jane again and hugged her. "I'm sorry. I'm so sorry. You don't deserve any of this."

"I hit him," Jane said.

"*He* deserved *that*," Gwen said.

"I'm so tired now. I can't ever remember being so tired."

"Should I go now? Do you want to be alone?"

"I don't think I have a choice anymore," Jane said. The idea seemed to steady her. "Yes. You'd better go. I'll be all right."

"Are you sure? I can stay the night. I'd be glad to. Really, Jane. I'll sing to you all night. I know some old Irish ballads and inspirational songs of the South. I'll fix you hot milk with brandy and rub your feet. I'll do anything you'd like."

"No." Jane shook her head emphatically and laughed. "Maybe some other time. But I'll call you in the morning. And thank you, Gwen. Thank you for everything."

She saw Gwen out. Although Jane had never been scared to stay alone before, she was now. She checked all the windows and doors. Because she feared what she would see if she opened the door to her own bedroom, she decided to sleep in Caroline's room. Before she slipped under the covers, she was sure she heard something. "Arnold?" she called out. But there was no one there. She lay down on her back, closed her eyes, and then wrapped her arms around herself.

Chapter Two

Daniel was Gwen's lover. Her married lover. It was a situation she had never anticipated, but she believed that everything happened for a reason. The reason for her relationship with Daniel had not, as of yet, presented itself to her, but she was still waiting.

Gwen had not been *in love* with anyone since Theodore. She did not even know if she could count Theodore, since she had been only seventeen when she loved him. Fifteen years older and far more experienced, he had shamelessly manipulated her emotions. But she counted him anyway. When her boys asked her if she had loved their father, she was glad she could say, "Yes. I loved him very much." It always pleased them and, therefore, pleased her.

The first time Gwen met Daniel, they were introduced by his wife, Sandra. Gwen and Sandra had briefly worked together on a committee that brought together teachers representing all five boroughs of New York. Sandra represented Staten Island. Gwen represented the Bronx. They spent several months preparing a report for the Board of Education that inevitably reinvented the wheel. Sandra and Gwen were laughing over their shared experience at a farewell party given by the Manhattan representative when Daniel approached them. Gwen had been certain he was heading for her even though he was more Sandra's age—sixtyish, Gwen guessed. Daniel's hair was almost entirely gray, but there was still plenty of it. A pair of reading glasses hung from a silver chain around his neck. On another man, this might have looked fussy, but not on Daniel. He placed the glasses on the tip of his nose as he closed the distance between them. From this new proximity, Gwen saw that his brown eyes were bloodshot. At first, she thought he might have had too much to drink, but his ponderous gait was so natural that she immediately saw it wasn't so. Daniel rubbed at his face, at the stubble that was so white it could not be called a five-o'clock shadow. She had opened her mouth to say something flirtatious when Sandra said, "And here's my Daniel. I've been wanting the two of you to meet. You have so much in common." When Sandra left them to talk, they fell easily into conversation.

Daniel was a superintendent of schools out on Staten Island. He and Sandra had a thirty-five-year marriage and three grown children. He missed teaching but felt he was really doing something as an administrator. Gwen listened, charmed by his genuine concern for his staff and students and flattered when he asked her what she thought made a good administrator. Then he asked her about herself. She was a single mother. She had two sons. Twenty years of teaching fifth-graders had diminished her enthusiasm, but not her hope. He touched her hand, the one holding her now empty glass.

"Refill?" he said.

They looked at each other bashfully and smiled. They were both too old to feel that surge of electricity reminiscent of adolescence, but they felt it anyway.

"Thanks, no. It's just club soda," she said. "I have to drive."

They talked more about how class sizes had become unmanageable and how materials were in short supply. As guests started to leave, Daniel cleared his throat and looked around for Sandra.

"We should talk about this some more," he said. "Some other time."

"Well, I'm in the book," Gwen said. "B–a–k–e–r, Gwendolyn."

He colored slightly, then raised one eyebrow in surprise and asked her to spell her first name. They laughed together, and Gwen felt that perhaps she had not been so presumptuous after all. When Sandra suddenly appeared, clearly ready to leave, Daniel and Gwen stepped apart and hastily said goodbye. Sandra kissed Gwen's cheek.

"I knew the two of you would like each other," Sandra said.

"Yes," Gwen said.

She barely looked at Daniel and hurried away to find the hostess. Gwen promised herself she wouldn't see Daniel if he called. It was wrong even if she hardly knew Sandra. Even if they hadn't known each other at all. Gwen didn't sleep with married men.

When Daniel called the next morning, she was flustered. "I think you might have taken my gloves by mistake," he said by way of excuse. She laughed because it was spring and neither of them had been wearing gloves. His discomfort consoled her. It was easier after that. They talked for a long time, mostly about education and their personal triumphs. He called again the next day, and then not for two days. Gwen fretted, wondering if he had come to his senses as she knew she should, but couldn't. They had intercepted each other in the middle of their separate lives, and it was impossible not to wonder where they were headed now. When he finally called late Friday night, he asked if he could see her. "Just to talk," he added, sounding very foolish. "All right," she said. "I promise to keep my hands to myself." He laughed when she did. Then she told him to come the next day. She gave him directions, telling him to take the Henry Hudson Parkway and where to exit. Riverdale was actually the Bronx, but no one liked to admit to that geographic reality. Gwen had moved there after Theodore left her and Manhattan prices became prohibitive. She had a spacious apartment with a view of the George Washington Bridge and didn't miss the city at all.

Daniel was prompt. At three o'clock, the doorbell rang. He brought her a fossil of a fish. He had prowled the galleries in SoHo that morning looking for something to please her. Gwen rarely found herself in a position where she didn't know what to do, but she found herself in one that day. She showed Daniel the apartment. *This is Matt's room. He's away at college. Middlebury. Yes, he loves it. Yes, it's very expensive. My parents provided for us after my husband left us. Both boys have substantial trust funds. And this is Ethan's room. He's a senior in high school. He's away for the weekend visiting his brother. They're both good boys. I've been very lucky.* She heard her voice and thought it odd that she sounded so unlike herself. She wondered who she wanted Daniel to think she was. Daniel admired Ethan's soccer trophies. Daniel had played soccer. They stood in Ethan's room and talked about sports. Soccer as opposed to football. Gwen extended her arm to point out the latest trophy, and Daniel grabbed her wrist. It hurt, but she hadn't been afraid. He pulled her to him with two hands—the way one might haul in a rowboat. She let him. She felt as if she would let him do anything. When he reached her upper arm, he held her by the shoulder with one hand and then pulled her into an embrace. She was still holding the fossil. Her fingertips were pulsing. She looked down to see if there was a live fish in her hands, but there was only the fossil wedged between them. Daniel pulled away and said, "I'm not very good at this sort of thing anymore. If I ever was, that is. Anyway, it's been a long time." She nodded and said, "For me too," meaning the desire. When he kissed her, she kissed him back. And there in Ethan's room, they had made love for the first time.

Gwen refused to give Daniel a key while Ethan was still living at home. It wasn't that she didn't trust Daniel to use good judgment, but it was a convenient way of avoiding the decision. When Ethan left for Yale, Daniel asked for his own key, and Gwen obliged.

He was asleep on the couch when she let herself in. She didn't wake him. It was still hard for her to come home and find him there. It frightened her. The television was on, but the volume was off. Daniel always did that, just as she liked to drive with the window open and the heat on full blast.

For the past two years the only thing Gwen had known was that nothing was the same. Daniel was usually available on Tuesday night, Thursday night, all day Saturday, sometimes Saturday night, and every Sunday night. She had never asked him what determined this schedule. He called every day, sometimes twice a day. She liked him more than she had liked any other man she had ever met. He was curious about most everything, asking questions about her childhood in the South, her marriage to Theodore, her friendship with Jane. He wanted to know why she had never married again, what she did when she was lonely, what comforts solitude offered her. But what she really liked about Daniel was that he wasn't stingy with his own confidences. He talked about his children, his failures with them and his achievements. With a complete lack of self-consciousness, Daniel shared how it felt to age. He was sixty-one, and his body often alarmed him. "What's this?" he would say, peering at a patch of dry skin that had suddenly appeared on his neck. And she loved his aging form. The vulnerability of his rounded shoulders, the loose flesh that she knew he tried to conceal in spite of himself. None of it bothered her. She loved him and saw it all as a bridge to the next level of her life. He made all that easier for her. He was an admitted hypochondriac, but cheerfully good-humored about it. They both laughed effortlessly at themselves and at each other. It never seemed to her that he would ever hurt her as other men had. Yet, they still held back, with a certain chagrin at their own cautiousness. It was only natural to restrain themselves somewhat. Daniel was still married, and Gwen chose to ignore it. She never asked him to leave Sandra. He never asked her what she saw in their future. If he had, she would have been evasive. The truth was that she told him as little as possible about the details of what she really wanted from him, and then told herself it was because secrets were a good thing to have.

She was in the tub when Daniel knocked.

"Come in," Gwen said.

He looked disheveled and sleepy. He smiled warmly at her and said, "I didn't even hear you come in."

"I know."

Daniel lowered the toilet seat and sat down.

"You didn't leave a note. Is everything all right?"

"No. Not really. Could you hand me my robe?" She waited for the robe before she stood. Daniel held it for her as she slipped into it. She tied the belt. "It's cold, isn't it?"

Daniel watched her and rubbed his chin as if gauging the hair growth. Gwen wanted him to grow a beard, but he insisted he would look like Father Time.

Gwen took the clip out of her hair and shook her head. She leaned forward and brushed her hair hard, with long, angry strokes.

"Are you going to tell me what happened?" Daniel said. "Or are you going to give yourself a concussion?"

She knew he had hoped to at least make her smile. Instead, she handed him the brush and sat on the edge of the tub. With her free hand, she touched his face. The lines around his eyes had grown deeper these last two years. He snored louder and slept longer after they made love, but it didn't matter. She had never been able to sleep with someone holding her, but it was different with Daniel.

He covered her hand with his own and then kissed her open palm. In return, she gave him a reluctant smile.

"Jane found Arnold in bed with a girl," she said.

"I see," he said.

It made her angry that his response was so dispassionate. She pulled her hand away and reached for a jar of face cream on the shelf behind him. He made no effort to help. As she smoothed the cream with an upward motion along her throat and then across her cheeks and around her eyes, Daniel waited in silence. She rubbed what was left on her hands and waited with him, hands clasped, head down, and thought about Theodore. He had taught ancient civilizations. The Egyptian funerary cult was his specialty. She had never forgotten the time he had told her that the ancient Egyptians believed that any part of a person could be used in a spell. During mummification the inner organs were removed and protected in special jars. The liver, intestines, stomach, and lungs were dried out, wrapped in linen, and each placed in a separate jar—canopic jars, they were called. "All except for the brain," Theodore had murmured into her ear. "They removed the brain through the nostrils." She remembered the chill she had felt on hearing that, and the way she had burrowed deeper into Theodore's neck looking for protection that he could not give. "What did they do with the brain?" she had forced herself to ask. "They discarded it," he said. "They believed that people thought with their hearts and that the brain had no function." Theodore had been incredulous at their stupidity. Gwen remembered that she had never felt the same about him after that night.

She put the cream back on the shelf and left Daniel in the bathroom. Daniel came into the kitchen as she was warming a saucepan of milk.

"I'm sorry," he said.

"About what?"

"About Jane and Arnold. I'm sorry for her pain. I'm sorry for yours."

She stared at him. She would have liked to take off her robe and pull him down to the floor on top of her. Quickly. She would have wanted it to be over quickly. Just enough to take away the sting of the day's events.

The milk boiled over, but Gwen didn't move.

"I'll get that for you," Daniel said. "Why don't you get into bed, and I'll bring it to you."

She nodded.

"What can I do to make you feel better?" he said.

As Gwen opened her robe and drew Daniel to her, she wondered if when her heart was weighed after she died it would allow her to pass through to the kingdom of Osiris. Theodore had told her that the ancient Egyptians believed that the heart of a dead man bore a record of all his past deeds. Forty-two assessor gods, one for each district of Egypt, would interrogate the deceased about various crimes. If the truth was told, Thoth, the god of wisdom, would write *true of voice*, and there would be nothing to fear. The awful alternative was the goddess known as the Devourer of the Dead. She would eat up the heart of the untruthful, and there would be no afterlife.

The first time Daniel stayed over, Gwen had not slept all night. She wanted to see if he would call her Sandy in his sleep. He had woken once that first night and murmured, "Gwen, I'm so glad to be here with you." Only then was she convinced that he knew exactly where he was and who he was with.

Daniel snored softly now in Gwen's ear. She couldn't see him, but she didn't have to. Her back was pressed against his chest, and his arms circled her waist. Daniel stirred and rubbed his chin against her neck. She pushed back against him and then turned toward him.

"It's late," she said.

He didn't answer. She kissed his closed eyelids and moved down to his lips. He kept his mouth closed, and she ran her tongue horizontally, back and forth, between his lips. It delighted her that he let her do these things without feeling obliged to reciprocate. She often teased him that he was a lazy lover. Her tongue circled his lips as her hands moved down his body. Although he had the body of a man his age, he seemed younger now than he had when they had first met. She had thought he was older than he really was. "Sadness ages a person," he said. Now he was happy.

"It's late," she said again.

It was not likely that they would make love again. He often worried that he didn't satisfy her enough. And she was still afraid to tell him that when he left, she often wept for just wanting his bulk in her bed night after night.

"Tell me about Jane," he said.

She put her arms around his neck and drew him tightly against herself. He repositioned himself and kept one arm around her waist. The other hand moved along her spine. His thumb pressed against each vertebra until he reached the small of her back and let his hand rest there, as if that had been its destination all along.

"Tell me," he said.

"She's so afraid."

"That's a pretty natural response. What does she plan to do?"

Gwen pulled away—not sharply, but suddenly. She didn't like it when Daniel behaved like an administrator. Then he wanted the facts. "Don't tell me how you feel," he implied when he was administrating. "Tell me what you think."

"You're angry now," he said.

"Yes," she said. "I'm angry."

"Why?"

"Because everything isn't always so clear. Because solving the problem quickly doesn't mean the solution will be better."

It was not a new argument. Daniel turned on his side and propped himself up with his head in his hand. He looked tired. Sometimes the tenderness Gwen felt for him was unbearable. It reminded her of how she felt about Matt and Ethan. Passion had many disguises. What she felt for her children was boundless. All the more so because she knew she could expect nothing in return for loving them. She would only be disappointed. But she wanted Daniel to know better. She wanted him to be more like her.

"I'm not trying to solve the problem," he said. "I have enough problems of my own."

There was something in his tone that made her afraid to look at him. She leaned toward him as if she might hear the echo of his last words and grasp his intent. But there was nothing.

"In their own bed," she said. "How could he bring a girl to the house?"

"Does it matter?" he said. "Are you angry because he was unfaithful? Are you angry that he brought the girl home? What's the point? Tell me, Gwen, what upsets you the most?"

She turned to get out of bed, but Daniel grabbed her arm.

"Oh no, sweetheart. You're going to finish this fight," he said. "I won't let you get out of this one."

"I'm hungry. Let go of me."

He pinned her down and straddled her body.

"Get off me," she said.

"I have something important to tell you."

She turned her face to the side. If he hadn't been holding her down, she would have covered her ears.

"Look at me, Gwen. I have something to tell you."

She looked. Her expression was impassive. He let go of her arms, and she pulled him down so that his head was on her breasts. She stroked his head and wound a piece of his hair around her finger.

"I told Sandy I was leaving her," he said.

Gwen had expected him to tell her that it was over between them. That he couldn't go on anymore. She would have understood. She wouldn't have had a choice. In fact, she had been practicing for the moment for the last two years. "Hand over hand," she kept telling herself. "You have the best control that way." It was what her driving teacher had told her. "Hand over hand," Marvin had repeatedly told her. He had demonstrated for her. "Hand over hand when you turn that wheel." Marvin had been a retired police officer who had never made detective. "Let me guess," he would say. "You're about a hundred and twenty-three pounds. Am I right?" Gwen always said yes. Even then she felt as if she owed him something more than his standard fee for teaching her to drive. He would try to guess things about her family, her friends, her perfume—anything to prove that he would have made a great detective. He wouldn't have, though. He was too earnest. Still, Marvin had demonstrated how to turn the wheel, moving his beefy hands with exaggerated simplicity. And to this day, Gwen wondered if Marvin had ever been able to transfer the majesty of that movement to anything else in his dull and predictable life.

Gwen tried to breathe evenly so Daniel wouldn't feel her heart pounding. An image of Sandra and the children flashed in front of her. The children were all grown now. Kate was married. Soon Daniel would be a grandfather. Samuel was in law school. And Rosie was in her junior year at Cornell. Rosie was Daniel's favorite. He denied it was so, but Gwen knew. She could tell by the way he always said "my Rosie." Gwen always asked about the children. But she had never asked about Sandra until this moment.

"How is she?" Gwen said. "Sandra. How is she?"

"I knew who you meant," Daniel said.

She suddenly felt the weight of his body and pushed against his chest with her hands. He rolled onto his back and lay still, with closed eyes. She copied his pose, but she kept her eyes open. She felt it was necessary to be watchful.

"Tell me," she said. "Tell me everything."

She thought about Theodore. She had been twenty-three when he had emptied his side of the closet to move in with the daughter of the neighborhood deli owner. Vicki was nineteen and infatuated with Theodore. She said "hi" as if it were a two-syllable word. Theodore was forever coming home with tuna fish on whole wheat or salami and provolone. The sandwiches had always seemed extremely generous to Gwen. Then one day she came home from grocery shopping to find Theodore packing. "It's a temporary arrangement," he said. "I just need some time to figure things out. I don't have any space here. I need some space." Gwen had listened intently, trying to understand each word Theodore said. When he spoke it seemed as if his voice was in slow motion, each word painfully dragged out, accentuating the terror that gripped her. She had no job and no money, and there was little possibility that her parents would be sympathetic. He left that evening, but he was back the next morning. "Let's try to work things out," he said. Theodore's lust was sparked by her helplessness, and he acted in accordance. She had complied because she had to know about Vicki and knew it was the only way to find out. She had asked all the questions that she had tormented herself with as she imagined Theodore coupling with the skinny girl whose face she barely remembered. What kind of underwear did she have on? Where did they do it? Did she talk to him? Was she a screamer? Did she pleasure him for endless minutes? He had told her everything. More, in fact, than she had wanted or needed to know. She had been helpless. It had reminded her of biting down on her newly tightened braces to intensify the pain, thinking, wishing, it would make it better. It hadn't worked with either the braces or Theodore. "Tell me," she had urged Theodore as they moved in discord. "Tell me everything." And she had bitten down, hard, and listened.

This time the pain was different. She had not invited the assault, and she was unprepared even though she had been waiting all along.

"It's not your problem," Daniel said. "I don't want to make you part of this."

"What did you tell her?" she said.

He rubbed his eyes with clenched fists. As they lay side by side, Gwen had an image of an old monster movie in which the energy from one body was transferred to the other. She looked up, half expecting to see an arc of electric current vibrating between them. When she reached out to touch Daniel's face, it was wet. She withdrew sharply, as if she had touched fire rather than a warm, salty fluid. But Daniel was wrong. He could not separate her from this. She rolled over on top of him and adjusted her body so that their parts were equally aligned. One rainy afternoon when the children were small, she had spent the day with Jane cooped up in the house and half crazed with boredom. Gwen had unrolled sheets of brown paper and instructed each child, one by one, to lie down while she traced an outline of each little body. She could still see the solemn procession as they waited first to be traced and then to watch as their bodies were cut out and then handed over for them to draw in their own features. "Do me," Jane had said. Gwen had outlined Jane's small frame in purple marker. And then Jane had done the same for Gwen. The children had been fascinated as they watched the familiar bodies take form on the brown paper. It had been a wonderful afternoon. Gwen now felt as if she were a brown paper cutout of Daniel. She pressed her cheek along his damp skin and wished to be a conduit for his pain.

"She cried," Daniel whispered into her neck. "I never saw her cry like that."

"What did you expect her to do?" Gwen said.

She had wept as Theodore left. "I knew you were going to do this," he had said. And she had stopped. She had watched from the window until the car became a speck of green that she wasn't sure had ever been anything else.

"She seemed so surprised," he said. "I don't know why I thought she wouldn't be."

Gwen had seen Sandra once after the fateful party. It had been almost a year later. "You're looking very well," Sandra said. "I hope *he's* being good to you." She was only being coy, but Gwen's face had burned with shame. Sandra never suspected it was her Daniel who was pleasing Gwen. "So tell me all about him," Sandra urged. Gwen had insisted there was no one. "Just the right shade of lipstick," she said. Then she pretended that someone on the other side of the room was trying to get her attention.

"Why didn't you tell me you were planning on leaving?" she said.

"Because I didn't know until it happened."

"How did it happen?" she said. She slid a hand between their bellies and shifted slightly.

"Don't go away," he said.

"I won't. Tell me what happened."

"Are you sure you want to know?"

"I have to know."

"We were having dinner, and I just couldn't swallow. 'Is something wrong?' Sandy said. I nodded. 'Everything is wrong,' I told her. She put her hand over my mouth and said, 'Just don't say it. If you don't say it, it won't be true. I don't want to know. I don't have to know. Just let it be the way it is.'" He held Gwen tightly. "It was awful. And I was so angry."

"Why?" Gwen said. "Why were you so angry?"

"Because it defined everything about the last thirty-five years of my life. And I let it happen."

"It wasn't so bad, Daniel. You had three children. They all turned out well. They felt loved. There must've been good moments with Sandra. It wasn't all terrible. You mustn't think it was all for nothing."

"That's what Sandy said. That's exactly what Sandy said."

They lay quietly, holding each other. Gwen understood what Daniel couldn't. She knew that women felt things that could not be easily translated into words men would understand. Women shared a language that effortlessly gave voice to even the most formless feelings. This puzzled men, for it was unlike any language that was familiar to them. "They speak male patois" was Gwen's wry description of their dialect. Even in her pain, Sandra had found some way to demonstrate the good she had shared with Daniel, some way to express her grief and still comfort Daniel. He would never understand what Sandra felt, what Gwen felt, what made women love men in spite of the persistent disappointment.

So when Daniel pushed her legs apart with his knees and eased her over onto her back, she didn't object. In fact, she understood it too. She thought about herself and Theodore. She thought about Jane and Arnold. And Sandra and Daniel. But just as a terrible sadness filled her, she stopped thinking, and matched her rhythm to Daniel's thrusts.

Chapter Three

For a very long time Jane had believed her grandmother's story about how babies were made. Her grandmother, Ida, revealed that a pinch of sugar on the windowsill would soon bring a baby. "A sweet dream," Ida said. "All dreams are sweet." When her daughter, Jane's mother, grew heavy with the child inside her, Jane had wondered what urge had prompted her mother to sprinkle sugar on the windowsill in the middle of the night. What had woken her and told her that it was time? When Jane's new baby sister finally arrived—Ellen was the name given to her, and Ellie was what she was called from the start—she didn't seem very sweet. Jane did not care much for her at all and began to wonder if perhaps a mistake had been made. Perhaps her mother had sprinkled salt on the windowsill and the result was the screaming red thing that sent a household of adults running in all directions for hot-water bottles and rattles. Anything to stop the screaming. Anything to soothe the colic. Ellie was passed from weary hand to weary hand as if she were a bomb set to detonate at any moment. Ellie grew up expecting to be happy and indulged. She married a banker, and they lived contentedly in Vermont with three children who were told that Daddy planted a seed inside Mommy that grew in her womb. Ellie felt that the word "belly" was misleading. Her sister, Jane, who had been a docile baby, "a really good baby," her mother always said (as if any baby could really be bad), grew up wondering why all dreams were not really sweet after all.

As Jane grew up, it seemed to her that life was a series of events to turn away from, much like a highway accident or a mutilated animal on the side of the road. She had always covered Caroline's eyes. "Don't look, darling," she said. Gwen had tried to warn her that it was wrong to shield Caroline from pain. "She won't be able to avoid it all her life," Gwen said. "She won't be ready for pain when it comes if you don't let her feel it now." But Jane couldn't do it. And when she could no longer elude Caroline's questions, Jane told her about the sugar on the windowsill.

She was sorry now. She should have listened to Gwen. Gwen had always told her children the truth. Oh, she had tempered it, of course. She had known it would serve no one's interest to tell the children that Theodore had taken up with Vicki and countless others because he was self-indulgent and heartless. Instead, Gwen had told them that love was not always enough. She had never told them more than they needed to know. "When they want to know more, they'll ask," she'd said. By the time they were grown, they seemed to have all the answers they needed. Gwen had never suggested baking chocolate chip cookies or making jewelry boxes from popsicle sticks instead of talking about why relationships fail and why people die even if they are good.

Jane knew that she would have to tell Caroline the truth now. All the evidence she had turned Caroline's eyes away from over the last nineteen years would have to be exposed. Jane would no longer be able to rearrange the outcome. She would have to pull Caroline through the muck and explain, "This is what really happened." It would be difficult to temper the truth now.

Jane thought about all this as she drank her coffee and watched the sky lighten. She had hardly slept, waking every hour, listening for Arnold's footsteps. It was just a little past six as she poured herself a second cup. It was probably too early to call Ellie, but Jane rummaged around in the drawer until she found the address book. She called so rarely that she could never remember the number.

"Hello," Ellie said.

"Ellie? Did I wake you? It's me. It's Jane."

"Jane? Are you all right?"

"I'm fine. I'm sorry. It's much too early, but I knew you'd be up. I just felt like hearing your voice. We haven't talked in such a long time. How is everything there?"

"Are you sure you're all right?" Ellie said.

"Yes. I have to get ready for work. I . . . well . . . I just wanted to know how everything is. How are the children?"

"They're fine. Susan is determined to get to the Olympics. She's already out skating with her coach. Peter has suddenly discovered girls, and Rachel is heavily into her self-hatred period. How's Caroline?" Ellie said.

"She's fine. She seems to be happy at school. She's taking two dance classes and a sculpture class. She loves her American lit class and hates math. How's Richard?"

"He's wonderful. And Arnold? Is he all right?"

Jane was sorry now that she had called. What could she say about Arnold? Richard was probably asleep under the heavy-weight down blanket. Jane imagined the sharp line of his jaw as he turned in his sleep, looking for Ellie. He wouldn't be upset to find her missing. He would know she was out in their kitchen. He could probably smell the coffee and the first whiff of the bran muffins Ellie had put in the oven. He would force himself out from under the warm blanket and pull on his robe. Ellie would be waiting for him downstairs. Maybe they would even have time to make love before he left for work. He'd pull Ellie upstairs back into the still-warm bed and lift her nightgown just enough to give him access. Jane knew her sister well enough to visualize the entire scene. Ellie would giggle into his ear and whisper, "Shh." He'd laugh at the wool booties she was still wearing and turn so that she was on top. He'd work her flannel nightie—Ellie used words like "nightie"—over her head. She would shiver in the cold, but would continue rocking. They would pull the covers over their heads until the heat became unbearable.

"Jane? Are you there?"

Ellie sounded more distracted than worried.

"I'm here. I'm fine. Everything is fine. Go ahead, Ellie. I'll speak to you soon."

"But you didn't tell me about Arnold. Is he all right?"

Jane imagined her sister with the phone wedged between her shoulder and ear as she prepared her children's lunches. Her blunt-cut brown hair fell oddly over one side because of her position. Richard was probably already in the kitchen with his arms around her waist. He was nuzzling her neck.

"I wouldn't know," Jane said.

"Hm? What? Yes. Well, I'm glad you called," Ellie said. "Come visit."

"When?"

"Hm? Oh, soon, Jane. Come real soon."

After Ellie was born, Jane had peered into the cradle to gaze at her sister's sleeping form. She looked angelic when she slept. She was swaddled in a pink blanket, and her full name, Ellen Barbara Kaufman, was stitched in pink across a tiny pink satin pillow. Jane took some newly folded bath towels from the closet and conscientiously stacked them on top of the baby. The towels were still warm from the dryer. Ellie slept on while Jane finished her work. Within moments, Ellie began to whimper. It sounded as if she was very far away, maybe at the bottom of a well. Terrified that what she had done could no longer be undone, Jane grabbed the towels and threw them onto the floor until her view of Ellie was unobstructed. Ellie gurgled and sucked at her hand. She was hungry. In a few seconds, she would be screeching for food again.

"Goodbye, Ellie," Jane said. "Have a wonderful day."

She closed her eyes and hung up the phone while Ellie was in midsentence. Jane was sorry now she had moved the towels. She decided not to speak to Ellie again for a long while. Maybe never.

"Jane?"

Arnold was in the house. She had known he would come back.

"Jane?"

Quickly, she closed the door to the bedroom and leaned against it with all her weight.

"I came to get some clothes for work. Please, Jane. We have to talk."

"I'm not interested," she said.

"You're going to have to talk to me sometime. C'mon, Janie, open the door."

Janie. She leaned her head against the wood. He always called her Janie when he wanted something from her. She thought she could hear him breathing on the other side of the door, waiting for her to relent. She opened the door.

"I'm going to be late for work," she said.

"I brought some Danish. Poppyseed. Your favorite."

Last year they had vacationed in Santa Fe. One morning at the buffet brunch offered at the hotel, Jane and another woman had reached for the same poppyseed Danish. The other woman was almost six feet tall and had a longer reach than Jane. "Go ahead," the woman—whose name turned out to be Katya—said. "I'm just as happy with prune." Katya was a healer. She studied Jane and said, "You are surrounded by a wonderful purple aura." Katya was performing a crystal healing that afternoon and invited Jane to observe. The client, a young man with severe lower back pain, lay quietly as Katya placed stones and crystals on the vital nerve points of his body. His back was resplendent with color. Jane thought that even if Katya was unable to heal him, he looked fabulous. Katya explained, "The ancient art of crystal healing is based on the belief that as light reflects off the crystals and stones, the aura—which is really the electromagnetic field of the body—absorbs the energy. This phenomenon allows me to become aware of the mental and emotional causes of the disease. Then, and only then, am I able to heal."

Jane was transfixed. The young man was blond and had beautiful skin. It seemed practically nonporous. He lay on his stomach, naked, covered with a towel. Katya asked him if it was all right if "my friend shares our energy during the healing." The young man, Blake, was extremely accommodating. "Cool, man. No sweat." Jane wished she hadn't heard him speak. She studied his body with interest. He was glorious. She watched as Katya held one crystal close to Blake's head and another near the source of the pain in his lower back. Katya's hands seemed to vibrate. She closed her eyes. Jane was envious of the boy. Envious of Katya. She had the power to heal. He had the faith to be healed. Jane was incapable of either. She slipped out of the room with a whispered "Previous engagement." She couldn't bear to know the outcome. If Blake was healed, Jane would have wanted to rip off her clothes and beg Katya to find the source of the pain that left her defeated and hopeless. And if Katya failed to diminish Blake's discomfort, if once stripped of the crystals and stones he eased himself off the table and was still an ordinary, though beautiful, young man with lower back pain, Jane couldn't have taken the disappointment. That evening, Jane saw Katya and turned away quickly before Katya could discover that Jane really did not have an aura after all.

Arnold might have benefited from Katya's table. Jane would have recommended to Katya that she use purple amethyst and rose quartz rather than yellow citrine. Yellow made his complexion sallow. Perhaps the bits of purple and rose quartz would make it possible to identify the source of his indifference. The place inside him that made him unresponsive to Jane. The hollow emptiness of something colorless yet dangerous that could only be detected against the brilliance of Katya's stones. Jane looked at him, half expecting to see some unrealized form hovering over his head like pictures of ectoplasm presumed to be the spiritual guides of those blessed to have such fortune.

"Boo!" Jane said, loud and close to Arnold's face. She waved her hands at him as if he were the apparition. "Boo! Boo!" she repeated.

"Are you crazy?" he said. He stepped back. "What's with you, Jane? I've never seen you like this before."

She smiled. It was the nicest thing Arnold had ever said to her.

She had thought about leaving Arnold many times, but something always happened. Arnold would cry and promise to change. Her mother would wring her hands and say, "What about the baby?" Jane always wondered why her mother never said, "What about *you?*" So Jane stayed. She did the laundry and shopped for groceries. She straightened the house and paid the housekeeper each week. Jane made waffles on the weekend and wholesome dinners at night. She helped Caroline with her homework. And there were always projects. Things that required chunks of time to organize. A sweet-sixteen party. A dinner for Arnold's colleagues. A family vacation. College applications. And the time passed in this way. It no longer seemed important to be happy. It seemed adolescent and impractical to want such a thing. But, still, there were moments when Jane felt a flutter of disquiet so faint it was like suddenly recognizing something familiar in a place she had never been before. The same disturbing feeling she had on waking and instantly forgetting a dream that had seemed so telling.

Arnold was waiting for her in the kitchen when she came down. She took some papers off the table and thumbed through them, feeling nervous. Arnold was a master of persuasion. It was possible he could convince her that he had actually brought the girl home for her pleasure. Jane could hear that conversation. *I didn't want to sleep with her,* he would say. *I did it for you, Janie. For you.*

"Sit down," Arnold said.

She shook her head. He looked so eager to satisfy. He reminded her of the boys in her class. They were always vying for her attention. *Look at this, Mrs. Hoffman. Did I do a good job? Did I get them all right?* They were sweet, really. But they were all so needy. Behind what they said, she heard the real questions. The ones they might never have the courage to ask. *Do you love me? Am I your favorite? Do you think I'm wonderful?* She touched their cheeks and the tops of their heads. She tried to teach them how to feel good about themselves and how to ask for the things they needed instead of hitting and shouting. Because she knew what would happen if they didn't learn now. They would grow up to be men like Arnold.

"I've had my coffee," Jane said. "And I don't usually eat in the morning." She smiled. "You haven't been paying attention. Not for a long time."

Arnold put his head in his hand and sniffled. Her back stiffened.

"Don't do that," she said. "I'm warning you."

Arnold wiped his nose with the back of his hand. Gregory Brewster always did that. *Take a tissue, please, Gregory. Don't use your hand. I'll be right with you, Mark. I'm busy with Madeline now, Jason, then I'll check your paper. Stop fighting, Michael.* Jane pictured Arnold in the front row of her classroom.

"What are we going to do?" Arnold said.

What should we do now, Mrs. Hoffman? Jason was waving his paper. Dancing in front of her even though she was sitting with another student. *Try to be patient, please, Jason. I'll be with you in a moment. Why don't you read until I'm done.* He became sullen. Petulant. *Pay attention to me now, Mrs. Hoffman. Now.*

"What do *you* think we should do?" she said.

It was the same question she would have asked Jason or Mark or Gregory. *What can you do while you're waiting?* The boys almost never had an answer. Blank. Waiting. *Heal me,* they seemed to say. Then they had to be cajoled out of their bad moods with promises of love and devotion.

Arnold blinked. He pouted. He stood and paced a bit. He waited.

"We should try to work things out," he said.

There. It was all done. He had taken care of everything. He smiled broadly. He had found the answer she had been looking for. Now he, too, could go out to play. He was a good boy.

"I don't think so, Arnold."

"No?"

Jane shook her head. Arnold looked frantic.

"Here," he said. "Wait a minute. I forgot what I wanted to show you." He pulled a piece of paper from the inside of his jacket pocket. "I called the inn. You know the one we saw from the road the last time we drove up to see Caroline? Remember? The one you admired? I made a reservation. For this weekend. So we could all be together."

He shoved the paper at Jane. She stared at what he had scrawled. Everything was a blur. She lifted her gaze from the paper to look at him. He was so sure of himself now. He had done the right thing.

"I don't think so," Jane said.

"Why not?" Arnold's voice rose an octave. "You said the place looked wonderful. You said it would be fun to stay there. Don't you remember?"

"No. I don't remember." She approached him so swiftly that he took an alarmed step backward. Fueled by his apprehension, she continued, "Do you know what I remember, Arnold? I remember you said, 'That dump? It looks as if it should have been condemned years ago.' That's what I heard, Arnold." She lowered her voice to a whisper. "That's what I heard, you no good son of a bitch."

Jane listened to the sound of herself panting and tried to quiet her breathing. Her chest was heaving. But she wasn't crying. She could feel the heat of her flushed cheeks. Her palms were sweaty. The ink on the paper Arnold had given her was smudged. But she wasn't crying.

Arnold was clearly shaken. He slumped onto one of the stools.

"I'm sorry," he said. "I'm sorry."

"What are you sorry about, Arnold? Are you sorry you got caught, or are you sorry you hurt me?"

She saw him searching for the right answer. The one that would please her.

"I'm sorry for everything," he said.

"For everything?" Jane said. "I don't think you even know what you've done. How can you be sorry when you don't even know what it is that you've done?"

"I'm sorry, anyway. I'm just sorry. Don't do this, Janie. We can fix it. We always do."

Jane wondered what it was about this hurt that made it so different from all the others. This wasn't the worst hurt. *Things will get better.* It had become a litany. And she, the chorus of one, had responded in kind.

"We never fix it, Arnold. Never," she said.

"Janie—"

"Never. And now it's too late."

"It can't be."

"I want a divorce," Jane said. "I have to go. I'm late for work already."

She took her briefcase and her purse and left the house. Just as she was about to turn around, she remembered the story of Lot. He had received a warning from God. It had been very clear. *Flee for your life; do not look back or stop anywhere in the valley; flee to the hills lest you be consumed.* Lot had argued with God. Lot had not wanted to flee with his wife and two daughters to the hills as God had suggested. It seemed too dangerous. Too close to the destruction that would soon be visited upon Sodom and Gomorrah. The little city of Zoar, farther away, seemed safer. God granted Lot his wish. But Lot's wife looked back. She had not been able to resist the temptation to see what she was leaving behind. She looked back, and she was turned to a pillar of salt.

Jane understood poor Lot's wife. It was hard not to look back. Perhaps if she had heard her husband's conversation with God, she might have acted differently. Perhaps if she had heard Lot's argument with God, she would have dwelled happily in the new land of Zoar. Lot had beseeched God. Lot had said, "...but I cannot flee to the hills lest the disaster overtake me, and I die." He had begged God, "Let me escape there...and my life will be saved." Lot had been worried about himself. *And I die. My life will be saved.* If only his wife could have heard that conversation. If only she had known that as Lot hurried on ahead of her, it was his life he feared for, not hers.

It occurred to Jane as she pulled the car out of the garage that maybe Lot's wife had been eavesdropping while her husband chatted with God. Maybe she had known that life would be no different with Lot once they reached Zoar. Maybe it was a way out of it all.

As she accelerated to move into highway traffic, she noted that she was calm. She was no longer panting. Her chest wasn't heaving. And her palms were no longer sweaty. Still, it was difficult to see through her tears.

Chapter Four

After Theodore left, Gwen started to read cookbooks. It became somewhat of an obsession, and although she felt in control—for really, there was nothing pathological about the pleasure it gave her—she chose not to share her new interest with anyone. There was something about the glossy photographs of beautifully prepared foods that made her feel as if perfection was more than a state of mind. She was fascinated by the suggested menus that offered one dish more spectacular than another. It seemed to represent the life she would have had if things had worked out with Theodore. Intellectually, she knew this was irrational. After all, she had not prepared such meals when Theodore had been home. Somehow, however, the food took on a life of its own, and she pored over countless cookbooks, looking for the answer to what had really gone wrong.

There had been little time to be sad after Theodore finally

moved out and consented to the divorce. He had wanted an *arrangement,* which basically meant he slept with whomever he wanted to, and she accepted it. Gwen refused to concede in spite of his attempts to convince her that she would never be able to survive without him. Even though she believed him, she persisted. She had her sons to think about and never wanted them to grow up believing that their father's deceptions were acceptable.

After it was all over, she dated occasionally—mostly to satisfy her mother. Sometimes Gwen would let one of the men kiss her, but it almost always left a brackish taste in her mouth. She had even considered marrying one fellow. He was a gardener, and five years younger than Gwen. He loved the children and her long legs. Every Saturday and Sunday he would stop over on his lunch break and play with the boys. When they napped, he would pull her into the bedroom and help her undress. Oh, she enjoyed those afternoons, but most of the time she couldn't remember his name when she was talking about him. Her mouth would open, and she would wait for the word to form. The day she told him that she didn't think it was going to work out between them, she called him Roger. "My name is Robert," he said. For a while, he continued to pursue her. One day, she called him Roy. She never heard from him again.

Then she began to borrow several cookbooks at a time from the library. "Are you a caterer?" the librarian finally asked. Gwen said yes. The lie came easily. Others followed. She said yes when dates asked if she was a model. And then she said yes to her mother when she asked if that "nice young man who took you to dinner" seemed promising. Gwen found her little lies made life much easier. *It's wrong to lie,* she heard herself tell her children.

Still, she couldn't help herself. Nor could she help taking refuge in the imaginary worlds she saw between the shiny pages of the cookbooks.

Gwen created a make-believe life for herself as it might have been had she been born a hundred years earlier. That life seemed so much easier. The boundaries were so well defined. She cast herself in a comfortable role. It was her job to do the billing for her husband's lumber business. But mostly, she imagined she would have stayed home and taken care of the house. There was a child on the way. It would be born nine months to the day she had wed. She would stroke her belly as she looked in the cookbook and wonder if her husband would like something new for dinner. She wanted to please him. He did not often touch her now, and she would be ashamed to admit how much she missed him. So, instead, she thought about the wonderful meals she could prepare instead of her husband's advances. Sometimes, when he reached for her in the night, she would need to clasp her hand over her mouth to keep from screaming with pleasure. He would not have approved of such conduct. She had suffered his reproach only a few weeks into their marriage when she had boldly grasped him in her hand instead of waiting.

The wine at dinner had made her giddy. It was his fault, really. She had warned him that wine made her feel peculiar. But he had insisted. And he was not the sort to be charmed by his young wife's lust. He had turned away from her that night and for several nights after that. And she would wake from a fitful sleep each morning, ashamed to find her own hand where she thought only her husband's should have been.

When the day seemed impossibly long, she would take down the cookbook from the shelf and say the names of the wonderfully strange dishes out loud. Suckling veal cutlets with truffles in red sauce. Roast quail with basil, nuts, and garlic. Mussels in wine sauce. Stuffed baked peaches. French cream. She would savor the words and imagine the foreign flavors. She had to swallow many times. She nearly swooned with longing. But she would put the book away before her husband came home and carefully set the table with the monogrammed napkins that had been a wedding gift from his aunt and uncle. There would be chicken and rice that evening. No unusual spices. No conversation during dinner. Both were bad for the digestion. She would go about her business never suspecting that she was not happy. It was this, more than anything, that Gwen saw as a blessing. It was easier not to know. Happiness was such an intangible, like the perfect man. She had allowed herself neither. Even in her reveries.

It seemed almost divinely inspired when Gwen woke in the middle of the night from a really sound sleep and smelled bread baking. She was a great believer in dreams and signs (though she hated to hear others tell about theirs) and knew there was something to all this. She pulled back the covers, shivered, and then hurried to the kitchen, where she had left a shopping bag on the counter. She had stopped buying cookbooks with a furtive compulsion after Daniel eased into her life. But today she could not resist the display in the shop window. It had been a mistake to go into the store. A mistake to think that she could just browse. Gwen reached into the bag and removed the cookbook she had bought that afternoon—it was on baking bread—and sat down to look at the pictures of the loaves of bread that seemed more perfect than anything in real life could ever be.

She read that in the days of pioneers, lumberjacks and gold prospectors had used a sourdough starter to make their bread rise. They created fermented dough by combining equal amounts of flour and milk. The mixture was placed in a glass jar or bowl and kept warm for several days. The batter bubbled and soured each time some of the starter was used. The starter always had to be returned to its original volume by adding equal parts of milk and flour. Although the starter improved with age, it was necessary to use it at least once a week. The key was always to put back what had been taken out.

The recipe said the mixture had to stay for several days before fermentation took place. The starter would make a wonderful sourdough French bread for Daniel. The bread would be so good it would not even need butter. As she broke off a piece of the crusty bread and held it to his mouth, she would explain about the gold prospectors and the lumberjacks. She would tell him her theory about the sourdough starter. The miracle of it all. The idea that as long as you put back what you used, there would always be more.

She would have told him all this if he had called. It had been days since Daniel told her he was leaving Sandra. Days and only one message. *I'm all right. Don't worry. I'll call soon.* He left it when he knew she wouldn't be home. She sat cross-legged on the kitchen floor and rummaged through the cabinets until she found a glass jar. Then she rinsed it and poured in a cup of milk. The recipe said to leave it uncovered for twenty-four hours. Then it would be ready for her to add the flour and leave it to rest for several days. She loved the idea of allowing it *to rest*. It was so kind. She knew she would sneak peaks at the mixture as it bubbled and soured. It would be difficult to keep herself from opening the oven door as the loaf was finally baking. But now she could do nothing but wait. Wait for the milk to sour. Wait for Daniel to call. She closed her eyes as she walked past the phone. With her eyes closed and her arms outstretched, she made her way to the bedroom. It reminded her of pretending to be blind when she was a child. Then it had been funny to bump into walls and to see the swirls of color behind tightly shut eyelids. Then it had been a game full of thrilling possibilities. Now it was just frightening. Lonely and frightening.

"What the hell is that awful smell?" Jane asked. She sniffed around the kitchen and stopped as soon as she came close to the jar. "For heaven's sake, Gwen, what are you doing? Making penicillin?"

"Don't touch it," Gwen said. "It's almost ready."

"Ready for what?"

"It's sourdough starter. The pioneers used to use it."

"For what? To keep away the Indians? It smells awful. How do you know when it's ready?"

"It's supposed to bubble." She came to stand next to Jane and study the contents of the jar. "It has to really sour. Then you put it in the refrigerator."

"The pioneers had refrigerators?" Jane said.

"State of the art."

They smiled at each other. The first time Jane had come for dinner, Gwen had been surprised to see her even though she had invited her. "Stop over any evening," Gwen had said. Then she had been living with the boys in a tiny two-bedroom apartment she rented in Mrs. Lombardi's house. Mrs. Lombardi also watched the children while Gwen was at work. It was an attic apartment.

Hot in the summer. Cold in the winter. But Mrs. Lombardi loved the boys, so Gwen stayed.

Jane had climbed the steep stairs and pounded on Gwen's door. "Here," Jane panted. She held out a casserole dish. "I brought dinner. The kids can eat it. It's not spicy. Arnold teaches late almost every night. I know you like to be alone, but I don't." Gwen had been startled by Jane's directness. Together they had scooped out bowls of the fragrant meat and rice for the children and poured them cups of juice. After dinner, Jane had cleared the dishes and offered to help bathe the children. "Let me," she begged. The two women, one so pregnant she could barely get her arms in the soapy water and the other so elegant she looked as if she were above such mundane tasks, bathed the boys with strokes so well orchestrated that the children, usually so boisterous and unmanageable, were docile in contrast to their usual selves.

Gwen remembered it as the night they had fallen in love. Yes, women do fall in love with each other. Differently, of course, than they fall in love with men. Falling in love with a man is a feverish experience. There is little control. But falling in love with a woman is much more serious. It guarantees so much more for the investment. For it is from other women that women are nurtured. It is from other women that they hear what they hope to hear from men. *I understand. I know how you feel. I'm sorry for your pain. I care about what you think:* Words that need no prompting. In that circle, women tell each other the things that men and women tell each other first with their hands and lips and tongues before they can tell each other with words. Women comfort each other with touch that is meant to heal, rather than to excite. The mysteries of love are less complex between women. The hidden passages are easier to negotiate. And the dangers do not seem as great as when the same journey is taken with a man. Around each dank and frightening corner, women hold out their hands to each other and form a human chain that is, quite simply, spiritually different. The lucky ones find men who (and it is a deep and well-kept secret between women) are more like women.

On this evening almost twenty years into a friendship, Gwen studied Jane's face as she popped a piece of cucumber from the salad into her mouth. Her lips were slightly thin, but she had learned how to compensate for this one minor flaw. She always outlined her lips with a darker shade of her lipstick color. It was the only makeup she used. Her skin was still good. She had started to have a rinse put in her hair last year but stopped after Gwen insisted on calling her Lucy. Jane's brown curls were tinged with gray now. It was still a flattering look, although Jane didn't know how much longer that would be true.

Jane was standing close to Gwen. The top of her head just barely reached Gwen's shoulder.

"You're too short," Gwen said.

"Thank you. I'll note that piece of information. I finished setting the table. Now I'll have some wine. Is it cold?"

"Chilled to perfection. Use the good glasses. I'll have some also."

Gwen had spent all of her Saturday morning preparing moussaka, Greek salad, and lemon poppyseed cake.

Jane poured the wine. "This was a good idea. I love a festive dinner. What are we celebrating?"

"Did you use that Mexican runner?"

"Yes. And I put the flowers on the table." Jane leaned against the counter. "Everything looks beautiful."

"Good," Gwen said. She broke up lettuce with her fingers. Her fingernails were painted candy-apple red. She had treated herself to a manicure earlier today. She liked to watch the water slide off the lacquered surface of her nails. She paused, momentarily transfixed. "Celebrating? Survival, I suppose."

Jane stood close to Gwen and patted her arm.

"Why didn't you call him?" Jane said. "You could have called him at the office."

"No. I never have. He'll call."

"What do you think happened? It's been days."

"I'm not sure." Gwen took the wineglass Jane held out to her. "I think he's in a lot of pain. People don't stay married for thirty-five years and just walk away. Especially if it hasn't all been awful. I mean, it isn't as if they hate each other. I'm sure they still love each other."

Jane looked away and fussed with a thread on her sweater.

"I know what you're thinking," Gwen said. "I never should have gotten involved with a married man. We've been through this a million times. I never asked him to leave Sandra."

"But you hoped he would. Admit it, Gwen. You wondered what would happen if he left her."

"Of course I wondered. I wonder about a lot of things. What if Theodore had never been unfaithful? What if there were no more wars? What if I had met Daniel instead of Theodore? What if I was short, like you? I wonder about lots of things. Don't you?"

"Don't change the subject. You always do that."

"I'm not changing the subject. Look, I didn't plan to fall in love with Daniel. I was alone for years. I dated. I slept with men. Good Lord, Jane. Don't you remember that teacher from the ESL department? After we had sex, he used to shake my hand. 'Thank you very much,' he'd say. 'It was a great pleasure to have inter-course with you.' It was like a Berlitz training course in human sexuality. So, please, let's not do this again. I wasn't looking for Daniel. I wasn't looking for anyone, and I certainly never believed in perfection."

"What about happiness?" Jane said.

Gwen wiped her hands on a dish towel and turned to face Jane.

"I don't think it's a valid requirement for having a good life," she said. "Don't you agree?"

Jane laughed.

"What else is there?" she said.

"Happiness is highly overrated," Gwen said. "I mean it."

"But you've been happy with Daniel."

"Actually, I'm not *unhappy* with Daniel. I consider that a tri-umph. Every other man I've ever known has made me unhappy. Do you understand?"

"Oh, I know a lot about unhappiness."

"I'll bet you do."

Jane carried the salad bowl to the table and poured herself another glass of wine.

"Not everyone wants the same things," Jane said. "I wanted security. A home. A family. I wanted a companion. Someone to share things with. And please, don't look so contemptuous."

"I don't mean to look contemptuous. I'm just always surprised."

"You don't know everything about my life with Arnold," Jane said. "We all have our secrets. I'm certain of that."

"You're right," Gwen said. "I'm certain of it, too."

Still, it was no secret to Gwen that certainty was not a guaran-tee of anything.

At seventeen, Gwen had been certain about everything. She was already in college and already in love. Theodore was her Ancient Civilizations professor. He taught to her even though there were twenty-five other students in the class. When he explained that the Egyptians had both a great belief in magic and a fear that the world might someday cease to exist, Gwen nodded. She believed in magic. The Egyptians developed rituals that would promise eternal survival. By preserving the body, they could be guaranteed an afterlife. *Guaranteed.* Theodore had said this as his eyes traveled the length of Gwen's body. She had been bold then. It was easy at seventeen. But she had almost stopped breathing when he said that the embalmers took the body to the Beautiful House. "There," Theodore had explained, "they made an incision in the left side of the body and removed the liver and lungs." Gwen had clutched her side. And when he explained the ritual of opening the mouth, she had wondered what it would be like to taste the inside of his. "One of the most important rituals of all was the opening of the mouth," Theodore had explained. "It made it possible for the mummy to eat, drink, and move around. They had special utensils for this purpose. There were vases and cups for holding and pouring the sacred liquids. There was even a separate instrument for touching the mouth of the mummy. They burned incense and recited spells during this most important funerary rite." Then he had smiled at Gwen.

He had seduced her with the single most romantic act Gwen had ever imagined. First, he had asked her to a movie. Her parents had objected. He was, after all, older. But he had charmed them. Assured them he would not hurt their daughter. Promised to be good to her. That evening as she called her parents from a phone booth, Theodore had kneeled in front of her and removed her shoe. It had neither straps nor buckles and slipped off easily. He kissed her bare foot so gently that she had cried. That had been the day she had been certain her life would be different from everyone else's. When she thought of that day now, she was moved. But she wasn't sorry. She knew that those isolated moments were worth having experienced. She believed that it was all important. The mistakes. The pain. The memory of the perfection she had believed in as she had touched Theodore's hair while he kissed the heel of her foot. She could still remember hearing her mother's voice coming from a great distance. It was a freeze-frame. The couples walking arm in arm as they left the theater. The smell of popcorn. And the feel of Theodore's lips on her foot was still so vivid that her skin tingled when she thought about it now.

Gwen had secrets of her own she had yet to tell Jane. Gwen had never even told her about the cookbooks. A week after she started seeing Daniel, she had told him. He had not laughed, although she had been afraid he would. It was so silly really. But he had not laughed. She had told Daniel because she had wanted to give him something that she had never given anyone else. She told him because he had seemed so sad that day. And she had understood. He told her that he had overheard a conversation between two elderly women in the elevator on his way up to her apartment. One woman said that her son had drowned last summer, and that both the dog and the cat had needed to be put to sleep. How terrible, the other woman said. We had to put our Bootsie to sleep too. It's such a hard thing to do. Daniel couldn't stop laughing as he told the story. He said it was really awful, but he couldn't help himself. And it made him so sad. The missed communication. The parallel conversations. And that was when they had fallen in love. For although he was already familiar with the soft flesh that was evidence of her two pregnancies, and she had traced the birthmark on his back with her fingertip, this was the first act of their covenant. She told him, and not Jane, about the cookbooks because some secrets were more easily first whispered in the dark.

"Coffee or tea?" Gwen said.

"Coffee, please."

Neither of them moved.

"Tell me about Arnold," Gwen said. "What are you going to do?"

"I think I'm going to do nothing for a while," Jane said.

"That's a big decision for you. I'm impressed." Gwen smiled. "And what about Caroline? She'll have to be told."

"I'll take a ride up to New Paltz next week."

"Alone?"

"Is there any other way?" Jane said.

Gwen shook her head.

"Very dramatic," she said. "I can go with you." She gathered some plates and motioned for Jane to leave everything.

"Thanks. I'll let you know."

"I just want to put up some coffee," Gwen said. "Leave everything."

"Did I tell you that I called Ellie?" Jane said.

"What on earth for?"

"Confirmation, I guess. You know, shared history and all that. I wanted to tell her my sad tale."

"And?" Gwen sat back down, dirty plates close to her chest, and waited for an explanation.

"I should've suffocated her when I had the chance," Jane said.

"There's still time, you know," Gwen said. "I'd be happy to help."

"Thank you."

Gwen stood again. This time, Jane ignored her and collected the silverware and glasses to take to the kitchen. Gwen was rinsing plates and stacking them. Jane came up next to her. They stood quietly for a moment.

"I miss Daniel," Gwen said. "I don't want you to think I'm so casual about it all. I miss him."

"Did you think you wouldn't?" Jane said.

"No. I didn't think I wouldn't miss him."

"I miss Arnold," Jane said. "And it terrifies me. Am I so afraid to be alone? Is safety so important to me?"

There it was. An offering. Something Jane would have had a difficult time admitting to anyone else. Now it was Gwen's turn.

"I used to imagine that I lived a hundred years ago. I had this whole fantasy life. Good daughter. Good wife. Good mother. Good *everything*. I did what I was supposed to do, and I asked no questions. It was always a relief to put myself there. It always felt so safe," Gwen said.

"When did you leave?"

Here they were again. The place they had been together so many times in the past. But now they were in a different part of the labyrinth, one requiring a new crossing.

"When it was time," Gwen said. "When I knew that being safe wasn't the most important thing in the world."

"Is there a message in there, my friend?" Jane said. "I hear prophecy coming."

"No." Gwen shook her head. "No prophecy."

Now the sourdough starter was ready to be used. When they went into the kitchen, they would find the mixture bubbling. Neither of them would consider this a coincidence. Gwen would rinse another glass jar and portion off some of the starter for Jane. Before the evening was over, Gwen would know that Jane had finally asked Arnold for a divorce. And Jane would know that during the hours in which all dreams seem real, Gwen was reading cookbooks again.

Chapter Five

Jane believed that everyone was attached by invisible pieces of string to a main spool of collective memory. A mass that represented the first conscious recall of everyone on the planet. She felt certain that everyone wandered through life looking for other willing spirits. Then they could be bound to each other the way she had once seen nursery-school children secured on a class trip. Rope had been pulled through the sleeves of their jackets to keep them from getting lost. Jane wanted to believe that when they moved they were forced to be aware of each other, comforted by the closeness of other bodies, and grateful not to be alone.

Jane did not like to be alone. She never had. Now she saw with alarming clarity what she had avoided facing since she first began collecting memories. Now she had to face the loneliness she sensed her parents had shared. Herself as a wife and a mother. And the nursery-school children who had to be restrained with a rope to keep them together. If she had really been able to separate all those moments, she would have seen herself surrounded by people as they moved through her life. And she would have seen that, after all, she had really always been alone.

Arnold seemed nervous when she opened the front door, but then so was she. Although it had only been a week, Arnold looked distraught. He hadn't shaved, and his disheveled appearance was so obvious she suspected it might be staged.

"Janie," he said. "I'm glad to see you."

"Come in, Arnold. You look awful."

"I've missed you," he said.

She allowed him to hug her, but then turned away and tried to ignore that the spot where he touched her felt like freezer burn—cold and hot at the same time.

"Janie. C'mon. I don't want it to be like this." He let go of her elbow and began to massage her shoulders. "Say you forgive me. Please."

Suddenly, she no longer wanted to talk. It was enough to lean back against his body. Her head fit neatly under his chin. He rested his cheek on her hair. They stood that way for a moment. But it was time enough for Jane to know what she would have wished to happen. Arnold would have told her that he was sorry for the pain he caused her. He had been a fool. And he was sorry. Truly sorry. He just wanted a chance to make it up to her. He loved her. She was so important to him.

But there was no time now. Arnold was impatient. She could feel him pressing into her. And it really did not matter anyway. She moved against him. Nothing would change, so she might as well satisfy herself.

"Ah," he said. "You do forgive me."

She did not say anything. She could not speak. It was so sad really. Then she pulled off her T-shirt and turned around. He thought everything was going to be all right. He did not understand that this was about something else. And she was wrong not to tell him. But she was lonely. She should tell him. And she would. Afterward.

She had not planned on screaming, but it was as if she were suffocating. Literally. It was as if she were being buried alive. So she screamed. Poor Arnold. It was almost the end of him.

"Jane! What is it? Did I hurt you?"

It had been a short scream, but it had been loud and piercing. And now she didn't know how to answer the question. *Yes.* He had hurt her. *Yes.* She was in pain. *Yes.* He was responsible for some of it. But she knew it wasn't what he was asking and shook her head.

"No," she said. She was surprised at how calm she sounded. "You didn't hurt me."

He ran his fingers through his hair and sat up.

"What the hell was that all about?" he said.

"I couldn't breathe."

"Why didn't you just tell me to stop?"

"It wasn't physical," she said.

"Then what the hell was it?" He took a deep breath. "All right. I'm calm. I'm willing to talk."

Jane waited.

"Go ahead," he said. "I'm waiting."

"So am I."

"For what?"

"You said you wanted to talk."

He was genuinely perplexed, scared really.

"What do you think?" she said. "What do you think happened?"

Arnold looked even more scared.

"What do I think?" he said. "What do I think? What do I think
about what?"

"About anything. What do you think about anything?"

He stood to pull up his shorts and bent over to pick up his
trousers from the floor.

"I think you're crazy. I think you need help, Jane. I think you
should see someone. And I think I'm going to leave," he said.

"You can't leave," she said. "I'm not done."

Decisively, she moved over to him and straddled his lap. With
one hand she pulled at his shorts and then raised herself slightly
so that he had to do nothing more but help them both keep
their balance. She squeezed her eyes shut. She did not want to
see him. She wished she knew of some other way to hold him
there, but there was no other way. There never had been. In the
final moments before nothing else mattered but the synchronization of their movements, she recalled the story one of the teachers
had told at work that morning. He was new to the staff. And he
was very young, in his twenties, most likely. A sweet young man
from Nebraska or Iowa or some such place. He told everyone that
he and his friends used to amuse themselves on a summer afternoon by cow tipping. The boys would wait until the cows were
asleep, jump the fence, and then tip over an unsuspecting cow.
The animal would cry as it struggled to get up off the ground.
But the boys, indifferent to the animal's plight, would run across

the field and over the fence. They knew that if no one discovered the cow, it would stay in that one spot and die. It simply could not right itself alone. But the boys didn't care, and neither did Jane. For now, she raced with the boys in her mind, shutting out the plaintive cries of the helpless animal and hurrying to get over the fence.

"What was that all about, Jane?" Arnold said.

She lay in his arms, wondering the same thing herself.

"I don't know," she said.

"Should I leave?" he said.

But he made no move to get up.

"It's late," she said.

"We didn't talk. We need to talk."

"Yes. We need to talk."

"Janie, do you remember the dance lessons?"

For their tenth wedding anniversary, she had bought them dance lessons. He had been surprisingly cooperative. Even excited. The dance instructors, Marilyn and Sal, were aged ballroom dance partners who seemed unlikely to exist without the other. At the beginning of each lesson, they would demonstrate the moves for Jane and Arnold. "Practice," Marilyn cautioned them at the end of each lesson. "You must practice." But they didn't. The best part of the lesson was watching Marilyn and Sal glide across the dance floor in perfect accord. The dance lessons became another failure. After several lessons, Jane and Arnold simply stopped going and never spoke of it again.

"We should've practiced," Arnold said.

"Practiced?" she said. "I don't understand."

"Dancing. We should've practiced dancing. I was wrong."

She didn't think she would be able to speak, but she swallowed hard and said, "Maybe our timing was off." She smiled. "You always said that timing was everything in life."

"I was wrong about that too," he said.

She moved away from him and searched for her clothes.

"I'll get dressed and walk you out," she said.

Arnold looked surprised, but she knew if she waited another moment she would tell him not to go. And she couldn't do that. If she did, she would remember all the times when Caroline was a baby and he had said, "Isn't it amazing how wherever we go, Caroline is the most beautiful?" Those were the moments when Jane had thought it was possible to love Arnold.

"Well, then," he said. "I guess I should get dressed also."

She dressed quickly and hurried downstairs. Arnold found her out on the porch with her arms folded across her chest.

"I always liked this porch," he said. "Growing up in the city, it always seemed like such a luxury to have a porch."

"A moon-watching platform," Jane said. "That's what the Japanese call a porch."

Arnold looked puzzled.

"It's all right," she said, touching his arm. "I didn't understand right away either."

"Understand what?" Arnold said.

"Nothing. Never mind."

"We need to talk. We were supposed to talk."

"We just did," Jane said.

Arnold looked puzzled again. Male patois. Gwen was right.

"I'll call you," Jane said.

"It's getting expensive staying in a hotel," Arnold said.

"Yes," Jane said. "I'm sure it is. You'll have to start looking for a place."

"Just like that?" he said.

"Just like that."

"It was just that once, Jane. I haven't seen her since."

"It's not the girl."

"Then what? Tell me what it is," Arnold said. "I make one mistake, and our marriage is over?"

Jane was momentarily too stunned to answer. Arnold looked so pained, so sincerely distraught over her callousness, that she could do nothing more for him than sustain his illusion. He would simply never understand.

"Yes," she said. "I'm afraid so."

She watched as he started the car and pulled away from the curb. He waved. When she was sure he could no longer see her, she waved back. Caroline used to love to wave at people in other cars, excited if someone returned the offering. Now Jane realized it was just another attempt to hang on to the rope that kept them all together. If it had been possible, she would have liked to pull the string taut around the people she loved and never let go. Instead, she stopped waving and put her hand down by her side.

Chapter Six

When asked if she believed in God, Gwen automatically said, "Yes, of course." But the Hindu belief that when the body died the Self did not die challenged her childhood memories of airless Sunday mornings spent on a hard wooden pew in the Methodist church her family had attended. *Get down on your knees and thank God you're on your feet.* Those were the Reverend Mr. Allsworth's favorite words. Death did not concern her then. It was not as if she feared death now. Nor did she find any special appeal in the notion of immortality. *The Supreme Self is hidden within the heart, and one who knows the Self puts death to death.* But karma made her believe in what she could not see. The simplicity of the notion that actions produced reactions was reassuring. And karma was always, always either good or bad. Good karma promised good results both in this life and the next. And while it was this life that mostly concerned Gwen, she was still troubled. Each soul was karmically conditioned to choose rebirth. Yet, when one could finally see with a spiritual eye, reincarnation was no longer a necessity. Those who became self-realized in life would not be reborn at all. They would be absorbed into the Brahma and find ultimate liberation from birth and death. But it worried Gwen. What if she was reborn again and again because she could not find what was in her heart? As the days passed without Daniel, it was clear to her that she might never be absorbed into the Brahma. Her spiritual eye seemed unable to see.

Gwen hated to come home to a dark apartment. As she turned the key, she tilted her head toward the cylinder and listened. Something felt different. A shift in her karmic sphere. A reaction to her actions. She closed her eyes and leaned against the door. Perhaps her apartment was no longer there. Perhaps she had found an opening to another world. She turned the key all the way and pushed open the door. There was only darkness in its disappointing blackness. For the first time all week, she felt defeated. She wondered what she had done in a previous life that made it necessary to find herself alone, in the dark, longing to alter her spiritual sphere.

Gwen had often found herself surprised at the shape a story took in the aftermath of a catastrophe. In the telling of the tale, it always seemed important to include what one had been doing in the seconds before the impact. The seconds before the room was engulfed in flames. The final moments before the gunshots broke the silence. The details might change with many retellings, but the way Daniel looked the night he came back and what he said would always be the same. He was waiting in her living room, silhouetted now by the light from the partially closed front door. He was wearing his suede jacket and the wool cap she had bought for him last winter. He had not shaved, and there was a scraggly beard taking shape. In the semidarkness, Gwen could only feel his weariness. It was vaporous, and she moved slowly through its thickness. Of course, there was nothing there. Yet, Daniel squinted as if he could not clearly see her. He held out a square of white paper, and she took it from him. It was one of those flyers handed out on the busy intersections of mid-Manhattan streets.

READINGS BY MRS. SABRINA
(Special on all types of readings)
You will not feel the Problems
of the World, or the Hurt of your Loved Ones,
After Just One Visit. For further information and appointment,
call (212) 888–6276.

"Did you call?" Gwen said.

"No," Daniel said. "I didn't call."

She wanted to tell him how angry she was that he had not phoned. How worried she had been. The unmentionable things that had crossed her mind. The horrible possibilities. But instead the day she and Theodore had taken the children to the street fair in Little Italy presented itself with fresh sharpness. Ethan had been asleep in the stroller. Matt was already walking. The streets had been dense with people. The sounds and the smells were overwhelming. One minute she had been holding Matt's hand, and then suddenly he was gone. The feeling still woke her at night.

The same chill of terror still gripped her when she thought of that moment.

We were walking. I was pushing the stroller with one hand and hold-ing Matt with my other hand. He was desperate to get an ice cream. "Hold on," I told him. "It'll be a moment. Daddy went to get it for you." And then he was gone. All that remained was the stickiness of where his hand had been.

She had told the story a thousand times. From the moments before to the moment after. Theodore had raged against her. She had been hysterical. A police officer had emerged through the crowd holding a tearful Matt by the arm. At first, Gwen had wanted to strike the little boy, whose face was streaked with tears and dirt. She had wanted to slap his face and shake him until he swore he would never, never again cause her such pain. But it would have been a foolish promise to ask him to make. One that could never have been kept.

It would still have been a foolish promise to ask of anyone. So she didn't ask Daniel anything. She allowed herself to be pulled into the circle of his warmth. It felt as if much more time had passed than actually had. Just as the minutes until Matt had been found had seemed like hours.

Daniel looked older than he had a week before. His hair seemed longer, and he appeared to be exhausted.

"You need a haircut," she said.

"Do it for me."

She led him to the kitchen and draped a bath towel across his chest, carefully tucking the ends of the towel into his shirt. She took a sip of tea and then began her work. First she snipped. Then she combed. Then she snipped again. They did not speak.

"Lean forward," she said.

He obeyed. She combed his hair straight and made a few final snips. Grooming. Like monkeys. She had always loved the way they groomed each other. Picking out bits of leaves and insects. Groping through each other's fur for what only another monkey could find. Stroking and fixing until each was satisfied with its work. And now she understood why. She undid the towel at the back of Daniel's neck and brushed at the stray hairs with her hand.

"Should I trim your mustache?" she said.

It was coarse and uneven, though not terribly long.

"Please," Daniel said.

She moved around to the front and touched his mustache with the tip of her finger. She could feel his breath on her skin. She cupped his chin in her hand and smiled. He did not smile back. She bent forward to trim the scraggly hairs along his lip and kept cutting as he reached over to undo the buttons on her blouse. She stopped cutting when his hands began to knead her flesh the way she had been taught to pinch the dough closed on the pastries they learned to make in her home economics class. Crimping, the teacher had called it. Gwen wondered what she'd think of her now. Half-naked and no hairnet. Daniel touched her everywhere. She pressed her hand over his as his fingers slid inside her and held them there, moved him first fast and then slow. "Gwen," he said, but she shook her head no. Not yet. With his free hand, he opened his trousers and drew her against him. "Like this?" she said. "Here?" But she did not wait for his answer. He pressed his face into her neck, and she held him there. There were no burrs to remove from her hair. No gnats to pick at. They touched and squeezed and crimped until they were properly groomed, and until both were satisfied.

"I didn't mean to worry you," Daniel said. "I'm so sorry."

"It doesn't matter," she said.

"Did you get my message?"

"I did."

"Sandy agreed to a divorce."

Gwen felt the change in his mood. The imperceptible shift that accelerated his heartbeat. He wanted something from her.

"I told her about you," he said. "I had to. I'm sorry."

"Don't be sorry. She would have found out sooner or later."

"I guess," Daniel said. "But she was shocked."

"It's been more than a year since I last ran into her."

"You never told me."

"There was nothing to tell," Gwen said. "We talked for all of five minutes. She told me I looked well and teased me about having a new romance."

"I wonder if she remembers that," Daniel said.

"Of course she remembers it. She probably remembers every word of our conversation, what I was wearing, the clues she overlooked."

"How do you know?"

"Because I know."

"This isn't your fault," Daniel said.

"Whose fault is it?" Gwen said. "I'm not sure. I went to a party, and I met another woman's husband. I flirted with him. I participated in the seduction. I let him come to my home and make love to me in my son's bedroom. I didn't ask you to leave."

"You didn't ask me to stay."

She pressed her palms flat against his chest and waited.

"I spoke to an attorney," Daniel said. "He recommended we see a mediator. Then I drove up to Ithaca to see Rosie and spent a few days with her. She was upset, but not surprised. She told me Sandy had known almost from the beginning that I was involved with someone. All this time, she knew and never said anything to me. That made me very sad."

Early in their relationship, Gwen had promised herself to ask him for nothing. What she suspected Daniel did not know was that those terms were more for her than for him. She liked their arrangement. And although Sandra and the children concerned her, Gwen had confidence in the laws of causation. Still, it was all terribly fragile. The rules. The feelings. The circumstances. And it was all about to change.

"I'm waiting for you to ask me to move in with you," Daniel said.

Several weeks after they had started seeing each other, Daniel had written her a letter. "I can't go through with this," he wrote. "It's wrong. I don't want to hurt you. I don't want to hurt Sandy or the children." She had read the two pages of his careful script, then replaced the letter in the envelope and hidden it away. If he hadn't called to say he'd changed his mind, she never would have called him.

Now her own heart beat faster, and she was frightened. She did not want to be released from the cycle of birth and death. The Brahma held no appeal for her without Daniel.

Chapter Seven

Caroline was two weeks late when Jane felt the first pangs of labor. She had known that Caroline would not make her entrance into the world easily. Jane had sat for long periods of time with her hands pressed against her swollen belly as if it were a crystal ball. She felt as if she already knew Caroline. When the doctor placed the bloody infant on her chest and she saw the apology in Caroline's eyes, Jane whispered, "It's all right. We don't have to talk about it now." And when the nurse tried to take Caroline, Jane said no. The baby yawned, and Jane was helpless with passion and understood everything. It was the first time she had ever been truly in love.

Unlike most other love affairs, this one was enduring. Caroline was a careful child. Jane often likened her daughter to the manatees they had observed on a visit to a wildlife park in Florida when she was thirteen. Caroline had insisted on taking a half-day course of instruction that would allow her to swim with the manatees. Arnold had been against it. He was afraid of animals and did not care much for nature. But Jane saw Caroline's expression when the instructor, Rick, told them, "You should never force an encounter with the manatees. Just be happy to be in the water with them." A spark of recognition crossed Caroline's face, and Jane convinced Arnold that the experience would be "educationally worthwhile." She watched as Caroline was given snorkeling gear. "Scuba gear is too risky," Rick said. "The manatees are very gentle. Even the sound of bubbles can scare them. Just make visual contact when you see one approach. Remember to float in place and let him come to you. If a manatee wants to play, he may nuzzle you or tug on your suit, or even roll on his back. It's a magical experience to be asked to play by these animals. It's not every day that an animal who is more than ten feet long and weighs more than a ton is so friendly." Jane tried not to think about those dimensions as she watched Caroline go underwater.

Of course, the first manatee to approach the divers went directly to Caroline. When Caroline emerged from the water she was so excited she could barely catch her breath. "I was scared at first," she said. "It was huge. He sort of pointed to his belly and asked me to scratch him. I didn't move. You know what he did then? He used his flipper to guide my hand to the exact spot he wanted scratched, and then he held it there until he got what he wanted." *Just like you,* Jane had thought. And just like the manatee, Caroline approached her mother, held her gaze, and then rubbed against her. Cautiously, gently, Jane waited for Caroline to give her the signal that it was all right to embrace her. "Thank you," Caroline whispered against her mother's skin. And her mother was happy just to be with her.

"What a surprise," Caroline said. "Is Daddy with you?"

"No, honey. He couldn't get away. I just felt like seeing you." Jane pressed her finger against her free ear to drown out the noise from the garage where she had stopped to phone Caroline. "I hope I'm not interrupting anything. I thought we'd have dinner. I'll drive back tonight."

"You hate driving at night."

"I'll be fine. May I come over?"

"Of course. Please. Do you remember how to get here?"

Jane was relieved that Caroline sounded pleased to hear from her. It had been an impulse. She had left work early on the excuse that she had a dental appointment. The children had a special assembly and another teacher was able to cover for that hour. The ride to New Paltz took a little over two hours. She stopped once for a cup of coffee that was surprisingly good and bought a pack of peppermint Life Savers from a vending machine. She also bought some Mexican jumping beans, a folding comb, and a plastic rain bonnet for Caroline.

"I think so. Go straight down Main, turn left after the Mobil station, and go three blocks in. It's the fifth house on the right."

"Perfect. I'll put up some water."

"See you in a few minutes."

Arnold had been against Caroline's wish to live off campus even though it was permitted in sophomore year. But Jane had supported Caroline. "She needs privacy. It's hard to have privacy in a dorm," Jane argued. He had finally conceded. They had driven up to approve the top-floor apartment in a Victorian house that rented to university students. The owner lived in a new development on the other side of town. Arnold mumbled about peeling paint and water damage, but Caroline was determined. Finally, Arnold wrote out a check for two months' security and the first month's rent. "Thank you, thank you, thank you," Caroline said as she twirled her father around. "Careful," he said. "The floor's likely to give way."

A produce stand caught Jane's eye. She stopped and bought some apples and three ears of dried corn. She added a small jar of honey and a loaf of homemade oat bread to her pile. At the last minute, she pointed to an apple pie that looked too good to pass up. She would add her gifts from the vending machine to these offerings.

It was already dark when Jane pulled into the driveway. She gathered together everything she had bought and closed the car door with the tip of her boot.

"Mom!"

It was very cold, even for November, but Caroline was barefoot and coatless. Jane forced herself not to say "You'll catch your death wearing that skimpy blouse and nothing on your feet." Instead, she smiled, placed everything on the hood of her car, and thought of the manatees and that long-ago summer. Caroline looked directly into her mother's eyes to be certain there was no admonition there. When she was satisfied, she entered Jane's open arms and returned her kiss.

"You look very well," Jane said. "What did you do to your hair? Turn around. I love it."

Caroline's hair was longer than usual. Her dark curls were held back with a wide band of blue spandex that made her look as she had in her fifth-grade class picture—innocent and hopeful.

"Let's go upstairs. I have a pot of tea ready."

"Sounds wonderful. I picked up some things at a stand down the road. You can freeze what you don't want to use right away."

They divided the packages and climbed the steep stairs to the top floor.

"Ta da!" Caroline said. "What do you think?"

"Well," Jane said. "It's spectacular."

It was true. Caroline had transformed the once bare and peeling walls. They were covered with hats. All kinds of hats—straw hats, hats with veils, bonnets. There was even a derby and a worn-looking top hat. Beneath each hat, Caroline had drawn a face. Each face was perfectly suited to the corresponding hat. But it was the ceiling that Jane could not stop looking at. There were large brown paper gingerbread people tacked all over the ceiling. Their faces were versions of the same faces on the walls, but either younger or older looking. It was eerie. Almost like a gallery of some whimsical ancestral heritage.

"When did you manage to do all this?" Jane said.

"You really like it?" Caroline said.

"I really like it."

And she did. *This is my daughter. This is my child.* Jane looked with wonder at this young woman who dared to do such things. Her body moved beneath the folds of the gauze skirt with assurance, in a way that made Jane lower her eyes. What she saw was too intimate.

Caroline laughed and pointed to the floor. She had painted feet everywhere. Some were bare, but some wore wildly patterned socks. Some feet had painted toenails and others were coarse and peasantlike. The effect was extraordinary.

"Won't the landlord have a cow?" Jane asked.

"I asked her first. She said I'd have to 'return it to its original state' before I moved out, but after she saw what I did she loved it!"

"I don't blame her."

"Come sit," Caroline said. "You look tired." She ushered Jane into a chair and poured the tea. "I'm glad to see you."

Jane placed her hand on top of Caroline's and squeezed.

"Mom?" Caroline said. "Are you all right? You sounded funny the last few times we talked. And when Daddy called the other night, you weren't around."

Jane patted her hand. "Oh, I'm just fine. Sit down with me. Where can we have dinner?" She poured herself a cup of the fragrant tea. "Hmm. It smells lovely."

"It's vanilla." Caroline sat down. "You don't look fine. You look tired. Is everything all right? Is Daddy sick? Are you all right?"

"No, sweetie. Daddy is fine. I just had this great desire to see you." She smiled and touched Caroline's cheek with the back of her hand. "You look fantastic. Really."

Caroline blushed and lowered her eyes. *And she likes it too,* Jane thought. *Whoever it is, he pleases her.* Jane was glad for her daughter.

"I brought you some things," Jane said. She picked her purse up off the floor and rummaged around until she found what she was searching for. "Here!"

Caroline took the rain bonnet, the folding comb, and the plastic box with the jumping beans and laughed.

"How did you know?" she said. "Exactly what I needed, especially the jumping beans."

She opened the plastic box and emptied the three decorated

beans into her palm. As she slowly tilted her hand, the beans moved as if they were a trio of weary acrobats. But Caroline was determined. First she tilted her hand this way. And then the other way. Each time she changed direction her head moved in synchronization. Jane watched in fascination. Caroline would persist until the beans performed.

"Tell me about him," Jane said.

The beans tumbled onto the table.

"Who?" Caroline said.

"Him. The one who's making you look so smug."

Caroline's lips parted slightly as if just the thought of him was seductive enough. She rolled the beans beneath her palm and took a sip of tea. When she turned to look at Jane her face was flushed with excitement and pleasure.

"He's wonderful," Caroline said. "He's a junior. An art major. Like me. He's from Arizona. He's the oldest of four children. He's smart and beautiful. And I love him."

"When do I get to meet him?" Jane said.

Caroline remained standing. She moved to the back of her chair and gripped the top with both hands.

"He should be home soon. Raymond has a class, and then he'll be home."

"Home?" Jane said. Her mouth felt strangely dry. She took a sip of tea. "He lives here then. With you. Just the two of you."

"Yes. He lives here. I was going to tell you, but I wanted you to meet him first. I was planning to bring him home for a weekend. I thought after you met him, you'd understand. Are you very angry?"

It was odd to Jane that her response mattered to Caroline. And then it occurred to her that this was about choice. Caroline had chosen Raymond, and now she wanted approval and acceptance. If Jane withheld those things from Caroline, she would not leave Raymond. Jane had to trust that Caroline had chosen well. That she had pulled into her circle someone who listened to what she could not say. Part of Jane (the part that really feared the courage she always hoped for Caroline to have) felt the urge to punish Caroline for leaving. But Jane knew it was her turn to dive underwater and to make her approach. Her turn to remember the warnings. She stood and drew Caroline to her. Slowly. Carefully. She did not want her to bolt. This woman who was still her child really wanted what Jane wanted, but they both knew it was no longer possible. No longer necessary. Caroline now told her secrets to a stranger.

"I love you," Jane said.

"I love you too," Caroline said.

Jane kept holding her, floating in place. And when Caroline was ready to be released, Jane let her go.

Jane heard him before she saw him. His voice traveled up the stairs. "Carrie! Carrie!" he shouted with such anticipation that Jane felt her own heart quicken.

His shiny black hair, high cheekbones, and coloring suggested an unfamiliar heritage. He was tall and elegantly built. Broad-shouldered and narrow in the hip. If he was surprised to see Jane, he didn't let on. He was already reaching for Caroline when he appeared on the landing. His hand was in midair and his upper body thrust forward in readiness for her. And she didn't disappoint. Although he paused when he saw Jane, Caroline did not halt her motion. With one joyful movement, she was near him.

Jane watched this girl, this woman, this once-upon-a-time baby of hers, press herself against this stranger with impatient force. And when he allowed it, even shielded Caroline with his arm from whatever he thought might be hurtful, Jane found the words that were needed.

"Raymond," she said. She held out her hand. "I'm Jane Hoffman, Caroline's mother. I sort of took Caroline by surprise." She smiled. "I'm very glad to meet you."

"Thank you," Raymond said. "I'm very glad to meet you."

He was shy. Jane could see that right away. But he did not look away from her gaze. He leaned into it, without threat, but rather with a need to overcome his own discomfort. Caroline put her hand in the one he had rested on her shoulder. Jane saw the ease with which their fingers laced, folding into each other as if in prayer. Caroline pressed her head lightly against Raymond's chest, and he relaxed.

"I was hoping to take Caroline out for dinner before I started back. Will you join us?" Jane said.

"Oh, don't drive back tonight. Stay," Caroline said. "Please. It's already late. You can leave first thing in the morning." She pointed to a couch in the living room. "It opens into a bed."

"I have to go to work tomorrow. I didn't bring a change of clothes."

"You can take something from me. Please stay." Caroline tilted her head up to look at Raymond. "You don't mind, do you?"

Jane watched the way he looked at Caroline. It seemed he would do anything for her. Say yes to anything.

"You don't leave him much choice," Jane said. She laughed. "I think I'll leave after dinner."

"No, please," Raymond said. "I can stay with a friend tonight."

Jane did not miss the grace with which he made the offer. She knew he was embarrassed. She also knew Caroline was ready to object, but Raymond lightly pressed her shoulder and she kept silent. Jane found their exchanges remarkable and touching. She had forgotten what it was like to be in love.

"That won't be necessary, Raymond, but thank you for the offer. I'll be happy to spend the night. I'm sure I'll be very comfortable on the couch."

Caroline squeezed his hand. Jane heard what it said. *I told you it would be all right. I told you it wouldn't matter. She just wants me to be happy.* And then he squeezed back. Jane heard the response as well. *It seems all right, but we'll have to see.*

Jane picked her purse up from the floor.

"I think I'll just go freshen up," she said. "Why don't you think of a place we could have dinner. Someplace where we can talk."

Caroline nodded. She had already turned away from Jane's voice. As she watched from the doorway, Jane saw her daughter fold herself into Raymond's arms as if she were a letter of great importance being tucked inside an envelope.

"Caroline tells me you're from the Southwest," Jane said.

"Yes," Raymond said.

Jane watched Caroline as she sketched on the tablecloth. Each table had a white paper tablecloth and a container of crayons. It was a clever gimmick.

"And you're an art major as well," Jane said. "What are you interested in?"

"Everything, really. My mother is a sculptor, so I've had a lot of exposure to that form. I'd like to try designing jewelry."

"Raymond's mom, Lily, was here last week. She had some business in New York, so she drove up to see us. By the way, she says they'll pay half the rent of the apartment. You'll like her."

"Oh," Jane said.

So there had already been a visit from Raymond's mother. She had already met Caroline. They had spent time together. Talked about art. Jane felt oddly connected to this unknown woman. She had also needed to make a choice. Jane envied the time that had lapsed for Lily. She had passed where Jane was now.

"I understand you come from a large family."

"Yes. I'm the oldest," he said. "I'm twenty-one. I have three sisters. My father is an executive with IBM. My mother is part Hopi and part Zuni. She taught me to keep a good heart, to have pure thoughts, and to avoid fights."

"What did your father teach you?" Jane said.

"He taught me to fight back and to disregard what other people think."

"That's quite a legacy," Jane said. "I'm sorry I didn't get a chance to meet your mother."

"I'm sure you'll meet her," he said.

"Lily tried to put my hair into a squash blossom," Caroline said.

"A squash blossom?" Jane said.

"When a Hopi girl reaches maturity, she has to prove herself marriageable by grinding corn into meal over a period of four days. Then her hair is parted in the middle and woven over a U-shaped bow. Lily decided to skip the grinding-the-corn-into-meal bit and just do my hair, but it was too short."

"My mother says that hair is the seat of the soul and often linked to a person's spiritual identity and existence," Raymond said. He ran his hands through his own sumptuous mass. "My father would prefer that I get mine cut."

Jane thought Lily must have offered to do Caroline's hair as a way of letting her know she approved of Raymond's choice. It was a clever woman who could manage such a feat and be convincing as well. For Jane knew about offerings. They did not always say what was really in one's heart.

Jane decided to drive back that night. But she could not leave before she told Caroline what she had come to tell her. And now there was even more that needed to be said. As soon as Raymond retreated to the bedroom, Jane moved closer to Caroline on the couch and took her hands.

"He's a very interesting young man," Jane said. "And I'm very happy for you. Really and truly, but—"

"We're careful," Caroline said. "I promise."

"Always?"

"Always," Caroline said. "And there isn't anyone else...for either of us."

She looked so sure that it broke Jane's heart to think of what Caroline had not yet felt. There was no way to warn her. And there was no point either.

"I'm glad."

"What about Daddy?"

"He loves you. He'll be fine when he gets used to the idea. Don't forget, I was eighteen when I met your father."

"Did you ever sleep with anyone else?"

"No."

"I can't imagine ever wanting anyone but Raymond." She pulled one hand away and placed it over her heart. "I love him so, Mom. I just love him so."

"I know you do."

It was late. If she left now, she might be home a little after midnight. But she wasn't finished.

"Caroline, I need to talk to you about something. There's no easy way to say it, so I'll just come out with it. Your father and I have separated. We need some time apart. We both love you very much, and we'll always be your parents. I know the right way to do this would have been for us to tell you together, but, quite frankly, I wasn't prepared to drive up and . . . well, anyway . . . now you know."

Caroline. Jane had wanted to name her something more exotic. Something like Eugenia or Isadora. A name that would alert everyone to how unusual she was. Caroline suited her just fine, though. It had from the start.

"Where is he?"

"He's staying at a hotel right now fairly close to Hunter. But one of the professors is leaving, going back to England, I think. He's not from the math department, but he wants to sublet his place, and—"

"It doesn't matter."

"Caroline, please try to understand. This isn't about you—"

"But what about me?" she cried. "What about me?"

"What about you? This isn't about you, Caroline. I know how upset you must be. I'm upset too."

"But what happened? I don't understand. Something must've happened."

"Lots of things happened, honey. Your father and I need to be apart right now."

"Where can I reach him?"

"I'll give you the number. I don't remember the name of the hotel."

"I'll get it myself."

"Fine," she said. Jane saw no point in arguing the matter any further. "I think I'll be going. It's very late, and I have a long drive."

Caroline did not protest this time. She stood and endured Jane's embrace.

"I'll call you tomorrow. I love you," Jane said.

Caroline said nothing.

"We can talk about this some more if you'd like," Jane said.

"No thank you. Not tonight."

Jane hurried down the stairs and stood in the vestibule. She opened the front door and then closed it, but she did not leave. She stood silently in the dark, barely breathing, until she heard Caroline's sobs, Raymond's footsteps, and then finally his voice asking, "What is it, Carrie? What happened?"

Too exhausted to drive, she stopped at the first motel, signed the register, took the key the attendant handed her, and found the room. She locked the door, pulled off her boots, and lay down on top of the chenille spread. In the morning she would not even remember falling asleep.

Sometime during the night, she was awakened by a baby's cry. There was an odd tightness in her breasts that had once signaled the readiness for her milk to let down. Often her blouse had been stained from the rush of fluid that was a response to Caroline's cry. The baby's muffled cries grew more insistent, and then suddenly everything was completely still. Jane wondered if Caroline had woken in the night, still crying. But there was nothing Jane could do now to comfort her own child. She touched the front of her blouse. It was dry.

Chapter Eight

Shortly after he moved into Gwen's apartment, Daniel became a grandfather. It was the first week of December. After Sandra learned that Daniel was involved with Gwen, he had found all his clothes on the front lawn. Still, Sandra had been careful to cover everything with plastic trash bags. When Gwen heard this, she wondered how long it took women to stop being wives.

It was a Sunday morning when the phone rang. It had been snowing since dawn.

"I'll get it," Gwen said.

She tossed the magazine section on the floor and uncurled herself from the couch. Daniel was in the shower.

"Hello," she said. There was silence on the other end.

"Hello?"

She was about to hang up when Sandra spoke.

"This is Sandra Dolger," she said. "May I please speak to Daniel?"

Gwen nodded into the phone. She had rehearsed this moment untold times, but now the words she had planned to say floated above her and out of her reach.

"Hello?" Sandra said.

"Sandra," Gwen said. "It's Gwen. I'm so sorry about all this. I—"

"Is Daniel there? I don't want to talk to you. I have nothing to say to you. Please, Gwen. Let me speak to Daniel."

"I just want to tell you how sorry I am."

"I can't take much of this. Is Daniel there? Please. It's important."

"If you would only just—"

Sandra's voice was careful and dispassionate when she spoke.

"Tell him Kate had the baby. Everything is fine. It's a girl. She weighed eight pounds. Her name is Elena. Elena Sandra. Tell him."

Sandra hung up. Gwen slumped to the floor and clutched the phone to her chest. She didn't cry. She was too sad to cry. It was like being overtired. *Too tired to sleep.* It had always seemed so odd that one could really be too tired to sleep. *Too sad to cry.* When she turned to look out the window, she saw that it was still snowing. The forecast had predicted a blizzard.

Daniel was out of the shower. The radio was on in the bedroom. *My bedroom,* she thought. She had made room for him on one side of the dresser, but it was not enough. There were suitcases and books. Shoes sticking out from beneath the bed. *My bed.* She knew he was trying to be neat. There were still boxes in the hallway. She could see them from where she was sitting. *If you'd like to make a call, please hang up and dial again. If you'd like to make a call, please hang up and dial again.* The alarming sound that followed recalled the fetal monitor that had been attached to her during

Ethan's delivery. She had been terrified then. She was terrified now. If she lay down now, stretched herself out on the carpet, her carpet, she would be asleep instantly.

"Gwen? Are you all right?"

Daniel was wearing a pair of brown corduroy slacks, her favorite, and buttoning a faded denim shirt. From where she lay, she could see his bare feet. His feet on her floor. Something was wrong. She closed her eyes.

"Gwen, honey. What happened?"

He dropped to his knees and peered anxiously into her face. She could see him through her almost but not quite closed eyelids. It was the game she had played with the children. *Close your eyes. Don't peek.* The children always assured her in solemn unison, *They're closed, Mommy.* But she saw everything. When they asked how she could see through closed lids, she told them, *Mommy magic!* Together they would roll around on the bed and laugh. Now she saw Daniel, but pretended she didn't. He took her face in his hands. If she opened her eyes, he would see the sadness, then the pain. But it was her sadness. Her pain. And her eyes. She kept them closed.

"Tell me what happened," he said. "Who was that on the phone? Did something happen to Matt or Ethan? Tell me."

Gwen opened her eyes. She hung up the phone and stood. *Goliath. Gulliver.* There were so few women giants. *Amazon.* That's what the boys had called her in high school. *Hey there, you big Amazon!* They were too stupid to understand overstatement. She had swept by them with disdain.

"Kate had the baby. They're both fine. The baby's name is Elena Sandra. She weighed eight pounds."

"Who called? Robby?"

Robby was Kate's husband. Gwen shook her head.

"Sandra called."

She looked down at him. He was hugging his knees. His glasses sat on top of his head. Soon he would be cursing and searching for them. *Grandfather Daniel.* It would make a lovely title for a children's story. *Grandfather Daniel left his wife and his children to live with a great big blonde in a new kingdom. Even though he had lived with his other queen for thirty-five years, the new queen was younger. He did not have to fight with this queen about the children or who should write out the cards for the holidays. The big blonde just had to tell him how wonderful he was, and he always came back. She asked him no questions. She told him no lies. The End.*

But that was not the truth. It never had been. Her fingers moved through his hair like five swimmers just below the surface of the water. His hair seemed to ripple. She slid her hand back and forth. His skull felt fragile, as if his fontanel had not yet grown together. In certain light she had been able to see her children's fontanels pulsating with the beat of their hearts. She had been so afraid of what could happen to them. Now it was she who felt vulnerable and afraid for herself.

"I'm going to call," he said.

Her arms circled her legs. She felt his lips against her skin. She wasn't even dressed yet. The storm was in full gear. And it was snowing outside too. She smiled at her little joke, but said nothing to Daniel.

Gwen had to stand on a chair to reach the smoke alarm. She had baked a sourdough loaf for Daniel. The dough had been alive under her hands as she kneaded it on the marble board bought especially for this renewed interest. So lovingly had she sprinkled flour on the board the first time that she had embarrassed herself. With the heels of her hands, she pushed the dough away and then pulled it back. The process made her feel strong. The muscles in her arms felt firmer with each movement. When she was done kneading, she turned the dough into an oiled ceramic bowl and covered it with a clean dishcloth. Then she had to wait for the dough to rise.

The waiting made her feel both liberated and anxious at the same time. It was identical to how she had often felt when the children were small. The push and pull of the kneading brought her back to the sensations of need and loss she had experienced early in motherhood. She could not wait for Matt to fall asleep in the afternoon, but an hour later she missed him. Sometimes she would purposefully make noise to wake him or bend over into the crib to sniff at his skin. "You're crazy," Theodore said. "Make up your mind." *Make up your mind.* As if such a thing were possible. *Make up your mind. Make up the beds.* As simple as pulling the sheets over the mattress and tucking in the corners. *Oh, if only it were so simple,* she often thought. *Make up your mind.* Put all these feelings here, and all those feelings there. Respond appropriately. Do what is expected.

She couldn't. Never could. The wait for the dough to rise seemed too long until it was over. Then she couldn't wait to shape the loaves and set the timer on the oven. The kitchen would become a sanctuary. The aroma as mystical as the incense burned in the Buddhist temple she had frequented for a time. A haven. A place of shelter and safety.

But this morning she had burned the bread. By the time she smelled it burning, the smoke alarm was sounding. The kitchen filled with smoke, and she tried to salvage what she could of the bread, scraping the burned parts off with the edge of a knife.

Daniel came into the kitchen, opened the window, and waved his hands in front of his face. She saw that he was wearing his insulated boots. His shirt was tucked in, and he was holding a sweater. She picked up the burned pieces and dropped them into the garbage.

"I'm going out," he said.

She scraped crumbs from the counter into her cupped palm.

"I had to leave this number," he said. "I left it with Kate and Robby. I gave it to Rosie too. I guess none of them wanted to call. Sandy just wanted to let me know about the baby. That's why she called."

Gwen stopped what she was doing. Her mother used to scrape crumbs into her apron and then shake them out in the yard. Gwen did not have an apron or a yard. She clenched the crumbs in her closed fist.

"No one else wanted to call," he repeated. He sounded as if he couldn't believe it himself. "So Sandy called."

"Congratulations," she said.

Daniel looked startled.

"On being a grandfather. You must be very excited."

"I am."

"You should be."

"I'll be back in the evening," he said. He looked out the window. "I'll take the subway. It looks too awful to drive."

"That seems sensible."

He looked at her and then looked away quickly.

"I'm glad everything is all right," she said.

She waited until she heard the door close, and then she threw the crumbs up in the air. Perhaps she had taken too much from Daniel and not put back enough. Perhaps it was the other way around. *Ask me no questions, I'll tell you no lies.* She took the broom and the dustpan from the closet and began to sweep.

By four o'clock the city was immobilized. There were ten inches of snow, and it had just started to taper off. She hadn't heard from Daniel and didn't know why she had thought she would. Both Matt and Ethan called. Matt said that ten inches of snow was light for Vermont. Ethan told her he missed her. It hadn't started snowing yet in New Haven, but they were supposed to be in for it by tomorrow. She blew kisses at him through the phone. He laughed, but would not do it back. She did not tell either of them that Daniel had moved in. For the rest of the afternoon she walked around Daniel's boxes and talked to them. "I don't know what to do with you," she said. "I don't really have room for any of you." She moved them slightly. Edged them with her toe. "You'll just have to be patient." By six o'clock she knew Daniel had slept with Sandra. Two new grandparents. How else would they celebrate their well-earned status. It was difficult to let go. Hard to break old habits. She was not angry. She just wanted to get through it.

For a long time after Theodore left, he would send her clippings from the tabloids. *World Exclusive Photo of Heaven. Woman Sleeps in Metal Grave to Escape Noises in Her Head. Unborn Baby Is Found Growing in Woman's Foot. Fed Up Dad Replaces Family with Dummies.* These articles were never accompanied by a note. Somewhere in the margin, Theodore would scrawl his first initial. She found the pieces frightening, not for their content but for the motivation that went into sending them. She felt compelled to save them for the boys, as if the articles represented information they would later need to have about their father. They were too small when he left to really miss him. Every so often Matt would pick up something that had belonged to Theodore and say, "Da Da?" Gwen would reassure him with hugs and kisses and throw the stray sock or book into the box that held the clippings. She. didn't know why she saved the items. She never allowed herself to really think about it.

Theodore was conscientious enough about his child support payments and kept his visitations with the children until one day he called to say he was off to Turkey for six months. He had been offered an opportunity to accompany a group on an archaeological dig. He sent postcards and phoned, but it was hard to hear what he was saying over the crackling sound of their connection. He must have told her he was coming back to the States, but she was still surprised to come home one afternoon and find him leaning against the building. He kissed Matt and held Ethan, and Gwen wondered if there was a place one could go to trade used feelings. A chance to be freed from what had already been felt.

He never planned on staying. Knowing Theodore, there was a reason for his coming that probably had nothing to do with her or the children. They were probably just on the way to something else. And she did not want him to stay. She liked it better without him. But she was lonely. He did not ask to spend the night, nor did he leave after helping her get the boys to bed. As he pulled her sweater over her head, he told her that it was likely only three hundred languages had a really secure future. In her ear he whispered that three thousand of the six thousand languages spoken in the world were doomed because no children spoke them. He licked her neck and lamented that along with the disappearance of the languages, traditional knowledge would disappear as well. He had to stop what he was doing, so overcome was he by this information. As she took him in her mouth, he explained that the loss of language would also mean the loss of information about healing and coping with the world particular to each native group. She persisted until he could no longer formulate coherent sentences. It seemed ironic to her that he was so distressed over the loss of languages when he himself could not communicate. Still, she understood about loss.

He was gone when she woke in the morning. He left an article on the pillow with his usual *T* prominently written in the margin. The article said that in the forests of north Borneo there still lived a few hundred Penans who held on to their nomadic ways. They were considered primitive by government officials. Penan souls were of much concern to the missionaries who sought to save them. Before their conversion to Christianity, they had practiced their animist beliefs from communal bases. Now, most of them extolled the practical benefits afforded by their new religion. Life was simpler. They no longer had to worry about the many taboos that had governed their existence. One old hunter said that everything had been a problem before progress reached them. Now there were no longer any taboos on women eating leopard, monkey, sun bear, and python. Medicines that involved spells were no longer used. And he no longer had to worry about going from place to place. His dreams had guided him before. He had listened to them in order to know which route to take. His dreams could foretell a successful hunt. "I no longer have those dreams," the old hunter said. Gwen had folded the article into

as many squares as possible and dropped it into the ~~~
she took the box and carried it out with the other garbage to
incinerator. She had thought wistfully about the old hunter as she
stirred oatmeal and scrambled eggs. She knew what it was like to
suddenly stop dreaming.

She had fallen asleep on the couch. When her eyes were finally
able to focus, she saw the boxes, Daniel's boxes, looming larger
than life. They seemed to surround her like the remains of a mys-
terious and ancient civilization, an urban Stonehenge of sorts.
The boxes looked like the awesome megaliths that continued to
confound archaeologists. No one really knew who had built the
massive stones spanned with horizontal slabs. No one really knew
why. She peered at the boxes in her living room and felt Daniel's
absence. Perhaps he too had disappeared without any explanation
of what it had all meant. Would a team of scientists appear at her
door with tools to help determine who Daniel was and why he
had positioned the boxes with a careful orientation to the sun?
She would make strong coffee and serve slices of freshly baked
bread to the men and women who scraped samples into plastic
bags and whispered among themselves.

She went into the bedroom and touched a folder of papers that
Daniel had left on the dresser. His briefcase was on the floor. Most
of his clothes had been put away. She saw his suits hanging in
the closet. His electric razor was in the bathroom along with his
toothbrush and a container of dental floss. Mint. He liked mint.
Whenever he had something flavored with mint, he would draw
her to him and say, "Taste it. Come on." He was determined when
he had a point to make. He would touch the tip of his tongue to

hers and stare into her eyes. "Taste it?" he said. She never did, but she liked to do it anyway. It made her feel as if she were a child closing a secret pact. Blood brother and blood sister forever.

She had never made friends easily. She was taller than any of the boys in school and prettier than any of the other girls. Secretly, she thought she was probably smarter than any of the teachers, but she never let them know. At the close of her junior year, her parents announced they would all be leaving Cedar Creek and moving to New York. Her father, a successful stockbroker, had been offered a position with a Wall Street firm that was too good to refuse.

There was no one she had to say goodbye to, no addresses to copy into the little leather book her mother had bought her as consolation. "We'll come back and visit," her mother promised. Gwen smiled for her. A brave smile. Her mother's name was Amanda. Her friends called her Mandy. Gwen thought it was a ridiculous name for an adult, and even though it wasn't her mother's fault, she blamed her for it. Amanda's bridge club gave her a goodbye party. They presented her with lovely stationery. Each one of the women had written her address on an envelope. There were many tears and promises to keep in touch. Gwen endured their comforting words and drank two glasses of sherry when no one was looking.

The move to New York was a turning point for Gwen. It confirmed what she already knew about her parents, especially her mother. Amanda (they were not friends, so Gwen never would have called her Mandy) had no idea who her daughter was. Moreover, Amanda did not seem to be interested in finding out. Each morning her father, Franklin, pecked Amanda's powdered cheek and patted Gwen's hair and went off to work. He admired his daughter's beauty and intellect, in that order, and was grateful not to be disturbed. He enrolled Gwen in a private school for her senior year. She graduated early, with high honors, and was accepted to Barnard College. She met Theodore the first semester. Amanda and Franklin were relieved to let someone else care for Gwen. She had always been a troublesome child, questioning everything, rejecting their values. And she was too tall for a girl, too outspoken, too everything for them. One of her mother's objections was that Theodore was "rather dark-skinned and foreign-looking." Still, Amanda felt Theodore would be able to "handle Gwendolyn." Soon after the wedding, her parents returned to North Carolina. New York turned out not to be right for them after all. But Gwen knew they just wanted to get away from her. With her married, they could return to the South without any guilt about leaving her behind.

When Theodore first left, she wondered how long she could wait before telling her parents. Three weeks later, she was out of money and phoned to tell them. Her father answered. "I see," was all he said. "Here's Mother." Amanda said, "Well, we should have expected this." They never asked her to come home. She would not have wanted to, but she would have liked to be asked. Instead, they sent money and clothes for the boys. Occasionally her mother sent something for Gwen. A pink sweater set or a silk scarf with hundreds of little American flags on it. Gwen always wrote the requisite thank-you note. She was grateful for the money. When the boys were old enough, they visited their grandparents and came home dressed in new suits and monogrammed ties. Their hair was combed back the way her brother, Warren, had combed his. Gwen was always startled by the smell of the hair ointment that Warren had used. For some reason, she felt as if the manufacturer would have stopped production after Warren died.

She knew her parents blamed her for Warren's death. They never said so in exact words, but they never said they didn't. He was older than Gwen by almost six years. He flirted with their mother and called their father "Sir." Franklin was always slapping Warren on the back and saying things like "Warren, my boy." Amanda and Franklin seemed to like Gwen a lot more in those days. On his first holiday home from college, Gwen begged him for a ride on his new motor scooter. There was only one helmet. "You wear it," Warren said. "We're just going around the block." He never saw the pothole. They both went flying. Warren did not have a scratch on him. Gwen was bruised and bloodied from the fall, but she did not die. Warren, on the other hand, did. When they found her on the side of the road, she was cradling his head in her lap and singing, "Ninety-nine Bottles of Beer on the Wall." She was down to number twenty-three when the police car pulled over. They knew the family. Everyone knew the family. They all came to the funeral. Amanda had to be supported by Franklin. Gwen walked in alone and left alone. Warren's friends were the pallbearers. They ignored her even though Warren had promised that it was only a matter of time until "they'll be falling all over you." Now he wouldn't be there to see it happen. The only sign that she existed was the minister's reference to "Warren's devotion to his sister." No name.

Six months later it was as if he had never lived. Every sign of him was removed from the house. His clothes were given away. His room was stripped bare of everything. Gwen managed to sneak out his favorite baseball trophy. Her parents never asked her if she wanted anything to remember her brother by. No one spoke of him. When Gwen tried to bring up his name, Amanda would run out of the room sobbing and Franklin would say, "Gwendolyn, please?" She always wondered why he said it as a question.

They offered to send her to boarding school, but she declined. Begged actually. She was terrified of being sent away and coming home to visit only to find that her parents had packed up, changed their names, and moved to another country. Although she often asked herself what the difference would have been, she was just a child and they were all the family she had. They mentioned it again a few times and then let it drop. She tried to stay out of their way. They barely spoke to each other.

When Matt was thirteen and Ethan almost eleven, Gwen was called to her father's deathbed. She could think of nothing to say. She held his hand and stammered, "Thank you for not sending me to boarding school." It was, all in all, a real tragedy. Amanda wore black well. She dabbed at her eyes throughout the service and beamed at her two grandsons. "They'll grow up to look like Warren," she said. Gwen nodded. The boys looked nothing like Warren ever looked—living or dead—but she kept silent. If she had said anything at all it would have been to comment on how her mother had suddenly started to mention Warren. No one else could, of course, but that was to be expected.

Amanda sold the house and moved to a retirement village. She seemed happier than she had ever been. At seventy, she was one of the youngest residents. The men pursued her. Within a year, she was living with a seventy-five-year-old man from Alabama, Kendall Johnson. Two years later Kendall died, and Amanda swore "never to get involved with any gentleman again." Gwen phoned every week and listened to Amanda talk about herself. She asked about the boys, of course, and never failed to mention the generous trust left to them by Franklin, which "will make it possible for them to go to college anywhere. I am so very proud of my boys." Gwen agreed with everything she said.

Amanda's last visit up North was to attend Ethan's high school graduation. Gwen invited Daniel for dinner. He brought flowers for Amanda and wine for dinner. She was charmed. They talked about bridge and the differences between the North and the South. Daniel had lived in Durham for several years after college. His wife's people were from there. As Gwen poured the coffee, Amanda smiled coquettishly at him and said, "And how many years have you been married?" Daniel inclined his head, took a sip of coffee, and answered honestly. "Thirty-five years," he said. Amanda nodded approvingly. "A good family man," she said. "Dependable." Then she turned to Gwen. "You've never been very smart about men, dear, but he seems quite stable." She never mentioned it again.

Jane found Amanda irresistible. Caroline adored her and loved the presents she sent. Little violet sachets for her underwear drawer, lace gloves, fabric-covered frames, chocolate-covered cherries, a leather-bound copy of the King James Bible. "I know you're Hebrews," Amanda told Jane, "but it's good to broaden yourself as much as possible." Gwen always felt excluded whenever her mother came for a visit. She took over with Jane and Caroline. She took over with the boys. But not so with Daniel. He held the upper hand with Amanda. He made her giggle. Only Warren had been able to have such an effect on Amanda. Even the swashbuckling Kendall Johnson was outwitted by Amanda's wiles. But Daniel made it very clear to Amanda from the onset that he loved Gwen best. Only Warren and her children had ever preferred her to anyone else.

Gwen missed Warren. Oh, not all the time, of course, but she missed him. Sometimes it was difficult to remember him really well. It was so long ago. In her dreams, she often confused him with other people. Sometimes she spoke to him aloud. "What do you think I should do about Daniel?" she asked. "Do you think I should let Matt live off campus?"

So now, on this evening so many years after Warren's death and well into her own adult life, Gwen still thought there was a chance her mother could be a mother.

Amanda answered on the second ring. Gwen could hear the television playing too loudly in the background. Amanda was partially deaf now, but she was too vain to wear a hearing device. She said she didn't mind people having to repeat themselves.

"Hello? Mother? Can you hear me?"

"Who is this? Speak up, please."

"Mother. It's Gwendolyn. Turn down the television set. Mother, can you hear me?"

"What's that? Gwendolyn? Hold on a minute. The television is too loud."

Gwen waited what seemed like a very long time. She heard Amanda's mules clicking on the tiled floor.

"Yes?" Amanda said.

Gwen knew she had forgotten who was on the phone.

"It's Gwendolyn. How are you?"

"Gwendolyn? Is everything all right?"

"Yes. I just felt like talking to you. I have some news for you. Daniel moved in with me."

"Daniel? Has he lost any weight?"

"No, Mother, he hasn't. But he moved in with me. He became a grandfather this morning. He went to see the baby."

"Aren't you too old to have another baby?"

"I didn't have the baby. Daniel's daughter, Kate, had a baby."

"Should I send something?"

"No, Mother. It's not necessary."

"I see."

Gwen was standing at the counter. She pulled some dead leaves off a plant that Daniel had brought with him. She had warned him that she wasn't very good with plants. "I run a hospice for plants," she told him. "They come here to die." He had kissed the tips of her fingers and said he could not imagine anything not coming to life under her touch.

"It snowed almost ten inches here." She crumbled the brown leaves between her fingers. "It looks so beautiful from the window."

"Everything looks beautiful from a distance," Amanda said. "I hate the snow."

"I miss Warren," Gwen said. "I miss him so sometimes. Do you still miss him?" She was practically whispering. "He would've been fifty this year."

"Who?"

"Warren, Mother. I'm talking about Warren."

There was silence.

"Mother? Are you all right?"

"Why did you call me?" Amanda said. "What do you want from me?"

It was so like Amanda to miss the point. *From me. What do you want from me?* Even Gwen's pain was about her.

"I just wanted to make sure you were all right," Gwen said.

"Yes. Well, I'm fine." She cleared her throat. "It's not good to dwell on the past. Chin up, dear. It doesn't do to cry."

"Yes, Mother. Thank you."

"I didn't plan on having a daughter. I knew I wouldn't be very good at it."

"It's all right, Mother. I'm sorry. I didn't mean to upset you."

"Yes, well. You're lucky to have boys. So much more sensible."

"Yes. I'm very lucky."

"Tell Daniel to lose some weight. He'd be a fine-looking man without that extra around the middle."

"I'll tell him."

"Goodbye, dear."

"Goodbye, Mother. Call if you need anything—"

Amanda had already hung up. Gwen would have liked to keep on talking for a while even though it was pointless. Even though her mother would not have heard anything. In a breathtaking moment of clarity, Gwen wondered how she had learned to love.

Sometime before dawn, Gwen heard the key turn in the door. Daniel did not come directly to the bedroom. She heard him fix himself something to drink. Probably herbal tea. Caffeine bothered him lately, though he did not like to admit it. She readied herself. Daniel had something to tell her.

It was already light out when he sat down on the bed. His coat was still on. His hands were wrapped around a mug.

"How's the baby?" she said.

Daniel didn't look at her.

"The baby is perfect," he said.

"Did you hold her?"

"Yes. I held her."

"May I have a sip?"

He offered her the mug. She sat up and took it from him, trying to reassure him with her whole self. He knew so little about separation. A novice yet to this kind of pain.

"Peppermint," she said. "It's good."

They passed the mug back and forth. Finally, Daniel took off his coat, then his clothes, and slipped under the blanket next to her. He took a final sip and set the mug on the floor. He did not offer her his tongue and ask, as he always did, "Taste the mint?" He couldn't. And Gwen understood that. He had just come from Sandra's bed. His bed, really. Still, she wished for his tongue inside her mouth and parted her lips as if she could draw him in with her breath. Her own tongue explored the ridges of her teeth and the moist skin, but it wasn't the same.

He was already asleep when she reached for his hand. Later, she would tell him about the call to Amanda. He would shake his head and laugh. And then he would tell her what she already knew.

Chapter Nine

Arnold had never wanted a child. He was very clear about that. Of course, he waited until after they were married to tell Jane how he really felt about children. She had felt as if someone had reached into her womb and closed it permanently. Her throat had ached from the effort of not screaming worse than if she had shrieked forever. *No baby. Ever.* It never occurred to her that she could leave Arnold and find a man who would be delighted to make babies with her. A man who would have kept promises long after they had been made. Jane never knew she was allowed. She did not know she was worthy of such privileges. She did not even know that they were not privileges.

The powers that be took matters into their own hands, and Caroline was born. And, for a while, things were better. Arnold fell in love with his daughter. He was more surprised than anyone. Jane watched the way he sniffed Caroline's hair after she had been bathed and kissed her toes. She received all the love Jane had thought she would be the one to get. Because she no longer loved Arnold anyway, Jane never felt jealous. Arnold's harsh words did not penetrate anymore. *I'm rubber, you're glue. What bounces off me, sticks to you.* When Arnold railed, she hummed to herself and said the words over and over. *I'm rubber, you're glue. What bounces off me, sticks to you.*

But he loved Caroline. And Caroline loved him. Jane was happy for them. She really was. It made her feel that she had not been completely wrong about her choice. Arnold *did* know how to love. He just did not love her. He did know how to show tenderness. He just never showed it to her.

Her own parents had barely spoken to each other. Jane and her sister, Ellie, tolerated each other out of need. They did not fight much because it was not allowed. When they did, it was in hushed tones through clenched teeth. But they depended on each other for what they could not depend on their parents for, and that included almost everything other than food and shelter. When it was time to ask questions about sex, Jane learned everything she needed to know from Ellie. One morning at breakfast, Ellie announced, "Cathy Rogers got her period yesterday." Their mother, Dorothy, sent to Kotex for a Personalized Kit for the Young Woman, and left it on Ellie's bed. Jane and Ellie solemnly read the instructions to each other and figured out what to do with the sanitary belt. Ellie, two years younger than Jane, was first at everything, including menstruation. When she told Dorothy, she slapped her once across the face. "To let the blood rush back," she said. Jane thought she had slapped Ellie unusually hard. It seemed as if Dorothy had been anticipating this moment since Ellie's birth. Ellie's cheek bore the mark of her mother's fingers for several hours. It was the greatest impact Dorothy ever made on her daughter's life. By her second period, Jane's best friend, Tammy Schwartz, came over with a pack of Tarrytons and a box of Tampax. Jane worried that Tammy might light a tampon and try to insert a cigarette inside Ellie. Fortunately, Tammy knew exactly what she was doing. She instructed Ellie to put one foot up on the lid of the closed toilet. Tammy did the same except she was not naked from the waist down the way Ellie was. "Now," Tammy said, "put your finger here, put the thing inside, and then push. Don't push too hard, or else. And hold on to that string." They had all heard horror stories about girls who had to have their tampons removed because they had been overzealous during insertion. Ellie was successful on the first try. Tammy said that was practically a miracle. She offered to teach her how to insert two tampons at a time and tie the ends together, but Ellie declined. She felt she needed to be more proficient before attempting anything quite that risky, but she accepted one of Tammy's Tarrytons. They became best friends.

Only weeks later, when it was Jane's time, she wouldn't allow Ellie in the bathroom. "Did you do it?" Ellie asked. Her mouth was pressed against the bathroom door. Jane fumbled only slightly, but on the second try the tampon slid in with little effort. She stood for a while with the string in her hand, wondering if she would be turned inside out if she tugged. Ellie knocked on the door. "Jane? Did you do it?" Jane dropped the string, pulled up her underpants and her jeans, and opened the door. "I did it," she said. Ellie looked impressed. Jane walked by her and sought out Dorothy to give her the news. When she raised her hand to slap Jane across the face, she grabbed her mother's wrist. "Have it your way," Dorothy said. Jane wished she could.

In those days, Jane was crazy about Keith. They spent their

afternoons groping each other and arguing. It seemed an equitable balance. Keith was forever talking about boners. And Jane, who had never seen a naked man (much less one with an erection), envisioned a bone uncurling itself like some anatomical party favor until the penis was fully erect. Keith begged Jane to use the hand he pressed against his crotch, but she knew her lines. Convention demanded that she protest and pull her hand away. It seemed odd to her, because she would have liked to do everything Keith asked, and more. But there was no one to talk to about how she felt. Ellie had already told her that she asked too many questions and worried too much. It was their mother's voice Jane already recognized coming from between Ellie's lips. It made Jane shudder with the thought of her own fate.

Ellie had skipped two grades. By the time Jane was a senior in high school, Ellie was her competition. After Jane had refused Keith countless times, he found relief with Ellie. Jane came home from her meeting at the Future Teachers Club to see Keith's bottom lighting up the bedroom she shared with Ellie like the moon on a clear night. She stared at her sister's splayed limbs and wondered how she had the nerve to screw her sister's boyfriend while their mother made meatloaf in the kitchen just two doors away. Jane closed the door and went to set the table for dinner. Keith left without saying goodbye to anyone, and Ellie ate half a box of Mallomars as she watched Jane pour tomato juice and add a piece of lemon to each glass. That night they tossed and turned in their respective beds. Finally, Ellie's voice reached across the darkness and said, "I enjoyed the Mallomars more." There was no apology in the words. Not a hint of regret. And Jane stared dry-eyed at the peacefully sleeping form that had a birthmark on the inside of the thigh identical to her own, and a laugh so like hers that not even their mother could tell them apart.

Their father died that year. He was sixty-three years old. Just two years away from the retirement he had been talking about as long as Jane could remember. "When I retire, I'm going to..." Abraham began almost every sentence this way. No matter what anyone asked him, he was waiting for his retirement. Then, and only then, would he take a trip to the Baseball Hall of Fame, see a show, learn how to play golf, reread *War and Peace*.

Two weeks after Ellie and Jane graduated from high school, Abraham Kaufman came home from the accounting office he had worked in since he came home from the service and died quietly in his green velvet wing chair. The newspaper was in his lap. Even his eyes were closed. He had spared them the pain of having to close them for him. Jane was setting the table. Ellie was on the phone with Tammy Schwartz, and Dorothy was mashing the potatoes. "Dinner's ready, Abe," she said. "C'mon, the fish'll get ice-cold. You hate it when it's cold." Jane wondered how her mother would have known such a thing. Abraham would have eaten it uncomplainingly whether it was cold or hot, cooked or uncooked. When Abraham didn't answer after the second time, Ellie hung up the phone and went into the living room. Jane followed her and stood watching from the doorway of the dining room. Ellie approached her father, gingerly touched his shoulder, called his name, pressed two fingers to the side of his neck, and stood staring down at him. Then she switched off the reading lamp that was next to the chair, folded the newspaper, and placed it on the table. She knew Jane was watching her. "He's dead," Ellie said. "Go tell Mom." Jane obeyed. Dorothy came to see for herself. When she had shaken him sufficiently to convince herself that he was, indeed, dead, she went to her room and closed the door, ending any expression of pain her children might have been inclined to show.

Ellie took care of everything. She made the funeral arrangements. She called all the friends and relatives. She ordered food for the mourners who would return with them from the cemetery. She ironed Dorothy's black dress.

In the funeral parlor, the rabbi ushered the three of them into a room. They made an odd trio. Composed and beautiful in black, Ellie stood between her mother and sister. Ellie held Dorothy's elbow. When Jane started to sway, Ellie took her elbow as well. The metamorphosis was complete now. Ellie *was* Dorothy. When the funeral was over, they would merge and become one formidable unit. The vision of her mother and Ellie with two almost identical heads attached to one black-clad body made Jane giggle. Ellie and Dorothy glared at her simultaneously. Jane felt a sudden attack of panic. Even though they had not talked much, her father had been her ally. In a moment of tension between Jane and Dorothy, it was a wink from Abraham that could calm Jane. When Ellie battled for the upper hand in a struggle, Abraham was the one to tell Jane, "Let her think she's in charge. She's just like your mother." Now Jane was left to contend with her mother and Ellie alone.

Rabbi Klein explained that in itself, death was not a tragedy. To be sure, the untimeliness of Abraham's death was tragic. But, he insisted, when a peaceful death follows a long life that has been blessed with good health and a sharp mind, then death is not a tragedy. "We must view this life as a doorway to still another world," Rabbi Klein said. "*Olam ha-ba* is where man is judged and where his soul continues to flourish. Abraham Kaufman will have a share in the world to come. Of this I am sure." With that he attached a small black ribbon to their collars. He made a small tear in each ribbon and explained it was an ancient sign of expressing grief and mourning. "It should be worn throughout the period of mourning," he said. He looked into their eyes and said, "Repeat after me: *Baruch ata adonai elohainu melech ha-olam dayan ha-emet.* Blessed art Thou, Lord our God, the true judge."

After the funeral, neighbors, friends, and relatives came home with them. The rabbi beckoned Dorothy, Ellie, and Jane to the table, where he urged them to eat. He made a special point of explaining that it was significant for the mourners to eat hard-boiled eggs. The rabbi held up an egg and said, "The egg has become a symbol for mourning and condolence. In a way, the roundness of the egg symbolizes the continuous nature of life. Perhaps the lesson for us is that from despair there follows renewal." Jane took the egg he held out to her and bit into it. She hated hard-boiled eggs. When no one was looking, she spit the bite into her napkin and tried not to worry about how it would affect the renewal process.

People she had not seen in years hovered around her mother. The immediate family were not allowed to sit on stools of normal height. Dorothy sat on a cardboard box that had been provided by the funeral home. Ellie sat beside her on another cardboard box. She was eating nuts and raisins. Jane watched her break the peanut apart with her teeth and insert a raisin between the two halves. This sandwich-making went on until David, the handsome son of their father's second cousin, engaged her in conversation. Poor David did not look happy about being dragged to the funeral of a man he barely knew, but Ellie with her cool gray eyes and dark blond hair was clearly an unexpected consolation prize.

Finally, Jane sought refuge in her parents' bedroom. She lay down on her father's side of the bed and turned her face to the wall. She inhaled deeply, hoping to catch a lingering odor of her father's presence. But there was nothing. It was as if he had never slept in the bed. For the first time since her father died, Jane wept. She pressed her face into the pillow and cried. She felt an unexpected hand stroking her hair and was surprised that Ellie would do such a thing. But when Jane turned, she saw David. He bent down and held his lips against hers. She immediately thrust her tongue into his mouth. It was as if she needed to do something to prove that she was still alive. David tasted of peanuts. Ellie must have made him some of her raisin-and-nut sandwiches. But he had come looking for Jane. Or so she told herself. Neither of them said a word. Neither of them moved their hands from their own sides. He sucked on her lower lip. She forced her tongue wherever it could reach. And then it was over. She half expected to hear the sound of the suction being broken, but David left as quietly as he had appeared. He left nothing behind except an awkwardness between them that would last forever.

That summer, Dorothy took them to a hotel in the Catskills. She said, "We need a vacation." She made them remove the torn black ribbon from their collars even though the period of mourning had not officially ended. She hired a driver to take them to the hotel and flirted with him the whole way. Ellie and Jane sat wordlessly for the three-hour ride.

The first night Jane saw Arnold. He looked smart in his waiter's uniform. His dark hair was slicked back from a wide forehead. Tall and muscular, Arnold made a good first impression. Even his dark brown eyes were deceptive. They exuded warmth and sensitivity where there was none to be had. He saw Jane staring at him and winked. She drank three glasses of water and never touched her food. When Ellie tried to follow the direction of Jane's gaze, she pretended to be looking at a blond waiter across the room. After dinner, Jane saw Ellie talking to the waiter.

Jane hurried back to their room and doused herself in Wind Song cologne. She changed into a blue off-the-shoulder blouse that tied just below her chest. She took off her bra and hid it beneath her pillow. She had watched Ellie enough to know exactly how to act. And there was no time to be wasted. Jane had to make her move before Ellie noticed. When Arnold walked out of the kitchen's rear entrance, Jane was waiting for him.

"I'm Jane," she said. But he didn't seem to care what her name was. He watched the way her breasts moved beneath her blouse and immediately tried to kiss her. Jane didn't resist. She had to stand on her tiptoes and stretch out her arms to reach around his neck, and that pleased him also. She would always be reaching for him. In his room, he held her bare shoulders and squeezed until it hurt. "You're hurting me," she said when she could catch her breath. But she saw only happiness for them. He wanted her, not Ellie. That was reason enough for Jane to be interested.

She took off her clothes while a fully clothed Arnold lay down next to her. "Let me put it in," he kept repeating, but she wouldn't even let him take off his shirt. He rubbed against her in desperation. "We have to keep our love secret," she said. "Especially from my sister." Arnold was not even curious enough to ask why.

The next night she waited for him again. This time he took off his clothes and asked her to "just touch it." She did better than that. All the while, she could not stop thinking about David and his salty tongue. It had been sharp and hard as it ran around the surface of her teeth. Arnold's kisses were wet and soft, but she pretended it didn't matter.

The rest of the vacation consisted of long nights in which she waited for him to say something more than "Where did you put the thing?" She would hand him the foil-wrapped condom and wait, her head turned to the wall, while he hastily put it on. After a while, she stopped waiting for anything more. She went back home with her mother and Ellie and sat by the phone. Arnold phoned every night at seven-thirty. Their conversations were brief. He said how's it going? And she told him everything was fine. He said he was tired. The work was hard and boring. She said she missed him. He said me too. It was the same conversation night after night until the summer was over, and he came back.

That fall, Jane attended City College. Arnold was teaching high school mathematics and beginning his graduate work at Brooklyn College. They saw each other every weekend, using her house or going to a cheap motel over the George Washington Bridge. He refused to go to his house. He lived alone with his mother, but said he didn't bring girls back there. Apparently his mother was some sort of a saint. Jane and Arnold had lots of sex and little conversation.

That was the beginning of always feeling something was missing. She tried to talk to Arnold, but Arnold didn't talk. She couldn't say he had changed, because he had always been the same. He asked her why she was always trying to complicate things with "a lot of questions." Or he said that she was never happy. And underneath she heard what her mother had always said. *Nothing is ever good enough for you.*

But Arnold never even noticed Ellie, so Jane loved him and

ignored the voice. *Something is wrong here.* She heard the voice whenever she was with Arnold. *Something is wrong here.* The voice grew louder. And when Arnold asked her to marry him and she said yes, the voice was deafening.

For the last month, Jane's fifth-grade class had been doing a unit called "Film and How It Began." The children were excited. Jane broke them into groups to work on special projects. One group presented a shadow puppet show with theater and play all of their own design. The parents had helped, of course, but the children had done mostly everything. It was a great success. And John Singer, who according to his classmate, Allison Tierney, was "one of the better boys," told everyone his uncle was a cameraman for a soap opera filmed in a Manhattan studio. "He's been to Africa at least a million times," John said. "And he collects real old toys about the movies." John said his uncle, Caleb Singer, would come to class and talk to them. John needed only to ask. Finally John reported back that Uncle Caleb would be happy to come. Jane wrote him a note: "We would be honored if you would join us on Friday." Caleb Singer wrote back that it would be *his* honor. The note made Jane smile.

Caleb was younger than Jane had expected. He was sweet, especially with the children. He told them something about a phantasmagoria show that had thrilled audiences at the turn of the century. A Belgian inventor used a special lantern to create frightening images of monsters that seemed to descend upon the unsuspecting audience. He kept his voice low and suspenseful. Next, he set up a complicated-looking contraption called a praxinoscope.

"Ms. Hoffman," Caleb said, "will you assist me?"

"Certainly," she said.

She was fascinated by the principle of the machine. Inter-changeable strips of paper with a black background showed a character in a sequence of twelve pictures with only slightly vary-ing differences. The strip was inserted in a circular drum where a mirror reflected the images. Different background pieces made it possible for the character to perform in as many places as an art-ist's imagination could invoke. The viewer had to spin the drum by hand to make the images move. A candle beneath an opaque shade provided the necessary light.

"Ms. Hoffman, would you look through the viewing window and tell us what you see?"

It was an awkward contraption. But when Jane looked through the viewing window, the black background of the strip appeared to be gone. She saw only movement that was smooth and delight-ful. Jane kept turning the handle. On the strip, in a pose that had hardly changed over the years, she saw herself. The backgrounds were all familiar. The home she and Ellie had lived in with their parents. The cemetery where her parents were together again in eternal silence. She saw herself lying quietly beneath Arnold, holding back the words she wanted to say in a bitter solution of rage and despair. Then the room where her mother had finally, and indignantly, died. Jane turned the handle until the class was so quiet she looked up in surprise. Couldn't they hear? The voice was the same, but the words had changed. *Something was wrong there.* She stared at the moving images and furiously turned the handle. Jane saw that without the backgrounds, the character was an isolated figure moving randomly through space. She held her breath and released the handle. When she looked at Caleb, he wore the same worried expression as the children.

"It's all right," she reassured them all.

The old Jane, the one who had endured the changing backgrounds with stoic acceptance, would have said nothing at all. But this Jane, the one who found the uncle's slow way of smiling remarkably attractive, thanked the nephew, dismissed the class, and invited Uncle Caleb home.

Chapter Ten

In the town of Cedar Creek, just ten miles outside of Fayetteville, North Carolina, where Gwen had been born, there had lived identical twin sisters who owned an egg store. The egg sisters, as they were called by the locals, were short and shaped exactly like the product they handled for the sixty-odd years they lived in the town. They were kind ladies. Cordial to their customers and friendly to the children who stopped in for glasses of water on a scorching summer day. It seemed to Gwen that the egg sisters must have been born in exactly the same way as the fragile brown and white eggs they sold all day long. Gwen pictured their mother lovingly lifting her bottom and gazing at the two perfectly matched daughters who would follow in the family business. The sisters could not have been more than in their twenties when they took over the store. They seemed ageless, their skin virtually without wrinkles as the years passed. If one was ill, a hand-lettered sign hung from the doorknob. *Feeling Poorly. Closed for the day. Help yourself.* It never said which of the two was ill, and no one ever thought to ask.

Long after Gwen's family moved up North, she thought about the egg sisters. Sometime after Ethan was born and her parents had returned to the town where the egg sisters conducted their business, Gwen received two clippings from the local paper marked *1* and *2* in her mother's ornate style. Gwen unfolded the first piece of newspaper and read, "Reynolds—Agatha. 92 years old. Died on September 24. She passed away peacefully and without anger. She is survived by her loving sister, Libby. In lieu of flowers, friends may make contributions to the Sanford Children's Home. At her request, there will be no service. Her ashes will be spread over the farm she loved so well." Gwen knew what the second clipping said without opening it. They could not have survived without each other. "Reynolds—Libby. 93 years old. Died on *their* birthday, October 5. She passed away peacefully in her own bed. At her request, there will be no service. She asked to join her sister." Gwen folded the articles and wept. But it was not for Agatha and Libby that she cried. She had not even known their given names, nor ever cared to learn them. Gwen wept for the love they must have felt. The comfort they must have given each other, the devotion that was even greater than anything they had shared in this world. And when she closed her eyes, Gwen saw not ashes, but millions of tiny pieces of eggshell scattered across the acres the egg sisters had watched, together, from the porch their father had built.

Two weeks had passed since Daniel had become a grandfather. He had barely spoken to Gwen and had not reached for her even once. She thought about the egg sisters and envied the certainty they had shared. The evenness of the days they had spent together. The countless egg cartons they folded on the surface of the worn counter. How many eggs had passed from identical hand to hand as they talked of secrets that mattered only to them. Once Gwen had fallen while playing behind the store. Blood ran down onto her cheek from the gash on her forehead. She had raced, in tears, to the egg sisters. They had ministered to her with few words. Gwen had watched as one wrung out a cloth dipped in a solution of witch hazel and water and passed it to the other. Then together they held the cloth against Gwen's wound. She had stopped crying almost immediately, entranced by the concordance of their movements and comforted by their touch. She remembered how she had felt no surprise that their hands were cool and smooth, exactly like the shells of the eggs they never seemed to break.

Gwen wished she could comfort Daniel as she had been comforted that long-ago summer day. But she could not even touch him. Instead, every night, when she was sure he was asleep, she crooned softly both to him and to herself, hoping to quiet the vague, yet inevitable, feelings of doubt that seemed to shape their time together.

The boys would be home soon for winter break, and Gwen had still not told them about Daniel. She didn't know what to tell them because she was not sure he was going to stay. Since Elena's birth, Daniel left for work earlier than necessary and returned later than usual. The first few times, he called. "I have a lot of catching-up to do. Don't wait with dinner." But she did anyway, hoping he might tell her what it was that made him look old again.

Still, she did not know what to do about Matt and Ethan. She almost believed Daniel would be gone by the time the boys came home. Sometimes she even hoped it would be so. He had still not finished unpacking, and although the boxes were in her way, she said nothing.

The week before the boys were due to arrive home, Gwen woke in the middle of the night to find Daniel missing and knew the time had come to talk. It couldn't wait another day. At first, she didn't see him sitting on the couch in the dark and gasped when he moved.

"Daniel! I didn't see you there."

"I'm sorry," he said.

"Sit," Daniel said. He patted the place beside him on the couch. "Please."

She sat with her bare feet curled beneath herself and shivered. He took the afghan that was always on the arm of the couch and wrapped it around her shoulders, holding the soft wool in place with his hands.

"Are you still cold?" he said.

She shook her head.

"I didn't mean to frighten you."

"I'm all right now," she said.

"Are you?"

The lines around his eyes had grown conspicuously deeper. She wished to take his face in her hands and press the pads of her thumbs against the lines as if he were made of clay. Then she could have smoothed away the past with a bit of water and gentle pressure. But then it would have been a different face, one she might only vaguely recognize. She rested her head on his shoulder. He laid his cheek against her hair and began to speak as if they had left off in the middle of a conversation.

"I can't seem to figure any of it out," he said. "When I walked into the hospital room that day, my whole family was there. Katie stopped smiling as soon as she saw me. Rosie had been in for a few days and hadn't even called me. Rosie, Gwen. My little Rosie." He shook his head. "Sam was there. He was holding a huge stuffed bear and didn't even put out his hand to me. 'Hey, Dad,' he said. Sandy was sitting on the bed. She was holding the baby. I saw the look that passed between her and Katie. I wanted to turn and run. Robby was the only one who came over to me. He hugged me and said, 'Welcome, Grandpa.' My own kids couldn't even congratulate me. I went over to Sandy and kissed her cheek. 'Well, Grandma. You look as if you could be the mother.' I didn't know what to say. I just wanted to break the tension. Sandy handed me the baby and said, 'She looks just like Katie, Dan. Just like Katie. I can't get over it.' And it was true. I looked down into that baby's face, and it was thirty years ago. Suddenly it was just the two of us in the hospital room with our newborn. I started to cry. Sandy started to cry. Then everyone started to cry. Except that baby. She slept through the whole damn thing."

Gwen took in Daniel's words with each breath she drew, listening and anticipating the outcome.

"...and I felt so bad, Gwen. I had caused all these people I loved so much pain. I hugged Kate with one arm. She was sobbing. My first baby. 'Don't do this to us, Daddy,' she said. 'We need you.' How do you tell your child that the woman who is her mother doesn't bring you joy anymore? How do you tell that child that you love someone else?" He tightened his arms around Gwen. "I really do love my children. And I love Sandy." He took a deep breath, held it, released it, and then said, "I went home with her. I slept with her."

"I know," Gwen said.

"I know you know, but I had to say it."

"Tell me the rest, but don't tell me about that night."

"I wouldn't do that." He shifted and pulled Gwen down so that he was almost cradling her. "I need to look at you." He kissed her forehead. "I'm going to move out. I looked at a few places this week, and I think I may have found something suitable. A one-bedroom. I haven't lived alone in over thirty years, and I'm afraid. I feel silly about that. But I have to do it. I know it's the right thing."

She had worried that he would go back to Sandra after the baby was born and had been afraid for him. She knew all about separation. It was compelling. It drew on familiarity and terror in an odd blend.

"Gwen?"

Her eyes were closed. He would be gone soon. She would have to relearn her route in the dark. For a while she would continue to walk around the boxes and step over the place where he put his briefcase. Items would disappear from her shopping list. She would do the laundry alone again, in the morning, when it was safer to be in the basement.

"I love you," she said.

He looked surprised, and she had to wonder what he had expected. She did not need to know details as she had so many years ago with Theodore. This was not about letting go of Daniel. This was about Daniel letting go. He was better now. She could feel it in her hands, through her skin. His flesh was warm under her touch. His color had returned.

"What about us?" he said.

"I think that should be my question. You're the one moving out."

"I just need some time to be alone. I never meant for us not to see each other anymore."

"Well, that's good," Gwen said. "I'm glad."

"Will it be all right?" he said.

The day Theodore left, Gwen had fixed dinner for her children, bathed them, read to them, and taken them into her bed for the night. She had stared into the dark as she stroked their little bodies and said over and over, "It will be all right. It will be all right," until the sun came up and she finally slept, reassured that the world had not ended.

"Yes," she said now. "It will be all right."

"I want you to be all right," he said.

"Oh, but I am."

Daniel stroked her back for a moment.

"Coming to bed?" he said.

"I'll be along in a minute," she promised.

Gwen gathered the afghan around her chilled body and turned to stare out the window. *Get down on your knees and thank God you're on your feet.* She shivered and decided to wait for the sun to rise. Just to be sure.

For the next two days, Gwen felt as if someone had handed her a package that she had thought would be heavy but instead discovered to be very light. She felt oddly unbalanced, and she frequently found herself touching the walls or grabbing on to the back of a chair as if she were about to fall.

Matt called and said he would be home Saturday. He was driving down with a friend. Could she pick him up in White Plains? That was as far as his friend was going. She asked him what she should prepare, and he laughed and said, "Lasagna. Meatballs. Chicken and rice. Chocolate cake. Anything and everything." Gwen promised it all and told him to wear his scarf, and to be sure not to speed, and to.... "And what about bears, Mom?" Matt teased. "Don't pick them up no matter what they tell you," she said. Matt agreed. "I love you," she whispered into the phone. "I love you," he said in a firm, strong voice. She couldn't wait to see him.

Ethan was due in on Friday night. Gwen would pick him up at the train station in Pelham. "I'll be in real late," he said. "I can take a cab." Gwen wouldn't hear of it. "I'll be there," she said. "Wait in the car," Ethan said. "I promise," she said.

Ethan was the worrier. He had planned to apply only to local colleges because he had not wanted to leave Gwen alone. She had insisted he look outside the city. She had assured him she would be fine. After Matt left for college, she often heard Ethan whispering to Matt on the phone about her. "She's all right," he said. "But I think she's lonely." And he had been right. It had been a lonely time in her life. She missed Matt. And she had anticipated Ethan's going off to college with dread. She hadn't been involved in a relationship in almost two years, and she couldn't even please herself anymore. Then she met Daniel.

It had been difficult to tell the boys that Daniel was married. She had insisted on telling them even though Daniel had tried his best to discourage her. "They'll understand," she said.

But she had been wrong. She waited until Matt was home for a visit. Ethan left the table. Matt followed him, but not before he turned and said, "I wish you hadn't told us. It would've been better if we didn't know." She had wanted to hurl her cup after him and shout, "How dare you judge me?" Instead, she splashed cold water on her face and knocked on Matt's bedroom door. She calmly explained that she also wished Daniel was not married. That she understood their feelings and shared them. That Daniel felt the same way. And then she reminded them of how it felt to stand on the shore and feel the sand pulled out from beneath your feet before you had to decide whether or not to run back. She had never before spoken to them so intimately about herself. And they listened. She told them about having hope and about disappointment. And she insisted that they see she was not without faults. That she could be angry and still love them. That they could be angry with her. And that she could live with their disapproval. She said everything she had tried to teach them by showing them in the years when words would have meant little. They said nothing. But when Daniel arrived later, they joined them in the living room and talked football as if nothing had happened.

On the day Matt had to go back to school, she huddled with both boys on the train platform. She already missed Matt's presence and tried not to cry. He kissed her cheek and said, "Watch those waves, Mom. Don't drown." When she put her arms around him, she barely reached his chin. Gwen hugged him tightly. "Never," she said. She knew he remembered that it was the same answer she had always given whenever either he or Ethan had asked, "Will you ever die?" It was the only possible answer to give a child.

⤇∼⤆

"Well," Daniel said, "I think I have everything."

All this past week, Gwen had refused to help him pack. His friend Charlie had offered his time and his van for the morning. She ripped off a piece of foil and covered the tray of lasagna. She had been cooking since dawn.

"That looks good," Daniel said. "Am I invited?"

Gwen slid the tray of lasagna into the refrigerator. A chocolate cake stood ready to be frosted on the counter. She fumbled in the drawer for a spatula and wished he would just leave.

"Gwen, I have to go. Charlie's waiting downstairs. I'll be back after we unload."

"I'm picking Ethan up at eleven-thirty in Pelham."

"I'll be back in plenty of time. I'll come with you."

"No. I don't think it's a good idea."

"Why not?"

"I just don't."

"You mean you don't want me to come."

"I didn't say that."

She was angry now and slathered the frosting on the cake with force. *Just leave. Just take your things and go.* She kept her eyes on the cake.

Theodore had whistled as he had packed his books and the clothes he had returned for. She had tried to keep the children out of his way, but Ethan had crawled into one of the boxes. "Can't you keep an eye on those kids?" Theodore said. She had scooped up Ethan and straddled him on her hip. "Can you at least make me a cup of coffee?" Theodore said. And she had. She had ground the beans just the way he liked them and heated the milk to a gentle boil in the red-enamel pot that doubled as a pitcher. Wordlessly, she served him the steaming mug of coffee and waited to see what would happen next. She had just wanted him to leave. She had just wanted him to stay.

"Gwen," Daniel said. "Please look at me."

"I can hunt for myself," Gwen said. "I don't need you."

"Ah," Daniel said, "but I need you."

She shook her head. *Daniel.* The first time he had wanted to enter her from behind, she had been surprised. It had been Theodore's preferred position. It wasn't long before she understood why Theodore favored that position over all others. From behind, she was anonymous. When she first insisted Theodore explain, he casually answered that five million years of evolution had done little to change women's greatest fears. "Desertion," he had whispered. "Abandonment." She had turned toward the sound of his voice, but he pushed her head down and held it. "You'll do anything not to be left alone." He moved her with his other hand, forced her to indulge his excitement. But she was terrorized. "You could never care for your young and hunt at the same time." The next night she had refused to accommodate him. He looked into her eyes and laughed. "It's likely that the first females grew earlobes, nostrils, lips, and breasts to entice their mates and guarantee their return from the hunt. Are you afraid, Gwen? Are you trying to entice me with your lips and nose? Do you think your breasts and nostrils will keep me here?" He rubbed her earlobes between his thumbs and forefingers. Then he smoothed her nostrils with his fingertips and bent close to lick her lips. By the time he reached her breasts, she was numb with dread. "Lovely," he murmured. "Almost worth all the trouble." But he would not acknowledge her any further. With one steady movement, he turned her and grasped her hips. "I never would have returned from the hunt. You could have promised to let me do anything to you, and I still would have stayed away."

When she told Daniel about Theodore's predilection, he had responded with embarrassed silence. "What is it?" she had said. Daniel had kissed her shoulders and back and said, "I would have stayed with you. I wouldn't have made a very good hunter." Then she had faced him and flaunted what had taken famine and ice and drought and destruction to finally create. She had rubbed herself against him, marked him with her scent and her touch. And Daniel had said that he would never have left for fear someone else would take his place.

From the street below came the sound of three short impatient blasts. Charlie was waiting.

"I have to leave," Daniel said. "Charlie has to get home. I promised him we'd be done by one."

"You'd better go then," she said.

"I'll speak to you later." He kissed her cheek. "I love you."

"Hurry," she said.

He hesitated only slightly over her cryptic final word. If he had asked, she would have been unable to answer. *She just wanted him to leave. She just wanted him to stay.*

She sat for a while at the kitchen table and tried to secure a position for herself in a space that no longer held Daniel. Some time after Theodore had left, she attended a lecture given by an acclaimed mystic. He was a devotee of anticipatory dying who practiced meditating on his own death to be reborn in God. He had sacrificed all his desires for worldly possessions for this single-minded purpose. She had sat in an auditorium filled with people like herself. People in search of something few could even define. But something. The follower of Krishna had spoken lovingly of the Ganges River. It was sacred throughout its winding course of fifteen hundred miles across the north Indian plain to the Bay of Bengal. He explained that at its source, high in the Himalayas, it formed pools of icy water from the surrounding glaciers. Bathing at the glacial source was an act of devotion that brought the pilgrim absolution for his sins. Holy men gathered there to oil their bodies and bedaub themselves with saffron. The sacred waters of the Ganges were believed to have once flowed in heaven. Gwen had been transfixed. *Acts of devotion*. She thought she had performed them all her life. After the lecture, he had approached Gwen and asked, "Are you alone?" The question had not startled her then, and the memory of her response brought her comfort now. "Always," she had said. The mystic, his skin the color of honey, had leaned on his cane with both hands, and looked pleased.

Ethan was the first one off the train. She had pulled into a spot that allowed her to view the platform without suffering either the cold or the eeriness of the deserted station. She saw him scan the platform until he spotted her half-emerged form and waving hand.

"Ethan! Over here!"

He had already seen her, but she had to be sure. She always had to be sure with Ethan and Matt. There was always the possibility that they could slip between the cracks of her uncertainty. They might detect her doubts about her ability to raise them. She spent her life waiting to be found out.

"Mom! Stay there. I'll come to you."

His voice was muted by the rumble of the train pulling out of the station. She watched him walk toward her. A duffel bag was slung over his shoulder. He was holding a book under his arm. *I love you,* she wanted to shout into the darkness. It was the only truth she really knew.

She sat across the kitchen table from Ethan and watched him eat. Spoonfuls of the potato and leek soup she had prepared disappeared between his lips. She broke off a piece of freshly baked herb bread and handed it to him.

"It's really good, Ma. Really good."

"I'm glad."

She filled his glass with more cider and pushed it toward him.

"What about Matt?" Ethan said.

"We have to pick him up in White Plains tomorrow. He'll call. Do you want some more soup? There's still some in the pot."

"No. Thanks. I'm stuffed. How's Daniel?"

"He's fine. He wanted to come with me, but I asked him not to. He'll be over tomorrow. He's looking forward to seeing you."

"How are things?"

Gwen smiled.

"What are you asking me?" she said.

"You haven't said much about Daniel lately. I was just wondering if the two of you were still all right."

"We're still all right, honey. He just moved into his own place. I think it'll be good for him."

Ethan rolled the soft part of the bread into little balls and then popped them into his mouth. He had always liked to do that with bread, and she had always reprimanded him. Now she said nothing.

"The bread is real good," he said.

"I baked it myself."

"You haven't baked in a long time."

He sounded concerned. Gwen knew he was remembering the years in which the aroma of freshly baked bread prevailed. The three of them now laughingly referred to that time as "our yeasty years." She felt compelled to reassure him.

"It's too much work. I can't believe I ever baked as much as I did."

Ethan looked relieved.

"Will it be good for you?" he said. "Daniel's moving out, I mean."

The eternal diplomat, Ethan would not ask if Daniel was leaving his wife. Ethan depended on euphemisms to maneuver the delicate boundaries of his mother's relationship with Daniel.

"Yes, I think it will be good for me," she said. "Tell me about yourself. Have you talked to your father?"

Theodore had moved out to California in Ethan's senior year, settled down, and finally married Arlene, who seemed to have turned his life around.

"You mean *Theodore*?" He doesn't want us to call him Dad anymore. He says it makes him feel too old. He's all right, though, you know. He sounds pretty happy. Arlene is still with him. They want us to come out to Berkeley in the spring. He's teaching again. He asked for you."

"Oh?"

"He wanted to know if you were still beautiful."

"I hope you told him the truth," she said.

"I told him you would always be beautiful."

Gwen reached across the table for his hand and stroked the hair on his knuckles. He looked so much like Theodore that Gwen was often startled at the resemblance. "Swarthy" was what Amanda insisted on calling Ethan's looks. Gwen preferred "Mediterranean." With his olive skin and almost black eyes, Ethan was conspicuous. He also shared Theodore's lanky gait and his interest in ancient civilizations, although Ethan had recently chosen to study cultural anthropology. He was not lured by the idea of sweltering, arid digs on foreign soil. "Dad thinks it's a good way to meet *chicks*," Ethan said, rolling his eyes in amused disbelief. "I told him I could do it on the basis of my good looks and great intellect. That seemed to satisfy him." Fortunately, Ethan had not inherited his father's arrogance. Ethan was unselfish and responsible. Gwen saw his greatest flaw as a compulsion to be honorable even when the situation didn't merit loyalty, but she attributed that to his youth and had hope that time would temper his views.

"I'm glad you're home," she said. "I've missed you."

Ethan squeezed her hand and yawned.

"I can't wait to get into my own bed," he said.

"Go ahead. I'll clean up."

She cleared away the dirty dishes and put away the leftovers. Ethan's snores could be heard throughout the apartment. She closed the door to her bedroom and tried not to notice how bare it seemed. At her insistence, Daniel had taken everything. Now she was sorry she had told him not to come with her to pick up Ethan. She had forgotten to tell him about the egg sisters and how they had spent their days together. She had been saving the story, knowing he would have understood about the ashes and why she had wept when the egg sisters died.

Chapter Eleven

Caleb was thirty-five, older than Jane had first thought. Both his parents were dead. He told her that Alice, his sister, still cared for him as if he were one of her children. He admitted that he didn't much mind. He had been briefly married to an actress. About a year ago, she had called him from location in Brazil to tell him she was in love with the director and wouldn't be coming back. Caleb had packed her things and put them in storage. He wanted to forget it had ever happened.

"I don't think that's possible," Jane said.

Caleb had recounted his history in the first fifteen minutes after they reached Jane's house. He followed her from the school in his own car while she kept checking her rearview mirror to be sure he didn't make a sharp turn in the opposite direction when she wasn't looking. Now he leaned his elbows on the counter and watched her pour boiling water into a teapot. He was wearing an Irish fisherman's sweater. It complemented his light coloring.

Jane thought his nose was a bit too fine for his round face, but he was definitely attractive. She liked his beard and mustache. There were already bits of gray that pushed through the dark red of his beard, making him look very wise.

"Sure it's possible to ignore the past," he said. "What's the point of thinking about it all the time?"

Jane shook her head and reached in the cupboard for teacups and saucers. She set them on the counter and turned away from Caleb. He had been rolling the delicate instruments he had brought to show the class in plastic bubble wrap when Jane had approached him and said, "Would you like to come over for a cup of tea?" He picked up a cord and began carefully winding it in a way she hadn't seen anyone do since her father had died. "What sort of tea?" Caleb asked. And when Jane had been unable to hide her bewilderment, Caleb had laughed, touched her hand, and said, "Oh, but I'd love it no matter what kind you're serving." She helped him carry some of the boxes to the car. "The children had a wonderful time," she said. He took the box from her hands, and she was shocked at the ache his touch produced. "You're a fine teacher," he said. She stood with her arms outstretched and felt momentarily defenseless. As she was about to withdraw her invitation, he said, "I'll follow you in my car." She had nodded and hurried off, cursing her recklessness.

Jane cut thick slices of date-nut bread and took some butter cookies from a tin and arranged them on the plate.

"Can you really control your thoughts?" she said. "I don't see how you can just put something out of your mind."

"Why not?"

"It just doesn't seem possible, that's all."

"I think we do it all the time. How else could we get through our lives?" He eyed the date-nut bread and cookies and said, "Do you have anything to eat? Real food, I mean. I'm hungry."

"Of course. I'm sorry. I should've asked. What can I get you?"

Caleb got up from the counter stool and came around and looked down at Jane.

"How long have you been married, Mrs. Hoffman?"

"Twenty-one years."

"I see."

"We're separated. About a month."

"That's not very long, but I didn't ask."

"I'm telling you anyway."

Caleb looked amused. When he smiled, he looked very young. When he smiled, he made Jane feel very young. She had an urge to grab hold of his beard and taste the skin on the smooth part of his cheeks. He pulled off his sweater. The shirt beneath it rose up a bit, and she stared at the red hair on his belly that was suddenly exposed. When he caught the direction of her gaze, he smiled. She blushed furiously and looked away quickly.

"Are you hungry?" he said.

"Yes. As a matter of fact, I am."

"May I make something for both of us?"

"You certainly may."

He was standing so close to her that the plaid pattern of his shirt made her dizzy.

"Don't make a mess," she said. "I'll be right back."

"I never do."

Arnold's clothes were still in the closet. She pushed them

to the side and refused to be intimidated by his good blue suit. The sudden shift of Arnold's wardrobe made his scent surface. The smell of Old Spice and medicated talcum powder, combined with her growing dread, left no doubt in her mind that she was about to be ill. She couldn't possibly take her clothes off in front of a stranger. The last time she had seduced anyone she had been scarcely eighteen.

Arnold's blue suit stood sentry as she directed the conversation going on in her head to its grave and silent form. *Mind your own business. He came home with me, didn't he? He knows how old I am. I know he's only thirty-five. Men do this sort of thing all the time, and no one thinks it's shocking. I know he hasn't seen me naked.* Jane leaned her face against the expensive wool. Then she took the suit off the hanger and rolled the jacket and pants into a ball. She stuffed both pieces into the back of the closet. When she was done, she went into the bathroom, splashed her face with cold water, sprayed herself with cologne, and reassured herself that experience must count for something.

In the kitchen, Caleb was slicing an avocado and whistling.

"I hope you weren't saving this. I helped myself to some tomato as well." He sniffed the air around her. "You smell good."

"Thank you."

She stood next to him and watched as he arranged slices of tomato and avocado on top of melted cheddar cheese.

"Any sprouts?" he said.

"No. I'm afraid not."

"Not to worry."

He sliced each sandwich in half and set the plates down on the counter.

"Tell me something important," he said.

"I have a daughter."

Caleb leaned against the refrigerator and waited for more.

"Her name is Caroline. She's nineteen. She's a sophomore at New Paltz. She's living with a young man. And she's very angry at me for not loving her father anymore."

"You don't love him anymore? Did you ever?"

"Well, not like I'm supposed to."

"*Supposed to*? What does that mean?"

"It means exactly what I said."

She felt foolish. She was too old for this.

"Maybe you should leave," she said.

But he didn't move. In fact, Caleb seemed not to have heard what she said.

"I said maybe you should leave. I'm too old for this sort of thing. It takes too much energy."

"Tell me what he did to you," Caleb said.

She was so surprised by the question that she could not control her voice. It shook when she tried to answer. And then she had to speak, as if there were some way to explain the heartache that had accumulated over the years she had spent with Arnold.

"He hurt me all the time."

"Poor Jane," Caleb said.

It was too much. The sympathy in his look. The shift in his tone.

"Yes. Well. I'm just as much to blame as he is. The door wasn't bolted," she said. "Why don't we eat?"

Caleb pulled his stool up close alongside hers and waited while she took her first bite and nodded approval. They talked between mouthfuls of food and sips of tea. He told her how much he wanted children. She told him how difficult it was to be a mother. He talked about his parents and what a shock it had been when they both died in an airplane crash. When she stroked his arm, he covered her hand with his own and smiled. He reassured her that the insurance money made his life easier than they ever had, and then he laughed when she looked horrified. He listened quietly as she told him about Ellie and the frustration that always came with speaking to her. He shouted "No!" when she told him about finding Arnold in bed with the girl. She covered her mouth with her hand and tried not to laugh when Caleb described finding his wife in bed with another woman who was wearing *his* boxers. They finished their sandwiches, ate most of the date-nut bread and half the cookies.

"Can I get you anything else?" she said.

Caleb took hold of the back of her stool as if it needed to be secured for her own safety. Then Jane braced herself, the way she might if she were about to jump from a great height.

"Twenty-one years between men is a long time," she said. "I don't think I can take my clothes off."

"Then don't," Caleb said.

Just as she had done as a child, she raised her arms over her head and waited. The sudden cold against her bare skin was a surprise. Then she felt the soft inside of her velour dress against her face. Caleb left her to finish pulling the dress over her head unassisted. His mouth was already on her, creating warmth where there had been none. Her cheeks were hot to her touch, flushed with the effort of freeing herself.

"Caleb," she said.

He lifted his face to look at her.

"More," she said.

Before Arnold met Jane, he had been dating a reflexologist, Amber, who was, according to her own testimony, "madly in love with Arnie." Even after Arnold and Jane were married, Amber kept calling and asking if she could come over and meet Jane. One evening, when Arnold was out, Amber phoned and Jane invited her to visit. Jane hadn't expected Amber to be quite so beautiful. It was clear to Jane that Arnold and Amber were a perfect match. They made such a striking couple, she with her alluring Swedish blond looks and Arnold with his chiseled profile and athletic presence, that Jane would have considered stepping aside if she could have thought of where to go.

Amber swept through the front door in a white wool cape. Her blond hair was shorter than Jane had ever seen on a woman in those years. Amber brought with her the heady blend of herbs and flower petals. "What do you know about aromatherapy?" Amber had demanded. And Jane had shrugged and watched as Amber unlocked her case and spread out bottles of lavender, rosemary, and rose essence. "I've been crossing over into new areas since Arnie left me." She held up a brown bottle and said, "Lavender is for relaxation." Then she held up a blue bottle and said, "And rosemary breaks up fibrous tissue when properly massaged into a woman's breasts. Are you fibrous?" Jane shook her head vehemently, and Amber chortled in disbelief. "All women with large breasts are fibrous," she insisted. "Look at me. I don't have a fiber in my body." And with that she had whipped off her white cape and revealed a remarkably thin figure clad in a black body stocking. "Very nice," Jane had politely offered. She just wanted Amber to leave before Arnold came home. But Amber had come with a purpose. She pressed her bony fingers into Jane's shoulders and whispered, "The body holds a lot of memories. If you know the right pathways, one touch can make a person cry." Amber had uncorked a brown bottle and poured a drop of lavender oil into her palm. Then she had rubbed her hands together and before Jane knew what was happening, she was having her feet massaged. "These are the control panels of the body," Amber said. Jane had felt her entire body relax under Amber's skilled touch. She manipulated Jane's toes and pressed her arches with a succession of moves that left Jane feeling light-headed. Later, she wouldn't even remember how this strange woman had persuaded her to remove her shoes and socks, but it didn't matter. Amber's touch expected nothing in return, and that was new to Jane.

Amber had been right. When Caleb kissed Jane, she remembered everything she had tried to forget. His tenderness almost broke her heart. He whispered to her as he touched her. Small words of encouragement. Praise for what her lips and tongue found. Blessings for the places her hands visited. He admired the softness of her skin, the taste of her in his own mouth. When Jane told him what she wanted, he listened.

She sat up and took him in her hands, pleased at the way he dropped her foot and his breath quickened. She pushed him onto his back and whispered to him about Amber and aromatherapy and reflexology and the silence that she had endured all these years. But as she spoke, she rocked back and forth until the words no longer mattered. When Caleb moved her hips and told her it felt good to scream, she threw her head back and did. And when it was over, she was certain that touch could heal what nothing else could.

If Jane had been disappointed that Caroline wasn't coming home for the winter break, she no longer felt that way. Caroline called to say that Raymond's family had sent two tickets to Arizona. "Will you be coming home at all?" Jane asked. Caroline answered, "Oh, do I still have a home?" Jane ignored Caroline's sarcasm and said, "I love you. Say hello to Raymond. If you decide to stop here on your way back, let me know." But Caroline promised nothing. That night Jane had not slept, remembering how she used to tell Caroline to press whatever part of her had been injured against her own flesh and transfer the pain, the discomfort to herself. "Press it into Mommy," Jane would say. And Caroline, trusting in that power, would shut her eyes and hold her bruised knee against Jane's open palm. "Better?" Jane would say. And Caroline would nod, not at all amazed.

Caroline would never love Jane as much again. But Jane thought she probably loved Caroline even more now than ever before. Now that Jane knew she could hold out to Caroline all that she had to offer and say, "Here. This is for you. Take as much as you need. More, in fact, if you want." Her offering would be genuine, not at all like Aunt Helen's had been. Their mother's only sister, Aunt Helen always encouraged Ellie and Jane to take the M & M's and halvah and chocolate-covered raspberry rings that she kept in crystal candy dishes on the coffee table. "Take! Take!" Aunt Helen always urged, but she never removed the plastic that was tightly wrapped around each dish. Instead, they practiced peeling navel oranges in one continuous piece and waited to go home.

After Aunt Helen died, Jane and Ellie had accompanied their parents to her house so they could pick up the personal items left to them in her will. Aunt Helen's daughter, Rona, had smiled, peeled back the plastic from the candy dishes, and said, "Here. Take as much as you want." Ellie had stuffed herself with some of everything, but not Jane. When Ellie wasn't looking, Jane had filled her pockets with as much as she could cram into them. After Ellie fell asleep in the car on the ride home, Jane kept patting her pockets, hoarding the secret they contained.

She had never eaten those candies. She had fallen asleep and forgotten all about them until the next morning, when they were stuck together and covered with pieces of lint. Then she had to covertly wash her slacks by hand, so her mother wouldn't find out. But Ellie saw. She had shaken her head and said, "You should've eaten them right away." Jane would have eaten them all now. She would have eaten her fill, piece by delicious piece.

Gwen refilled Jane's cup and sat across from her at the kitchen table. Matt and Ethan were still asleep, even though it was almost noon.

"So she's not coming in at all?" Gwen said. "The boys have been asking for her. They'll be disappointed."

"I'll mention that to her," Jane said. "Not that I think it'll matter much. She called to let me know they arrived safely. Lily, Raymond's mother, insisted on speaking to me. 'We're so happy the children will be here for Christmas,' she said. I wanted to remind her that Caroline doesn't celebrate Christmas, but I kept it to myself. She assured me that Caroline was very welcome. The children looked right together, she said. I invited her to visit the next time she was in New York, and she said she would. I have a feeling she really will too."

"You don't sound pleased about it."

"Pleased? No, I'm not pleased. She seems nice, but it feels more serious than I'd like it to be. Why do I have to meet her? I don't want Caroline to marry Raymond. I think it's the first time she's really been in love. I'm happy for her. I really am. It's just that they're so young, and I so want her to live first."

"Because you didn't?"

"No. Because it's right."

"Right?" Gwen said. "I see."

She rested her chin in her hand and smiled. Jane narrowed her eyes and put her hand over Gwen's.

"Go ahead," Jane said. "I haven't got all day."

"Lily said they looked *right* together. Whose *right* is correct?"

"I know what you're saying, Gwen, but not everyone is as confident as you are in the karmic balance of cause and effect. I'm not willing to sacrifice my child's future to the possibility that she has to go through another life cycle to work it out."

Gwen laughed and reached across the table to kiss Jane's cheek.

"I love you madly," Gwen said. "But you've never done anything that you didn't think about for days. Consequently, I refuse to trust your judgment."

"You're certain of that?" Jane said.

"Absolutely," Gwen said.

"Well, my know-it-all friend, I'm about to shatter your little cycle of birth and death. Come closer, so I can poke my finger in your spiritual eye once and for all."

"Go ahead. When was the last time you did anything because it *felt* right?"

"Yesterday," Jane said.

"Oh? What did you do? Leave the laundry? Eat out of the ice cream container? That doesn't count."

"How about sleeping with someone? Does *that* count?"

Gwen snorted.

"Don't tell me you slept with Arnold again," she said.

"I slept with Caleb Singer," Jane said. "I took him home from school and to my bed."

"You don't say," Gwen said. "One of your students?"

"I do say, and he's one of my students' uncle," Jane said, clapping her hands in delight at Gwen's astonished expression. "Well, big mouth, now what do you say?"

"I'm speechless," Gwen said. "Why didn't you tell me right away? Why didn't you call me?"

"He spent the night."

"The great lesson of life, I suppose," Gwen said, "is to trust our instincts. Damned if I know why it takes so long to do that. Bravo. I'm really impressed."

She stood and poured herself another cup of coffee. She held the pot out to Jane and looked at her questioningly. Jane shook her head.

"Tell me about this Caleb," Gwen said.

Jane looked up, and then held her coffee cup aloft. "I think I will have some more."

Gwen refilled Jane's cup and then kneeled beside her.

"You're not in love, are you?"

"Oh, no. But I'd like to be."

"With him?" Gwen said.

She leaned against Jane and took both her hands in her own. She turned Jane's hands palms up.

"You didn't answer my question," Gwen said. "Would you like to be in love with him?"

"He's smart, funny, and rich. He's also great in bed. I didn't know it could be so good. Forty-four years old, and I just had the best sex of my life," Jane said. She sighed and looked into Gwen's eyes. "He's thirty-five years old, you know. What do you think about that?"

"Well, eventually he'll be forty-four."

They both stared into Jane's open palms and laughed. Jane moved her hands slightly and pointed at them with her chin.

"What do you see in my future?" she said.

With dramatic intensity, Gwen peered at Jane's palms.

"I see us getting older. I see our children not needing us anymore. I see discouraging relationships with men."

"It sounds positively grim," Jane said. "Don't ever count on making a living as a fortune-teller."

She moved her hands and placed them beneath Gwen's, turning her palms upward to expose the secrets of her lines and indentations. Jane's thumbs slowly traced the grooves, pretending not to already know what she foresaw. But Gwen pulled away and stood, pressing her hand into the small of her back and groaning before Jane could offer her own prediction.

"I don't count on anything anymore," Gwen said.

"I think there are some things you can count on."

"Now *you're* a soothsayer. So what do you see?" Gwen said. "When you look into our future, what do you see?"

"I see you," Jane said. "I see me."

Many years ago when both women were very young, they had pushed their children in strollers and fed them crackers and juice. Huddled close together, they sat on park benches and watched their toddlers run through flocks of pigeons, scattering them in a tumultuous show of human strength. Then the women were confused and angry. They had obeyed the prescribed customs. They had carried out the rituals, and they were still bereft of the love that had been promised. They talked of witchcraft and sorcerers and speculated about the future.

On one especially beautiful morning, Jane and Gwen fed crackers to the pigeons. "Run for your life," Gwen urged. "Destruction is near." It was summer. It had rained earlier, and the smell of the concrete rose in a way that reminded Jane of the sizzling steam iron against the freshly washed cotton in the Chinese laundry where her father's shirts had been carefully starched and boxed each week. When she turned to Gwen, she was leaning back on flattened palms, and her face was tilted up toward the sun. Her eyes were closed, and she was breathing through her mouth. Before Jane could ask what she was thinking about, Gwen said, "We didn't do anything wrong." She sat up very straight and then opened her eyes. Jane saw that she was crying and wanted to say something profound, something that Gwen would tell the children when they were older, but nothing came to mind. Gwen kissed

Jane's cheek and said, "You don't have to say anything." They had sat quietly, holding hands, watching their children and wondering why they couldn't find men whom they loved as much as they loved each other.

Chapter Twelve

The only childhood friend Gwen ever wondered about was Rowena Otis. They had been classmates for several years. Rowena was from a deeply religious family. Her father, a deacon in the church, was a grim but handsome man. The mother, a homemaker and seamstress, was cheerful and ugly. Rowena had her father's personality and her mother's looks. Gwen had never wanted to be friends with Rowena, but was drawn to her because she was different from all the other girls. Gwen had never wanted to be friends with any of the girls in her class. They were all versions of each other, except for Rowena and Gwen. "Beauty and the beast," the girls called after them. Rowena's freckles would fairly shimmer against her flushed cheeks. She always clutched her books to her chest and bent her head low against the taunts.

Once, in her hurry to escape the others, she dropped her books. They were held together by the sort of strap that was the fashion then, a thick rubber affair with a metal buckle. Rowena's books came undone, and she sank to her knees. "What's the matter?" the girls shouted. "Did your daddy forget to hook it right after he used it to beat you?" Gwen stood off to the side and watched the horrible scene. After the last words, she was covered in goose bumps even though it must have been ninety in the shade that day. She always made it a point to mind her own business. But Rowena was crying. Her thin lips were stretched tightly over her gums, and she wiped her eyes with the back of her hand. Streaks of dirt marked her face and created an odd pattern against her freckles. "Shut up!" she screamed at them. "You just shut up. You're nothing but a pack of filthy whores." The girls were silenced. They smoothed their carefully sprayed flips and patted their pageboys. Except for Rowena and Gwen, everyone wore her hair in one of those two styles. Rowena's shoulder-length hair was pulled back into a ponytail. Gwen had often watched her spend an entire class period with her ponytail over one shoulder as she pulled apart split ends. Gwen's own hair was extremely short. "She looks like that model, Twiggy," the girls whispered among themselves.

Gwen felt sorry for Rowena that afternoon and watched as she gathered her papers and books. Rowena piled her things and gently laid them on top of the red rubber strap. She held one end in each hand and tried to make the buckles meet. The rubber was worn, and the pile of books too high. Gwen could hear Rowena's breath come in deep, jarring gulps. Gwen knew what had to be done. If she failed to go to Rowena's aid, the regret would be unbearable. "Can I help you?" Gwen said. She crouched down next to Rowena and smiled. "No!" she said. "Just leave me alone." After several failed attempts, she strapped her books. Then she stood and stared down into Gwen's face. "You are beautiful," Rowena said. "You really are." Gwen watched her walk away.

On the back of Rowena's thin legs were marks exactly the width of the rubber strap. Ashamed of what she had seen, Gwen turned her head and buried it in the crook of her arm.

That night, long after her parents were asleep, Gwen lay awake and thought about Rowena and the beatings she endured. Gwen knew that Rowena probably thought she deserved to be beaten. Her father probably believed the same thing. When the phone rang in the middle of the night, Gwen reached out to grab the receiver before her parents could be disturbed. She suspected it might be Rowena. "Hello?" Gwen said. She listened to Rowena's breathing for a while and then said, "Rowena? Is it you? What do you want me to do?" After a brief pause, Rowena said, "Repent. Repent for your sins." Then she hung up.

At school the following day, Rowena slipped a folded piece of paper into Gwen's hand. *Fast for three days each week on bread and water. This will be medicine for your soul.* Gwen flushed the paper down the toilet. Rowena called again that night. Gwen tried to reason with her. "I haven't done anything wrong," she said. "I just thought we could be friends." Silence followed, and then Rowena hung up. At school the following day, she slipped another message to Gwen. *If anyone commits fornication with a virgin, he shall do penance for one year. If with a married woman, he shall do penance for four years, two of these entire, and in the other two during the three forty-day periods and two days a week.* Gwen tore the paper into as many pieces as possible and threw them away with the remains of her lunch. *Crazy,* she thought. At night, she waited for the phone to ring. Rowena called and said nothing. It became a ritual. They listened to each other breathe until, finally, Gwen would say, "Good night," or "Goodbye," and hang up. For a while, there were no more phone calls, and no more pieces of paper. Then one day, Gwen found a folded paper in her sweater pocket. *If a woman practices vice with a woman, she shall do penance for three years.* Gwen's face flushed a deep red, and she hastily shoved the paper back into her pocket. Rowena called that night. She came right to the point. "I want to touch you," she said. Gwen shook her head no into the phone. She was only fourteen and still a virgin. Rowena described what she wanted to do to Gwen with words that created heat only her own hands had been able to produce. She had French-kissed with Daryl Thompson, but he smelled of the phenolic resin his family used in their paint factory. Once she had even let Kyle Lowry put his hand under her sweater, but she saw a chicken feather on his shirt and couldn't stop wondering if he had washed his hands after doing his chores.

Gwen invited Rowena over after school. They walked together in silence. Gwen knew her parents were out. They were hardly ever home. Rowena followed her to her room and closed the door behind them. That afternoon they began a routine that would last for months. They would talk for a bit and look through some of Gwen's teen magazines. Rowena was especially fond of *Seventeen* and *American Girl*. Then she would slide her hand along Gwen's thigh and work her way up under her blouse. Gwen always kept her eyes tightly shut. She did not want to see Rowena's lust.

Rowena always had to make up a story. They were in a limousine on their way to a ball at the governor's mansion. Or they were in a movie theater in the back row. She always said, "I'd never hurt you, Gwen. You're so beautiful." And she never did. She would unbutton Gwen's blouse and fondle her while she pressed her legs together. Rowena never tried to touch Gwen anywhere else. It was as if they understood that anything more would make what they did real instead of a harmless game.

The other girls continued to mock them. "Beauty and the beast are in love," they said. Little did they know that their derision kept the relationship going. Gwen fancied herself a martyr. Rowena was her cause. If she could bring pleasure into Rowena's life, then there was some purpose for her own existence.

On the last afternoon they would ever spend together, Gwen touched Rowena for the first time. The end was imminent. They both knew that they looked forward to their meetings with too much urgency. With a quivering hand, Gwen pressed her fingertips against the welts at the back of Rowena's leg. It was the welts Gwen thought about each afternoon as Rowena sighed against her chest. It was the welts Gwen thought about when she turned away from her own reflection in shame. "Why do you let him?" Gwen whispered. Rowena's expression was eloquent. There was poetry in her eyes and grace in the angle at which she held her head. Then with a force Gwen would not have expected from someone as slight as Rowena, she felt her own hand trapped, felt the pain of her bones being crushed. "Because that's what it feels like," Rowena said. "Because his power is greater than God's."

They didn't go home together the next day, or the day after that either. They barely acknowledged each other anymore. And Gwen was relieved. By the end of the school year, Rowena's family had moved away. Gwen heard different stories. One was that they had been forced to leave by the local officials. Word had gotten around enough so that *everyone* knew the deacon beat his wife and children. *Everyone*. Another story was that Rowena was pregnant with the deacon's child. There were lots more stories, but Gwen stopped listening after a while. That summer was her fifteenth birthday. She breathed through her nose instead of her mouth and let Daryl Thompson have his wish in the back of his father's Chevy. The whole time she kept thinking about how Rowena had looked that last afternoon.

That was the year Gwen's family moved north. She never even said goodbye to Daryl. After they were already settled in their new home, a letter arrived. It had first traveled to their old address and had been forwarded along with the rest of their mail. The postmark said Alabama, but there was no return address. The letter inside was written on lined paper. There was no salutation, no closing signature, but Gwen knew who it was from.

Women who commit abortion before the fetus has life, shall do penance for one year or for the three forty-day periods or for forty days, according to the nature of the offense; and if later, that is, more than forty days after conception, they shall do penance as murderesses, that is, for three years on Wednesdays and Fridays, and in the three forty-day periods. This according to the canons is judged punishable by ten years.

Perhaps it was knowing that the great, terrible secret of her life was not what she had done with Rowena, but what she had not done to help protect her from her father that made Gwen feel she should repent. For three days, she ate nothing but bread and water. Her parents either didn't notice or chose not to say anything. The way the officials, and the ministers, and the parents of their town had done when Rowena walked past them.

Gwen had never told anyone about Rowena. Not even Jane knew about those afternoons with Rowena on the pink-canopied bed in the room of every girl's fantasy. Daniel never suspected that Rowena's adolescent hands had been where his hands now touched long before either he or Gwen knew enough to hope for each other. *Secrets.*

Gwen was glad she remembered Rowena. Some secrets were meant never to be shared. But now it was her children and their secrets that frightened her. The subterfuge they must have already been part of. The tacit pledges they had sworn to strangers. She did not want to know. And she did. That made her too much like her own mother. The sameness frightened her. Between herself and Rowena. Between herself and her own mother. And between herself and her children. They all had secrets that would never be shared. If she could have, she would have wedged herself between the space that separated everyone and held the future in abeyance.

Theodore always teased her that she was really a witch. She always woke just seconds before Matt's wails pierced the stillness. She always knew when he was ill or unhappy. Her touch alone could soothe him. "You're a witch," Theodore insisted. Once he had even frightened her by running his hands along her body looking for the mark of where the devil had grazed her body. "His touch would leave a thing like a teat," Theodore said. "They were found on the bodies of witches all the time. The devil created them so the witches could feed their familiars." Theodore pulled back the covers with such force that Gwen had stifled a scream. "They're no bigger than half a finger. And they always look as if they've just been sucked," he added. She looked down at the dark flesh of her own nipples, still erect from having just finished nursing Matt, and shuddered. Theodore measured his bent pinky against one of her nipples. "Just the right size," he said. "Perhaps Matt is really your familiar. It's usually a cat or a dog, but it could be any small creature. Matt's a rather small creature." Gwen had pretended to find this funny, but Theodore hadn't even smiled. She reached for the blanket, but he held it away from her. "I'm cold," she said. "I'll warm you," he whispered against her breasts. "I'll be your hungry familiar." As he licked at whatever remained of the thin, bluish milk, Gwen had a revelation. *There will be nothing left over for me after he's done. He will take everything inside me for himself.* She endured Theodore's voracity. She even helped bring it to a finish when her own nerve endings warned her that Matt was seconds away from waking again. Theodore didn't protest when she pushed against his chest with her hands and slid out from beneath him.

Stealthily, she had made her way to Matt's room and stood at a distance from the crib. She could almost smell the intoxicating sweetness of his breath. He stirred and made sucking noises, although he had eaten just a short time before. The Mother Goose night-light was enough to cast her shadow on the wall behind the crib. She was transfixed by the reflection of her nakedness. Her image did not reveal the sticky fluid that ran down between her legs, teasing her, urging her to impede its progress. But she ignored it. Matt paused and took a deep breath, and Gwen scooped him up in her arms before whatever had woken him compelled him to cry. "Shh, baby, shh," she chanted. "Mama is here." She nuzzled his face, rubbed her cheek against his, and gave him her knuckle to gnaw. "Still hungry?" she asked. His gums and tongue desperately sought some fulfillment, and Gwen, not really understanding her own motivation, waited for his frustration to peak before giving him what he really wanted. "There now," she whispered. "Hold on a minute." She stepped back, leaned against the wall, and then slithered to the floor. She sat Indian-style and waited for Matt to soothe himself back to sleep. The night air dried the sticky patches of her skin to a hard glaze, but she didn't move. She wanted the same thing Matt wanted. The same thing Theodore was looking for when he gripped her wrists and held them above her head because he was too foolish to understand that he could never be affirmed in this way. And she obliged them both. She gave them what they wanted and needed. In return, Theodore had given her Matt. For that, she had waited in her bed night after night and never let Theodore know that he was giving her something in exchange. Still, her baby would grow into a man. He would empty himself over and over again into women Gwen might never even meet. He would forget that it was his mother's touch that had been the first to produce the delirium of pleasure.

Certainly, neither Matt nor Theodore was likely to remember the night Gwen now recalled. But she did. She remembered it all. They had slept, replenished by her body and her touch. And she had lain awake beside Theodore in readiness for dawn and wished hard for someone to take care of her.

Daniel was angry because she still refused to see his new apartment. They had argued about it constantly, but Gwen wouldn't relent. Daniel brought it up again a few days before Christmas. He came to her place and brought the winter inside. His hands chilled her flesh as he reached under her sweater.

"The boys are here," she said.

Her sweater was wet where the snow from his hat had fallen. Daniel's hands made her shiver.

"It's so cold," she said.

"Let me," he said.

"Later."

"Then you'll come home with me tonight? I even bought a small tree. I want you to help me decorate it."

"I don't know. The boys are—"

"All grown up. They can be left alone."

He took her by the shoulders and shook her a little.

"You're running out of excuses, Gwen. I miss you. I want you to see the place. I want you to be there with me."

"Has Sandra been there yet?"

"Is that what this is about?"

"Has she been there?"

"No," he said. "And I haven't invited her either."

Gwen rested her head on Daniel's shoulder and picked at a piece of lint on his coat, grooming him again. Making him hers. Something she wasn't even sure she wanted.

"What is it?" Daniel whispered against her hair. "What do you want me to do?"

Take care of me. I want you to take care of me.

She put her hands inside his coat and clasped him to her body. All the secrets of her life would be lost if she didn't tell them to someone. Rowena Otis and her tragic life. Theodore's hands searching her weary body for telltale signs of the devil's touch. If she told Daniel her secrets, there would be no going back.

"Promise to listen to one of my secrets," she said.

"I promise to listen to all of them."

"No. Just one."

Maybe she would tell him that one night Theodore had oiled her body and told her it was an ointment that contained aconite and belladonna. "You may experience an irregular heartbeat and some incoherence," he said. She was always somewhere between terror and desire when Theodore touched her. She felt sleepy, but was afraid to succumb. There was really nothing in the scented oil, but his power of suggestion was great. "Don't, please. I'm too tired," she had begged. She had closed her eyes and slept. But in the morning, she remembered the rhythmic contractions that had made her call out and hang on to Theodore in spite of herself. "What happened?" she asked him as she shook him awake. "Your spirit made love to me all night," he said. "It only just returned to your body." She had hurried from the bed, eager to be away from him.

Perhaps tonight she would tell Daniel about the time her spirit left her body and brought back a complete memory of everything she had done the night before. She would not deny any such knowledge as she had with Theodore. She had lied to Theodore because she had been afraid of what he might do to her next if he saw her as an accomplice.

"Which one?" Daniel said.

Take care of me. I want you to take care of me.

And because she was still afraid, she lied again.

"I'm not sure," Gwen said.

Chapter Thirteen

The night before, Caleb had asked Jane what the unhappiest day of her life had been. "The unhappiest day, Jane," he said. "What was it for you?" She almost told him that there had been so many unhappy days it was impossible to choose, but she didn't think a few weeks of casual sex, no matter how extraordinary, should exact that sort of confession. And anyway she was afraid the truth might frighten him. "The unhappiest day?" she finally said, and then flirtatiously added, "It was the day before I met you." Although it was dark, she could tell he was considering the significance of her response. When she said, "What about you?" and he didn't answer, she pulled the blanket to her chin and curled her body into herself. It wasn't so much that she was hurt, but she wanted him to at least counter her remark with one of his own. Instead, Caleb slept. His beard rested on top of the blanket as if the dark gold hair were not part of his face. *Grandma has a habit of chewing in her sleep. She chews on Grandpa's whiskers and thinks it's shredded wheat.* Some foolish boy whose name she could no longer remember had scrawled those words in her autograph book when they completed middle school. Perhaps the boy who had written those words to her had been in love with her. He might have been as surprised by her disregard as she was by Caleb's careful silence. If she could have remembered the boy's name, she would have whispered an apology into the darkness.

Caroline was wearing a yellow sundress and red sandals. She was kneeling by the pond and watching the ducks. Jane held out a handful of bread and urged her to feed them. "Am I afraid?" Caroline asked. She needed to be told what to feel until she learned to trust herself. Jane shook her head and fit Caroline's hand into her own. Together they offered the bread and waited. Jane saw Caroline's little body quiver with excitement and fear. "It's all right," Jane reassured her. "Just keep your hand steady." Caroline was taut with apprehension until she saw that they only wanted the food. Only then did Jane slip her hand out from beneath Caroline's and watch her revel in her own daring.

"Mother?"

Jane opened and closed her hand. There were no cubes of bread left. The sun was so bright she could not open her eyes.

"Mother!"

Now Caroline's voice was insistent and demanding. It forced itself upon Jane. She bolted upright and was surprised at how much Caroline had grown.

"Caroline?" Jane said. "Where are the ducks?"

"The ducks?"

Jane looked down at herself. She was naked. Caleb stirred and reached for her thigh under the cover.

"What ducks, Mother?" Caroline said.

Then Jane was fully awake. She covered herself with the blanket with one hand and shook Caleb awake with the other.

"Who is that?" Caroline's voice trembled. "Who is that man?"

"Please wait outside," Jane said. "I need a moment."

By now Caleb was awake. He reached for his glasses and wrapped the wire stems around his ears. Then he stared stupidly at Caroline.

"Who is that?" he said.

Jane ignored him.

"Please, Caroline," she said. "Just give me a few minutes."

Caroline was stubborn. She always had been.

When the ducks were finally glutted and waddled off, Caroline pursued them and tried to entice them to eat more. "They've had enough," Jane said. But Caroline could not be convinced.

"What's going on here, Mother?"

"I wasn't expecting you," Jane said. "You're supposed to be in Arizona."

"I suddenly wanted to come home. I thought we'd surprise you."

"Well, you did. Now surprise me again and wait outside."

As soon as Caroline left, Jane put her face in her hands and shook her head. Caleb squeezed her shoulder.

"Poor Jane," he said. "I guess that was Caroline."

"I wish I had a back door we could use to just run away," she said.

"I wish you did too."

"Would you run away from me or with me?"

She had saved the white page in her autograph book for Simon Kramer. He had mattered to her more than anyone else. For months she planned something clever to write in his book. *If I were a head of lettuce, I'd cut myself in two. I'd give the leaves to all my friends and save the heart for you.* But he never asked. Simon had passed her book back across rows of giggling girls and never even bothered to turn around. *Roses are red. Pickles are green. My face is a holler. But yours is a scream.*

Now she had made the same mistake with Caleb. He tied his shoes and carefully double-knotted them. Jane liked the way he concentrated on even the simplest tasks. When he stood, he shrugged apologetically.

"I'm not sure what you want me to say," he said.

If you love me as I love you, no knife can cut our love in two. She had hoped Simon would write those words in her autograph book. She would stare at the back of his head and say the words over and over. *If you love me as I love you, no knife can cut our love in two.* If she really concentrated, she might bore through his skull and bend his will to hers.

"What do you want me to do?" he said.

Caleb's will was impenetrable. She could see that now.

"I don't think there's much to do."

Caleb sat down beside her and took her hands in his. He kissed her fingers, one at a time.

"You know I care a lot about you," he said. "You're splendid in bed."

Love many, trust few. Always paddle your own canoe. Cheryl Morris had written those words to her. Cheryl had been wise beyond her years.

Jane pulled her hands away. Simon Kramer. Arnold Hoffman. Caleb Singer. *Sugar is sweet. Coal is black. Do me a favor and sit on a tack.*

Raymond was sniffing at cartons of Chinese food when Jane walked into the kitchen. Jane and Caleb had feasted on Chinese food and abandoned everything halfway through the meal. The containers were scattered over the counter in greasy recognition of appetites that lo mein and fried rice could not satisfy.

"I wouldn't eat any of that if I were you," Jane said.

He looked up and tossed the containers into the trash.

"Well, hello," he said.

"Hello yourself. Where's Caroline?"

"She went up to her room."

He collected the rest of the containers and threw them away without bothering to look inside.

"Please," she said. "Leave everything. I'll do it all later."

"All right, Mrs. Hoffman. If you insist."

"It's Jane. And, yes, I insist."

Raymond washed his hands and then dried them on a piece of paper towel. He balled up the paper and made a neat shot into the trash. Jane found his composure irritating.

"How is your family?" she said.

"Very well, thank you. They look forward to meeting you and . . . well, you." He scratched his head. "I'm sorry. I guess we should've called first."

"I guess."

They both turned when they heard Caleb knock on the wall. Neither of them had heard him enter.

"Sorry," he said. "I didn't want to interrupt. I ran into Caroline upstairs. She was pretty upset."

Just then, Caroline materialized as if from a magician's cloud of smoke. She pushed past Caleb and immediately flew into a rage.

"Well, Mother, I just introduced myself. He's charming. A bit young, but I'll bet he can go two or three times a night without stopping. You did very well for yourself."

"That's enough, Caroline."

"Enough? I don't understand," Caroline said. "How could it be enough already?"

"I said that's enough. This is my house, Caroline. I won't have you insult my friends here."

"Friends? No. I would never do that, Mother. But Caleb is more than a friend. Isn't he more than a friend?"

Caleb removed his glasses and cleaned them. They all turned to him and watched as he wound the stems around his ears, riveted by his every motion. Raymond took the opportunity to move closer to Caroline. She was breathing so hard that her chest was heaving. She had closed her hands into fists and looked ready to pounce.

"Caroline, please," Jane said. "Why don't we sit down and talk. I know it must be very difficult for you. I realize what a shock it must've been for you, but—"

"Why would I be shocked? At least now I understand why Daddy left."

Raymond came up behind her. Jane watched as this hulking stranger overpowered her daughter with tender force. Finally, Caroline relinquished her rage and broke into a heartbreaking lament that had no words. Raymond led Caroline, weeping and limp, from the room. Caroline had nothing more to say. She never even glanced at Jane. If Caroline had turned around, even for a moment, she might have seen her mother serenely gazing off into the distance. Caroline could not know that Jane was searching for the little girl in the yellow sundress and red sandals.

~~~~~

When Caleb asked if he should phone later, Jane said it would be best if she phoned him. It was a relief when he finally left. She hurried to find Caroline and found Raymond instead. He was sitting at the top of the stairs, staring at nothing.

"Are you all right?" she said.

He nodded and moved over to make room for her next to him.

"Carrie's asleep," he said. "She knocked herself out."

"Well, that's good. That she's asleep, I mean."

"I knew what you meant. I need to talk to you. Carrie's pregnant."

When you are married and have 1, 2, 3, name the prettiest after me.

"Mrs. Hoffman...Jane?" Raymond said. "We're going to get married. I love Carrie."

"Did you tell your parents?"

"Yes. My father didn't say much, but my mother offered to take care of the baby while we finished school. She suggested that we transfer out there to make things easier."

"Did Caroline agree to move out there?"

"No. She said it was too far away from you."

Jane patted his knee and then used him to pull herself up. There was an ache in the small of her back and all the warning signs of a migraine. Her body would pay the price for her restraint. *How could you?* The words made her quiver. *Why weren't you more careful?* She wanted to beat his head against the wall.

"Is Caroline all right?" she said.

"She's afraid."

"Does her father know?"

"Not yet."

"I think I'll go rest for a while," Jane said. She looked down at his dark hair, so straight and shiny that it almost looked wet. It would be a beautiful baby. "I'm suddenly very tired."

"I'll do my best to take care of Carrie and the baby," he said.

"I believe you," Jane said. "I really do. It's just that I wish things were different."

"I'm sorry," he said. "I don't know what else to say. I'm really sorry."

He had not meant to cause anyone pain. Jane could see the sincerity in his expression. That made it all the more surprising that she felt nothing.

When you are sick and going to die, call me up and I will cry.

"Me too," she said.

"Caroline's pregnant," Jane said.

Gwen's sharp gasp seemed to linger in Jane's ear as she waited for a more complete response.

"Oh, Jane," Gwen said. "How did you find out?"

"She's here. With Raymond. They showed up this morning."

"That must have been quite a surprise."

"Oh, it was a surprise all right. I was in bed with Caleb. We were asleep. Caroline walked right into the bedroom."

"No! I'm so sorry. It must've been awful."

"It was awful, Gwen. Caroline was out of control, and I was enraged. She blamed me for destroying the marriage. Can you believe it? Well, that's the least of it. She's pregnant. Caroline is nineteen and pregnant. What a mess. I wish I had been more sympathetic. But I didn't know she was pregnant until Raymond told me. Still, I should have handled it better. She must have been horrified to open the door and find me in bed with Caleb."

"If she's old enough to get pregnant, she should be old enough to knock on a closed door."

"She wanted to surprise me."

"And she did. And now you feel guilty. Now you blame yourself because you couldn't read her mind. You couldn't anticipate her every feeling and predict her reaction. If you were a *really* good mother, you would've been able to do all that. Right?"

"Yes. Yes to everything. Exactly right."

"Do you really believe you have that much power?" Gwen said.

"I don't know. Everything is such a mess now. What should I do? Tell me what to do. You're so good at this."

"At what, disaster? I guess I do have a knack for it. Oh, Jane, my dear, dear friend whom I love very deeply, I don't think there's anything you can do now except be there for her. Tell her you love her. Tell her you'll help her. And tell her you also have a right to be happy. And if she doesn't buy that, then it's her problem and not yours."

"I know, but she has an awful lot to deal with at one time."

"She needs you now, Jane. You'll help her," Gwen said. "Where's Arnold? Does he know?"

"He's in Florida," Jane said. "We were supposed to go together. I'm glad he's away. He'll be back Monday."

"Well, that worked out. I'm almost afraid to ask, but what happened to Caleb?"

"Oh, him." Jane laughed. "Poor man, I almost feel sorry for him. He couldn't wait to leave."

"That's it?" Gwen said. "I don't even get a chance to meet him?"

"It doesn't matter now," Jane said. "Will you come for dinner tonight? Bring the boys. I think Caroline would love to see them, and I need to see you."

"Daniel wanted to take the boys out for dinner tonight. He's going to Kate's for the holiday. It's the baby's first Christmas. I think it'll be fine anyway. What can I bring?"

"Wine. Lots of it. And some dessert. Something with chocolate."

"It'll be all right, Jane."

"I'm in no mood for optimism," Jane said. "If you can't be miserable with me, I don't want any part of you."

"I promise to be miserable all evening."

"Bless you," Jane said.

Jane had once heard that it was possible to heal a burned finger by placing the injured flesh behind the earlobe. She was told that the skin would burn intensely for a few minutes and then stop. There would be no blisters. No sign that there had ever been a wound. She never remembered to try this remedy, and thought of it only at the oddest moments. Like now, when it seemed that nothing in the world could make the pain better.

Caroline's face was buried in the crook of her arm, her body curled up into a tight ball. The shades were still drawn. Raymond said she was awake, but she didn't stir when Jane called her name.

"Do you want me to leave?" Jane said.

She stood in the doorway. Caroline did not answer.

"I've invited Gwen for dinner. She's coming, with Daniel and Matt and Ethan. They've been asking for you. Raymond's downstairs. He's worried about you."

Jane had the sense of speaking to someone in a coma and had the urge to say, *Move your toes if you hear me.*

"I know this morning must've been awful for you. I know it was for me. I'm sorry you were so upset. I didn't want it to happen."

"I didn't want it to happen either."

Caroline still didn't turn around. She spoke to the wall, her body turned away in a deliberate statement of rejection.

"Caroline, if only we could talk about this."

She sat up and swung her legs over the side of the bed. They barely touched the floor, and Jane smiled because the scene was so reminiscent of a different time, a different argument. A resolute child who liked to linger over her anger until she was thoroughly satisfied that she could take it no further.

"Raymond told me about the baby," Jane said. "I want you to know I'm here for all of you. I love you, Caroline."

Caroline's eyes were red and her cheeks blotchy from crying. She touched her earrings, two small gold suns against the dark sky of her skin. The earrings had been a birthday present from Gwen. Caroline loved them. Jane kept her distance and waited. Caroline cleared her throat several times before she began to speak. It was evident that she had given a lot of thought to what she wanted to say to her mother. When Caroline finally spoke, her voice faltered a bit. She breathed deeply, giving herself a chance to recover, and then proceeded with clear intent.

"I've been thinking about us," Caroline said. "I've been thinking about all the picnics we used to take with Gwen and Matt and Ethan. Remember them?"

"Of course I remember."

"But there was one when I was eleven or twelve. We went to an outdoor sculpture garden. I remember we drove for a long time."

"Storm King," Jane said. "I remember."

"Gwen made peanut butter and jelly sandwiches with some of that good bread she was always baking. You made pinwheel cookies. Gwen braided flowers into my hair. Matt and Ethan said I looked stupid, and Gwen got mad. They teased her, and she looked so sad. She said, 'I should have had a daughter. Every woman should have a daughter.' It's funny, because that's what Lily, Raymond's mother, said. She said the very same thing. That's why I came home. I wanted to be with you, with Gwen. I suddenly missed you both so much. I remember that day I told Gwen that she did have a daughter. She cried and hugged me. You cried and hugged both of us. The two of you held me like I was some valuable piece of china. Sometimes I measure a good day against that day, but not too many come close."

"That was a real good day, sweetie," Jane said. "A real good day."

"You know what made it such a good day?" Caroline didn't wait for an answer. "I knew exactly what to say. I was only a kid, but I knew just what to do. And I felt so loved."

"You're still loved that much. And you'll have lots more days like that. I promise."

"How can you be so sure when I'm so unsure?"

"Because I already am a mother," Jane said.

She started to walk toward the bed, but Caroline put her hand up and shook her head.

"What is it, Caroline?" Jane said. "Why won't you let me hold you?"

"I can't, Mother. If you touch me, I'll fall apart."

Jane took several steps back and leaned against the wall.

"I'm at a loss," Caroline said. "I don't know how to make anything better anymore. Nothing is working out the way I planned. I've made a mess of everything."

"Oh, big deal," Jane said. "You'll get used to it."

It was good to hear Caroline laugh. Jane crossed the floor and reached for her. Not surprisingly, she burrowed into the nest of her mother's warmth and did not fall apart.

~~~

Gwen arrived with Daniel, Matt, Ethan, and two bottles of wine. Daniel held up two bakery boxes. "Pastries and a chocolate mousse cake," he said. The introductions seemed endless. Matt and Ethan kissed Caroline. Raymond shook hands with Daniel, Matt, and Ethan and then blushed when Gwen pushed his hand aside and kissed him instead.

"Why don't you all get acquainted while Jane and I tend to things in the kitchen. Daniel, you can be in charge."

"For once!" Daniel said. "What a treat."

"Now, you stop it," Gwen said. She playfully slapped Daniel's arm. "I'm just trying to be nice to you."

"She's trying to get rid of us," Daniel said from behind his hand.

"Go ahead, now. Go sit down," Gwen said. "I'll bring you a glass of wine in a minute."

She took Jane's elbow and steered her toward the kitchen.

"Why didn't you just push them into a closet and lock it?" Jane whispered. "It would've been less obvious."

"I know," Gwen said. "It doesn't matter. How are you?"

"I think I'm all right."

Gwen opened a bottle of white wine and poured them each a glass. She raised her glass.

"To the baby," Gwen said.

"And to us," Jane said.

"I'd drink to both those things if I were drinking these days."

Caroline stood in the doorway.

"Is this a closed party or can any girl join?" she said.

"Well, not *any* girl," Gwen said. "Only special ones. Come here. Let me touch you now that we're alone."

Caroline went to her and placed her hand over Gwen's as she rubbed her belly.

"Anything yet?" Gwen said.

"A few flutters, but no real movement. I just feel tired and scared."

Gwen kissed her eyelids and pulled her hair away from her face.

"We'll take care of you and the baby," she said.

"Promise?" Caroline said.

She turned around and looked at Jane.

"Promise," Jane said.

Caroline took her place between the two women. Jane raised her glass and took a small sip of wine. Then she set the glass down, turned, and moved in slowly toward Caroline. Arms outstretched, Gwen reached for Jane's hands and completed the circle. Caroline closed her eyes, smiled, and held her belly as Jane and Gwen swayed back and forth with her between them. And as so many years before, Caroline relaxed in their hold and found just the right words. "I'm not afraid. I'm not afraid," she murmured until it seemed it might even be true.

Chapter Fourteen

The boys asked to be dropped off at a party on the way home from Jane's house. "We might spend the night," Matt said. "Just call," Gwen said. It only felt late, although Caroline had almost fallen asleep right after her herbal tea. She was in her first trimester, when sleep was as essential as air. "I used to pass out in the middle of a conversation with Arnold," Jane said. "Yes, but I don't think that had anything to do with being pregnant," Gwen blurted out. She was on her fourth glass of wine by then. Caroline had glared at her, but Jane laughed so hard that Gwen had to slap her on the back. "Sorry," Gwen said. "It's the wine talking." Caroline excused herself and left the table. As she bent down to kiss Jane's cheek before leaving, Gwen whispered, "I should've told the wine to shut up. I'm really sorry." Jane patted her hand reassuringly and said, "Please don't apologize. It's the most I've laughed in ages." Still, Gwen couldn't forget the way Caroline had looked at her, as if she couldn't believe the betrayal.

"That last glass of wine put me right over the edge," Gwen said.

Daniel was driving, lost in his own thoughts.

"What was that?" he said.

"I was just thinking that I hope Caroline isn't mad at me because of that crack about Arnold."

"Well, my dear, your witticisms are often a bit sharp." He glanced at her sympathetically and added, "I'm sure you'll fix it with her tomorrow. Don't worry. It'll be all right."

"You think?"

"I know," he said, and reached over to pat her knee. "What about Raymond? You haven't said anything about him."

"He seems like a nice boy," she said. "I like him."

"That *boy* is going to be a daddy soon."

"You were a daddy at his age."

"You were a mother at Caroline's age."

"And look at us now," Gwen said.

Daniel's expression was so anguished that it made her ashamed of her part in his pain.

"Can you stay for a while?" she said.

"Am I invited?"

Gwen would have liked Daniel to lie beside her as he read aloud to her from the newspaper. He always chose bits of life she might otherwise have disregarded.

"You're always invited," she said.

She was already responding to the touch of his large hands against her drowsy flesh. Whenever she was tired, Daniel's grazing fingers left her with nothing to do except dream.

During dinner Raymond had told them that the Iroquois believed that certain dreams had to be obeyed. It was risky to let too many dreams pile up without heeding them. She had listened, hard, and known for certain she was in danger. For a long while now, she had been neglecting her dreams, inventing reasons for their recurrence, telling herself that she would know when it was time to confess to Daniel that she was afraid to lose him.

"I am a selfish little thing," she said now to Daniel. As soon as they were inside her apartment, she had taken him to bed. His flesh seemed so much more real to her than anything else in her life. "Mother was right about me," she said, predicting that Daniel would object to such a slur against her character.

You're a selfish little thing, her mother had said from time to time. Amanda had known it was an inherited trait and always savored the opportunity to show Gwen she could not escape who she really was. *Selfish little thing,* Amanda would repeat. Her voice was so filled with derision that Gwen had to wonder if her mother loved her at all. *I'm not a thing!* she had shrieked back. They sparred with hateful words that left Gwen crippled with resignation and Amanda pacified by her own keen insight.

"It's not true," Daniel said. "You're not selfish."

"Oh, but I am."

She took hold of him with one hand and lowered herself over him, teasing him for her pleasure alone.

"You *are* a selfish thing," he said.

"You see?" she agreed.

"Why?"

"Why am I selfish?"

His hand closed over hers and guided her.

"Yes," he said. "Why?"

"Because I like it," she said.

He gasped when she forced his hand away and lowered herself in one quick move.

"You do too," she said. "Say you do."

"I do."

He started to say more, but she covered his mouth with her hand.

"Why do you like to be selfish?" he said.

She felt his muffled question against her open palm and moved faster, so her answer wouldn't matter quite so much.

"Because," she said. Her breasts flattened against his chest as she bent low and whispered against his ear. "Do you hear me?"

"Yes. I hear you."

"Good," she said. "Very good."

She slowed him down for her own fulfillment, waited a moment, and then began to lift herself up.

"Don't," Daniel said.

He gripped her firmly, but without force. Still, she was aroused by the desperation in his voice.

"All right," she said.

She suddenly wanted to tell him about a photograph she had seen of pepper fields in Macedonia. She had tucked the image away to share with him, and was surprised to think of it now. But there it was, the red in the photograph so red it had been almost impossible to trust. She reached down now between their bodies, searching for the place where they met, whispering in his ear about the pepper fields until his voice was no longer desperate.

When the phone rang shortly after the sun rose, the official-sounding voice at the other end identified himself as "Lester

Clark, the new director of the development where your mother has graced us with her charm and wit." Gwen had never met Lester Clark.

"What happened to Paula Chapman?" she said.

It seemed very important. Mother had never mentioned a new director.

"Miss Chapman retired, Miss Baker. I'm sorry. I phoned to share the sad news that your mother passed on during the night," Lester Clark said. "She died peacefully. We found her in her bed. There was no pain."

"How do you know?" Gwen said.

"Excuse me?"

"How do you know it was peaceful? How do you know there was no pain?"

"Well, we can only assume, of course, but it's apparent that she didn't suffer. She clearly had no time to call for assistance. She went to sleep and never woke up."

"But how do you know she never woke up?"

By this time Gwen was almost shouting. Daniel was awake now and trying to make sense of what was going on. He had spent the night after the boys phoned to say they would be staying over.

"Miss Baker, I'm sure you're distraught, and we really want to make this as easy as possible for you. Your mother was a delightful woman. We were all very fond of her—"

"Where is she now?"

"Her body has been taken to the hospital. It's routine procedure. We have to notify the authorities that there's been a death and—"

"You had no right to move her. No right at all. No right at all. . . ."

Daniel fumbled for his glasses on the night table and then took the phone from her hand. She slid back down under the blanket and shivered. He jotted down a few things on the back of an envelope and asked some questions in his best administrator's voice. Gwen watched him with unblinking eyes.

"Yes, thank you very much," he said. "You've been very kind. Yes. I'll phone back as soon as I know."

When he finally hung up, Gwen raised one side of the blanket and then lowered it after he lay down beside her.

"I'm cold," she said. "I can't seem to get warm."

He rubbed her arms and pulled the blanket even tighter around her body.

"What can I do?" Daniel said.

"I have to tell the boys. They'll want to come along."

"I think they have bereavement flights. We'll check. Is there anyone you have to call?"

"No. Nobody. I'm all alone now."

"But I'm here," he said.

Daniel stroked her back and kissed her hair. She burrowed into the space between his shoulder and chin and wept, afraid to grow old alone. Daniel would go back to Sandra. They would retire to Florida and play golf. They would never talk about what had happened. Every so often Sandra would find Daniel standing at the kitchen sink, staring off into space with a glass of water in his hand, a half-smile across his lips. "Is everything all right?" Sandra would ask. He'd turn to her and shake himself out of his reverie. "Yes," he'd say. "I'm just a bit preoccupied." Sandra would never ask him what it was that seemed to absorb him as nothing else could. She knew the answer without having to ask. And every few years, as fate would have it, they would meet someone or watch a television program in which the name Gwendolyn was used. Neither Daniel nor Sandra would acknowledge the connection. If the arrangement seemed odd, at least they were together. Each day they would perform immeasurable kindnesses for each other. He would fix tea in the afternoon and bring it to her in the mug that said "World's Best Grandma." When his eyes grew too weary to read the newspaper, she would read to him. If she pressured him to tell his dreams, he would lie. *Foolish old man,* he'd tell himself. *What's happiness, anyway?* And Sandra would ask, "What did you say?" and insist that he had spoken aloud.

"Give up the apartment and move back in," Gwen said. "I don't want to be alone anymore."

She had held back the words for so long that they sounded foreign to her now, some exotic idiom haphazardly strung together.

"You're not alone," he said.

Perhaps he had not understood what she meant.

"I'll stay with you as long as you need me," he said. "I'll go down with you to take care of things."

No. He had understood everything. She made her voice light with indifference, making it seem as if she had never said anything at all.

"Don't be silly," she said. "Leave it to Mother to die just before Christmas and screw up everyone's plans. Don't you worry. You go on and see the baby. It's her first Christmas."

Then she turned her face away from him and licked at her own salty tears. Her body was rigid with anger and shame against his refusal. He had given his answer.

She decided not to phone Matt and Ethan. They had promised to be home before noon. For three hours, Gwen was on the telephone. The first call was an apology to Lester Clark. He was gracious and understanding. Next, she phoned the funeral home where both her father and her brother had been taken. It was a family-run business into its fourth generation of funeral directors. Gwen spoke to the son of the Mr. Richardson who had helped make the arrangements for her father. She remembered this Richardson heir as a boy no older than Ethan. "You sound just like your father," Gwen said, and he said, "Thank you. We take great pride in our work."

Jane cried when Gwen gave her the news. "I'll be there as soon as I can," Jane said.

"Hurry," Gwen said. "I don't know how long I can hold out."

Amanda's attorney had to be contacted. He was a friend of the family. Reginald Fisher was from old money. His law practice was mostly for his own amusement, although in his day he had had a fine reputation in the county. His son, Junior, ran the firm now. Gwen and Junior had been classmates from kindergarten on up. She had not seen or spoken to him since her own father had died. She gave her name to his secretary and waited impatiently for him to pick up.

"Gwen? I can't believe it's you. How are you?"

"I'm all right, Junior. How are you? How's Annabelle? And the children?"

Junior had married Annabelle Thorton right after high school. Actually, Junior had *had* to marry Annabelle even though every-one pretended she had just put on a little weight because she was "so deeply nervous" about her Junior possibly having to go off to Vietnam. Well, Annabelle had nothing to worry about. The senior Reginald knew people in high places, and the Thorton family was from even older money. Amanda had told Gwen that Annabelle wore an Empire waist gown that hid her protruding stomach very nicely. Three hundred and fifty guests came to the club and sipped imported champagne and dined on lobster. Annabelle fed cake to Junior and stuck her tongue in his mouth when they kissed. "It was very common," Amanda said. "You could see her iced tongue darting in and out of her mouth. For the first time in my life, I felt truly sorry for Candida Thorton. Truly sorry. First that awful gown Annabelle had to wear, and now this." Gwen remembered that her mother hadn't sounded the least bit sympathetic about Candida's humiliation, but by that point in her life Gwen knew better than to challenge Amanda's intentions.

"Annabelle is just fine," Junior said. "The youngest, Conrad, is just sixteen. And our oldest, Roxanne, made us grandparents last year. Can you believe I'm a granddaddy?"

"Well, that's just fine news, Junior. I'm real happy things worked out for the two of you."

"I heard you got divorced. I'm real sorry about that. Your mother said he was a foreigner."

Somehow that statement more than anything else that morning made Gwen feel the loss of her mother. It was so like Amanda to offer that as an explanation for the divorce.

". . . but she said you had two fine boys," Junior said. He cleared his throat. "I hope I didn't offend you."

"You didn't offend me, Junior. It's just that, well, I'm calling with some sad news, and, well, I need to tell you that Mother passed on last night."

"Oh, Gwen! I'm so sorry. So very, very sorry. She was an

unusual woman. I just spoke to her last week. She was as alert as could be. It's funny, she wanted to be sure her will was in order."

"Really?" Gwen said.

"Why, yes, she was very exact about everything. I'm sure you'll see for yourself. When will you be down?"

"Tomorrow, I hope. I still have to make the arrangements. But I would appreciate it greatly if you would see to it that Mother is appropriately dressed. I know she'd hate to be seen in anything less than her best. I'll leave it to your good judgment."

"I'll take care of it immediately. But you must promise to call me when you know your arrival plans for certain. I'd like to meet you at the airport...if it's all right with you."

"You're very kind. I'll be sure to call as soon as I've made my plans."

"Well, that's just fine, Gwen. I'm real sorry about this. I don't look forward to giving the old man the news."

Gwen knew the senior Reginald was still spry and as lecherous as always. "Why, he makes a pass at me every time we see each other," Amanda had said. "Ridiculous old coot. Doesn't he know Gloria was my friend? It would be unthinkable." But Gwen could tell it pleased Amanda that he still found her attractive enough to make a pass at over lunch at the club. "The crab salad isn't as good as it used to be," she said, "but they still make the best damned Bloody Marys in the South." Gwen was going to miss those stories. Now she would never know what color table linens they were using this month at the club or the new dishes they had added to the menu. She wouldn't be privy to any more of the local gossip or Amanda's distinctive commentary.

"Please be sure to call," Junior said. "Annabelle will be disappointed if you don't."

"I'll call. There's just one more thing," she said.

"Yes. Anything."

Gwen was going to tell him that Theodore wasn't a foreigner and that their marriage had failed because she had been too young and he had been too cruel. Then she thought about Amanda leaning intimately across the table and divulging the "supreme truth, I swear" to someone she could count on to pass the information along and clear Gwen's name. It didn't even matter that Amanda was relentlessly unforgiving toward Gwen in private. To everyone else, Amanda was inculpable. Gwen had married a foreigner. The rest was to be expected.

"I'd like you to say a few words at the service," Gwen said. "I know Mother would've liked that."

"I'd be honored," Junior said.

Actually, Amanda had never had much use for Junior. "Preposterous to call a blockhead *his* age Junior," she always said. "In addition to which, I've never met anyone as insensitive as Reginald's boy in my life. Annabelle will regret her indiscretion for the rest of her life. That's for sure." Gwen decided to keep that bit of information to herself as well.

Matt and Ethan sort of tumbled through the door and then froze when they saw Gwen's pale face. She had been resting on the couch when the sound of their voices made her sit up and try to look as if nothing was wrong.

"What's the matter, Mom?" Ethan said.

He pushed past Matt and came right to Gwen's side.

"Are you sick? Did something happen?"

She took his hands in hers and pulled him down next to her on the couch.

"Sit," she said. "You too, Matt. Come sit with me."

Although Matt was the older one, he often deferred to Ethan. They had grown to look so much alike that people often mistook them for twins. Matt sat quietly and leaned against her. Braced by her boys on either side, she was ready to speak.

"Grandmother died last night. I've been assured it was a peaceful death, so I'm encouraging that view. I'll have to fly down tomorrow and probably spend a few days taking care of business. I know you'll both want to come to the funeral, but you don't have to stay if you'd rather not. This interferes with our Christmas plans, but it can't be helped. Daniel and Jane have offered to accompany me and to stay down as long as I need them to, but we haven't made any definite arrangements yet." She felt slightly nauseated and took several deep breaths before she continued. "Grandmother loved you both very much."

"Are you all right?" Matt said.

"I will be."

Matt kissed her cheek and stood.

"I got a letter from her last week," he said. "She sent me five dollars. All singles."

"What did she have to say?" Gwen said.

"She told me she hoped I was practicing safe sex and should use the money to buy condoms if I had reason to use them. She also told me to have hot water with lemon juice every morning and an occasional glass of buttermilk. 'Both extremely beneficial to the digestive system' were her exact words. I didn't get a chance to write back."

"It's all right, sweetie. She was more interested in what she had to say than in what you had to say, anyway."

Matt laughed and said, "I guess."

"Well," she said. "Daniel's on the phone with the airlines. I'll be going on ahead of you, so you'll need to be sure your suits are clean. Don't forget you'll need real shirts, preferably white. Grandmother would insist on ties. You can skip the hair cream." She smiled. "I'm going to see how Daniel's coming along. Are we all right?"

"Yeah," Matt said. "We're all right."

"Should we call Dad?" Ethan said.

"If you'd like," Gwen said. "There was no great love between him and Amanda, but I'm sure he'd appreciate that you wanted him to know."

Ethan kissed her hard on both cheeks, and she hugged him tightly. A sudden image of herself as a little girl trying to cuddle with Amanda emerged as if it were only just happening. "Careful," Amanda had said. "My nails are still wet." She was waving her hands around to prove her point. Then she thrust out her chin and proffered her cheek. "Fresh coat of lipstick, but you can kiss me." The anger at the memory was so immediate it took Gwen by surprise. She had thought it would be easy to forgive Amanda everything in death.

Gwen sat quietly on the bed, listening to Daniel make the arrangements. He turned the page of the pad and paused before writing something else. She leaned over and could see he had scrawled, *3:30—LaGuardia—Delta*.

"Thank you," he said. "I'll call back before eleven to confirm.

You've been very helpful." With the receiver still in his hand, he rubbed his eyes. "Well, I think that's the best fare so far."

"Thank you."

"I booked three seats on tomorrow's flight," he said.

"Three? Why three?"

"You. Me. And you said Jane wanted to come."

"You don't need to leave with me tomorrow."

"But I want to."

"It's not necessary," she said. "I won't be alone. I'd like to go on ahead with Jane. You can follow after Christmas with the boys."

"How do you know Jane will be able to leave tomorrow?"

"I just know."

"This is my punishment, right?"

"That's not true."

Daniel tossed the pad onto the bed and pulled himself up.

"This isn't about you," he said. "It's about me. I need time to make things all right with my kids, and with Sandy too. I wish you'd try to understand."

"I am trying to understand. I just don't know what I want anymore. It's been a long time since I've been so afraid. I don't care for it much."

"Gwen, please. Let me come with you tomorrow. I want to be there with you. Please."

"I need a few days to be alone. I'll call you as soon as I've made the final arrangements. You'll come for the funeral."

"I want to be with you," Daniel said.

"But this isn't about what you want," Gwen said. "It's about me and what I need. Now you try to understand."

"Hello?"

Jane's voice from the other side of the door forced a standoff neither of them was reluctant to accept. Gwen said, "Come in," and hurried past Daniel to open the door.

"I'm interrupting," Jane said. "I'm sorry. Matt told me to—"

"It's all right," Gwen said. "We were finished."

"I'll leave," Daniel said.

Both Gwen and Jane turned to him as if they were surprised he was still there. Jane hurried to Gwen and embraced her.

"I'm so sorry," Jane said. "Now we're completely alone. We're both orphans."

"No, no, we have each other," Gwen said.

Over the top of Jane's head, Gwen saw how the truth brought both grief and outrage to Daniel's expression.

Chapter Fifteen

Jane's own mother had died in the guest room. When nothing more could be done, the doctor had advised Jane to take Dorothy home from the hospital. "I'm taking you home," Jane told her mother. "It's time." Dorothy was already only intermittently lucid, but she seemed to understand the implication of Jane's message and sighed in relief. After fourteen months of resisting breast cancer, she was ready for the end. For the rest of the morning she appeared to sleep peacefully. When the ambulance attendants lifted her from the bed onto the waiting gurney, she opened her eyes and said, "Home." Jane was enraptured with her mother's enthusiasm. It was a good sign, she told Gwen. The doctors were wrong. It meant things could only get better. Gwen rode with them in the ambulance. All the way home, Jane held Dorothy's thin hand and chattered on in a whisper about Caroline's nursery school and the tulips that would be coming up soon. "Jane," Gwen said, "try to relax." But Jane started up a fresh monologue about the new wallpaper she wanted to get for the guest room. "Something cheerful," she said firmly. "Pink and green, I think. Soothing, yet bright. What do you think, Mother?"

But Dorothy had already spoken her final word. For the next thirty-six hours, hospice nurses came in shifts and sat by Dorothy's hospital bed and read. A jar of unopened baby food was so evidently a perfunctory gesture that it seemed pathetic to everyone except Jane. Dorothy moaned, but she never opened her eyes again except in unexpected bursts that were both startling and disturbing. "Is she in pain?" Jane asked the nurse. "I don't think so," was the cautious answer. But when Jane asked, "When will she wake up?" the nurse looked at Gwen in confusion. "Doesn't she know?" the nurse whispered. "She knows a lot of things," Gwen said defensively. Then she turned to Jane and drew her close. "She's not going to wake up. The doctor explained all this. I was there. He sent her home to die. There's no more medication. Only what's needed to keep her comfortable."

Jane was frantic. "She's sleeping," she insisted. "The painkillers make her drowsy. I'll call the doctor and have him phone in something less dramatic to the pharmacy." She tried to wriggle out of Gwen's grasp, but Gwen held on. "Listen to me," Gwen said. She caressed Jane's hair. "This is your last chance, Jane. Talk to her. Touch her. Tell her how much you love her even if it isn't true. She'll be gone in a few hours. Do it now before it's too late. Hurry."

Jane couldn't hear what Gwen was saying. She wrestled free from her grasp and opened the jar of baby food. "You see?" she said. "This is for her to eat. That's why it's here. Why else would it be here?" Dorothy's breathing was hoarse, and there was a sporadic rattle from her open mouth. "They wouldn't have brought this if they didn't think she was going to eat." She took the spoon and gently scooped out a scant amount of food. "Here," she said. "Have just a bit, Mama. Just a tiny, little bit for me." Jane placed the spoon by Dorothy's lips and waited for a miracle. When there was none, she turned to Gwen, held out the spoon, and said, "She's not hungry. It's the medication. It makes her lose her appetite. That's why she's not hungry."

Gwen took the spoon from Jane's hand and held her so tightly that Jane was sure there would be bruises on her arms. "I'm so sorry," Gwen said. "So sorry for you, for all of us." Gwen knew that Jane and Dorothy had never been close, but it didn't matter. Now Jane was out of time. She had to forgive her mother for a lifetime of withheld emotions and careless disregard, and it had to be done without any delay.

Together Jane and Gwen kept a vigil through the long night. They sang to Dorothy and stroked her arms and her face. Gwen twirled whatever was left of Dorothy's hair into soft curls. Jane pressed her lips to her mother's warm flesh and cried, "She doesn't even know I'm here." Gwen shook her head. "It's not true. She feels you through her skin. She knows. She knows you're here." Every few hours through that final sad night, Arnold popped his head in to ask, "Is everything all right?" He never approached either Dorothy's bedside or Jane; both seemed equally inaccessible to him. The fifth or sixth time he came to check, Gwen, without masking her irritation, said, "We'll call you when she's dead." Arnold left quickly. The hospice nurse, who had been dozing in the corner, woke in time for this last stellar performance.

Henrietta was a large, very dark-skinned woman with a Southern drawl that immediately endeared her to Gwen. "Well," Henrietta said, "I guess they all alike. No matter what color skin they have, they all alike. Bunch of big foolish children." She shook her head and added, "I hope you don't mind me talkin' like that about your husband, but I suppose you already know the truth. We always know the truth." Gwen started laughing first, and, of course, it was infectious. The three women laughed so hard that Arnold came running in. "What is it?" he said. "Have you all gone mad?" Jane walked over to him and put her arms around him. "This is what you're supposed to do to me when I'm in pain," she said. "Hold me. Rub my back. Like this." She moved her hands along his stiffened spine. "Ask me how I feel. Tell me it's all right to cry. You can do it." But she was wrong. "Jane, please," he said. She still hoped his "please" was meant as an apology rather than as a rebuke. But she knew better. She knew Arnold.

Arnold handled things. It was the only way she could describe his function in the days that followed. "Yes," Jane said to everyone. "Arnold's handling everything." He made the funeral arrangements. He called friends and family with the news of Dorothy's death. "Jane's being very strong," she heard him say again and again. Arnold handled everything. There was nothing for Jane to do but mourn.

Ellie had been on vacation in the Bahamas when Dorothy died. As soon as Dorothy's death was imminent, Arnold had consulted Ellie's itinerary. Still, Ellie was too late. She didn't have a chance to say goodbye, and blamed Jane. "Why did you let her die?" Ellie shouted. She arrived at the funeral home deeply tanned and dazzling in a black linen suit. She insisted on viewing the body alone and came out dry-eyed and even angrier than when she went in. "A shroud, Jane?" she said. "For goodness' sake, she looks like a fucking Pilgrim." Jane walked away and stood quietly next to Gwen. Arnold asked Ellie to help him with some "last-minute arrangements," and the two of them left already debating the advantages of buying disposable paper goods over using real china.

Dorothy's funeral was scheduled for ten the following morning. Gwen drove Jane home from the funeral parlor and waited while she undressed and stretched out on her bed. "I'm so tired, Gwen," Jane said. "I just want to sleep." She closed her eyes and listened to the sounds of Gwen drawing the shades and picking up around the room. Gwen left only to return minutes later with a sleeping Caroline cradled in her arms. She was only a toddler then and very sweet. Gwen placed Caroline on the bed next to Jane and covered them both with the quilt. Caroline opened her eyes and smiled. "Mommy," she said, and slept again. Gwen sat in the rocking chair in the darkened room and hummed softly to them. And as Jane inhaled the scent that was distinctly Caroline's and no one else's, all the anger rose and then ebbed in waves that left her faint with apprehension. Once, long ago, she must have slept beside her mother and known the peace she saw in Caroline's repose. There had been no anger then, none of the rage Jane felt over Dorothy's negligent mothering. None of the abandonment she felt at being left to negotiate the world alone. Gwen came over to the bed and lay down on the other side of Caroline. The two women laced fingers over the sleeping child. "She was never the mother I wanted," Jane said. "I still want *that* mother." Gwen gripped Jane's fingers and said, "We all want that mother." Jane turned away toward the window. Gwen had left the shade only partially down, and Jane saw a moth fluttering wildly against the glass. She watched its crazed dance, but couldn't tell which side of the glass it was on.

"I'm sorry about Amanda," Caroline said. "I liked her."

"I did, too," Jane said. "She was a real character."

"How's Gwen?"

"She's sad. You should call her, Caroline. It would mean a lot to her."

"I will. Of course, I will. I wish I could go to the funeral."

"I'm sure Gwen understands."

"I know, but still," Caroline said. "What time is your flight?"

"We decided to take the evening flight. Six-thirty."

They were in the kitchen putting away the groceries Jane had stopped in for on her way back from Gwen's. Caroline and Jane maintained the sort of rhythm that came with repetition. It was something they had done countless times before. Caroline's job was to empty the bags and arrange all the items in order on the counter—frozen foods, paper goods, cleaning products, pasta and rice, jars of spaghetti sauce, perishables. Then Jane put everything away while Caroline folded the paper bags.

"Microwave dinners?" Caroline said. "I'm shocked."

"The joys of living alone," Jane said. She regretted her words instantly. "I'm sorry. That was thoughtless of me."

Caroline shrugged and read the ingredients on the side panel of a frozen vegetarian meat loaf dinner. She made a face and tossed the box back on the counter.

"It sounds awful," she said.

"I'll let you know."

Caroline yawned loudly and sank into a chair. "Don't bother," she said. Her face was pale. She looked exhausted, like a little girl who had played too hard and was up way past her bedtime.

She's too young to be pregnant, Jane thought.

"I asked Daddy to come over," Jane said.

Caroline immediately shielded her belly with both hands.

"He's back?" Caroline said.

"Seven days. That's a week. He got in last night," Jane said. "With all the commotion this morning, I forgot to tell you. He'll have to be told sooner or later. Delaying the telling won't make it any easier."

"I'm afraid," Caroline said.

"Well, he likes Ray. At least, that's what he told me after he drove up to meet him. You don't have to be afraid. Daddy loves you. After the initial shock, he'll be there for you."

Jane walked over to Caroline and cupped her chin in the palm of her hand. Caroline nuzzled her momentarily, and Jane bent over and kissed her cheek.

"Don't worry, Caroline," Jane said.

"I'll tell him," Caroline said.

"I think that's best."

"I think I'll go take a nap."

After Caroline pulled away, Jane left her hand in the same position. She was certain she could still feel her child's skin against her own, pressing with the weight of unmet needs.

"Hello, Jane," Arnold said. "It's nice to see you."

Jane had fallen asleep on the couch. She opened her eyes to see Arnold standing over her, leaning in for a kiss. As she sat up, she pushed one hand against his chest.

"That's not being very friendly," he said.

"I didn't hear the doorbell," Jane said. "How did you get in?"

"I used my key."

His tone was confrontational, but Jane thought it best to

ignore the invitation to quarrel. They had more serious matters to address in the hours ahead.

"How was Florida?" Jane said.

"Hot," Arnold said. "I hate Florida. I don't know why I always go back."

"You love Florida. You're just afraid to die. Whenever you get back from there, you say the same thing, because the old people scare you." Jane placed her hand on Arnold's arm. "We're all going to die, you know."

Arnold laughed and said, "Not in Florida, I hope. But you're right. I played a lot of tennis. It was a good vacation. I needed it. It's a shame I had to go alone."

"You look very well," Jane said. "You had an extra ticket. You could have taken someone."

"I wish you had been with me, Jane."

"*I* hate Florida," Jane said. "I have some news. Amanda died last night. I'm going to Cedar Creek with Gwen tomorrow."

"I'm so sorry," Arnold said. "How's Gwen?"

"Overwhelmed at the moment, but she's coping. Let's go in the kitchen. I'll make some coffee. Have you eaten?"

She hurried off to the kitchen before Arnold could answer, but he followed close behind.

"Coffee sounds good. I'm glad you asked me over," he said. "What's going on with Caroline? How come they didn't stay in Arizona?"

"Caroline wanted to come home. She needed to be with us."

"Is she sick?" Arnold paled. "She's not sick, is she?"

"God, no. She's not sick—"

"You didn't tell her about me, did you?"

She stepped back toward the sink, as if she feared he would strike her. But it was only his words that threatened her.

"Give me another chance," he said. "We can go for counseling. I'll do whatever you want me to do."

She had bathed Caroline in this sink. The little plastic infant tub had fit snugly across the width. She had used the sprinkler, first testing the temperature of the water against her own skin. Caroline had trusted her to keep harm away forever.

"I would like you to tell Caroline the truth," she said. "I want her to know what really happened, and I want her to hear it from you. But that's not our priority right now."

"I can't tell her," he said. "Anything but that. *Anything*."

Caroline walked in and studied them with hopeful eyes.

"Anything but what?" she said.

"Anything but nothing," Arnold said. "Come here and give me a kiss. You look tired, Caroline."

"Thanks, Daddy." She kissed him and returned his bear hug with some squealing and giggles. She could have been a little girl again if someone were listening with closed eyes.

"So, where's lover boy?" Arnold said.

Jane and Caroline looked at each other and quickly looked away. Arnold didn't even notice.

"Ray went to the library," she said. "Anything but what?"

She was as suspicious as she had been when she found their bedroom door locked on a Saturday morning. *What are you doing in there? Open the door!*

"Your mother and I were just talking," Arnold said.

Gwen had tried to persuade Jane to tell Caroline the truth about Arnold's infidelity right off, but Jane had refused. The truth would have to come from Arnold, she insisted. Now she realized that she should have listened to Gwen and told Caroline. Sweating and pacing, Caroline was evidently out of control.

"You told him, didn't you?" Caroline said. She approached Jane menacingly, hurling accusations. "You couldn't wait. You never keep your promises! Never!"

"Caroline!" Jane said. "Don't. I haven't said a word."

"What is it?" Arnold said. "What's going on?" He drew Caroline to him and said, "Tell me what has you so upset."

Caroline pressed her face into her father's chest and sobbed softly as Arnold patted her back. Jane saw the girl who had sat on her father's lap, trying not to cry. *Don't cry, sweetie. C'mon, give Daddy a big smile now. Don't cry.* Caroline always gave him a smile that was hollow with unstated regret. At night, she would crawl into bed next to Jane and sob, finally safe from reproach. Through the night she whimpered and sniffled while Jane consoled her. "Daddy just wants you to be happy." Once Caroline had said, "*All* the time? He wants me to be happy *all* the time? I don't think I can be." Jane understood the quandary of wanting to please others as well as yourself.

"Tell me what's wrong, baby," Arnold said. "Tell Daddy."

"I think we need to sit down," Jane said.

Caroline moved away from Arnold and blocked Jane's way.

"Mother has a lover. Did you know that?"

"Caroline!" Jane said.

The girl was all grown and ready to vindicate her own imprudence by placing the blame elsewhere.

"Well, it's true. Isn't it true?" Caroline whined.

And then Arnold surprised them both. He did the decent thing.

"Whether it's true or not, Caroline, I think you're mistaken about what your mother divulged. Now, what is the news I'm really not supposed to hear?"

"I'm pregnant," Caroline whispered.

Arnold looked so shaken, so thoroughly frightened, that Jane hurried to his side and put her arms around him.

"I'm so sorry," she murmured. "There was no easy way."

Caroline cried into her hands. Her words were muffled, but distinguishable.

"I'm sorry, Daddy. I'm so sorry. I didn't mean to let you down."

"Why don't you sit?" Jane said. "I'll get you a drink."

Caroline froze while Jane steered Arnold into a chair and then went into the living room for the brandy. When she returned, neither Arnold nor Caroline had moved. They looked like a display of macabre wax figures in *Ripley's Believe It or Not*—disappointment and anguish captured in their expressions for eternity.

She poured Arnold a generous glass of brandy and handed it to him.

"Here," she said.

He reached for it and hesitated, unsure what to do next without explicit instructions.

"Drink it," she said. "It's all right."

"How can it ever be all right again?" Arnold said.

He drank the brandy and set the glass on the table. Jane saw that he was crying, and watched with growing curiosity his outpouring of emotion.

"It's all my fault," Caroline said. "Everything is my fault."

Arnold and Caroline both looked to Jane and waited for her to make it better. She always had before.

"We can get through this if we don't fall apart first. We have to stay calm. Right now, however, I have to pack," Jane said. "I'm going to Cross Creek with Gwen tomorrow, and I need to deal with that first. This will still be here when I get back."

Arnold stared morosely into his now empty glass of brandy.

"I'm really sorry about Amanda," he said. "Even though she never liked me, I'm sorry she died."

"No. She never did like you, Arnold."

"Why is that?" he said. "She liked *you*."

Jane recalled Amanda's judgment. *I'm surprised that a smart Hebrew like you married such a childish man. At least, if he had some money. Gwen's father, Mr. Franklin Baker, wasn't much better, but he had money, bless his soul. He had lots of money.*

"I guess we'll never know now," Jane said.

Jane went up to her bedroom to pack. Within minutes, Arnold entered the bedroom without knocking.

"I wish I'd knocked that day," Jane said, "but you didn't even have the decency to close the door."

"Is there really someone?" Arnold said. "You didn't waste any time."

"It doesn't matter."

"It matters to me."

She dropped an armful of underwear and sweaters into the suitcase.

"I don't want to talk to you about anything that doesn't concern Caroline," Jane said.

"I am sorry. No matter what you think or how this turns out, I am sorry. I hurt you. I hurt Caroline, and I hurt myself."

Jane folded a sweater and rested it on top of a pile of clothes she was preparing to pack. He sat on the bed, shoulders slumped, head down, as quiet as she had ever seen him. The classic pose of repentance. When he finally realized that she wasn't going to say anything, he lifted his head and spoke.

"Tell me about the boy."

"Ray?"

"Yes. Tell me about Ray."

Jane folded another sweater, held a skirt against it to see if it was a good match, and then sat next to Arnold. The skirt rested on her lap like a blanket, and she smoothed its creases with light strokes.

"He's a good boy. He loves Caroline. I think he'll do his very best. I like him a lot."

"Can he support a family?"

"Of course not. He wants to finish college. I think he has another two years, maybe a little less. His parents seem to be taking the whole thing in stride. I don't know what plans he and Caroline have made. I think they're still awfully stunned by the whole thing."

"How could this have happened to our baby?" Arnold said. "When did everything go so wrong?"

She set the skirt aside and took him in her arms. He wept against her while she rubbed his back with the same lack of concentration she had used for the skirt. Arnold just did not move her anymore.

"I'm sorry, Mom."

Jane was organizing things in her suitcase. Arnold was downstairs speaking with Ray. Caroline sat on the bed and began to sort through the panty hose that were in a pile next to the suitcase.

"I believe you," Jane said.

"I don't know why I did it."

"It doesn't matter."

"These have runs," Caroline said. She tossed two pairs of black hose to the floor. "I got scared."

"I don't blame you," Jane said. She kicked the rejected hose to the side. "There's a lot to be scared of."

"Remember when I was having all those bad dreams, and Amanda sent me that monster spray? She called me and said, 'Read the warning label, missy.' It was marked 'Caution. Monster Spray. Keep out of the reach of children.' She told me it was imported from the great state of North Car-o-lina and was very dangerous. She told me to spray my entire room from top to bottom. I didn't have any bad dreams that night or for a long time after that. I never knew it was water and food coloring. I thought it was magic."

"It was."

Caroline nodded.

"I wish I had some of that spray now."

Jane patted Caroline's hand.

"It was Daddy, wasn't it? He had an affair."

"I wouldn't call it an affair, Caroline. It was more of an act of spontaneous carelessness."

"I'm scared again, Mommy."

"I know."

I'm scared, Mommy. Check everywhere. Under the bed. In the closet. Everywhere, Mommy. Everywhere.

Jane had done a thorough search of Caroline's room every

night for months until Amanda sent the monster spray. Arnold had laughed at the whole notion. "It's ridiculous," he said. "She's too old to be afraid of monsters." But Jane had faithfully sprayed the room with the bottle Amanda had sent until Caroline stopped being afraid.

"We're never too old to be afraid of monsters," she said.

"I guess not," Caroline agreed.

But, secretly, Jane wished there were some sorcery, some enchantment, to make both her own and her child's fears evaporate.

Chapter Sixteen

"She never wore orange lipstick in her life," Gwen said. "And that dress. It's all wrong."

Amanda had been outfitted in a red-and-white polka-dot dress with a wide white belt and white gloves.

"She would never wear a summer dress in the winter," Gwen said.

"They should've dressed her in one of her lounging outfits and a pair of mules," Jane said.

"I never should've asked Reginald to select something, but I knew she would want to be dressed immediately."

They stood quietly for a few more minutes and looked into the coffin. It was strange to see Amanda so complacent. Even when she had withheld her opinion, it had been impossible not to know what it was. Now she looked like an old lady. Gwen had never thought Amanda looked old before.

"I was always angry when I was with her," Gwen said. "Everything she did was wrong. She'd look me over and say, 'Is that a new outfit, dear?' When I said it was, she'd say, 'Oh.' I could never help myself. I always had to ask, 'Do you like it, Mother?' Then she'd say something like 'Did it come in any other colors?' I always got angry, and she always said, 'Then why do you ask me?' It was incredible."

Jane linked her arm through Gwen's and laughed.

"Maybe they're all the same. My mother used to introduce me to people and say, 'This is my daughter, Jane. She's just a school-teacher. My other daughter, Ellie, married a wealthy man.' It got to me every time. And if I said something to her about it, she'd say, 'You make such a big deal out of everything. Don't you think I wish you could've married a wealthy man also?' I could never make her understand."

"I know," Gwen said. "But look at her now. I really loved her. No matter how outrageous she could be, I really loved her. I hope she knew that."

"She knew it. I'm certain of it."

"You know what she said the last time I told her? She patted my hand and said, 'That's nice, dear. You were always such an emotional child. I don't think it's served you well at all.'"

"And what did you say?"

"I said, 'You're probably right, Mother.' That seemed to make her happier than anything else."

"Gwendolyn? Gwendolyn Baker?"

They both turned to face a rather handsome man dressed in a dark blue suit and a red-and-blue-striped tie. He had a full head of gray hair that was cut short and severe. His broad smile seemed out of place under the circumstances, but Gwen smiled back.

"Reginald? Can it be? Why, you're still a handsome devil. The years have been very kind to you."

He came toward her with outstretched arms and embraced her warmly.

"Not as kind as they've been to you, my dear. You're still the most beautiful girl this town ever knew."

They hugged and stood back from each other, still holding hands.

"Reginald, this is my very good friend Jane Hoffman. She's come down from New York with me to help me through the next few days. Jane, this is an old friend, Reginald Fisher, Jr. He was the best kisser in high school. All the girls were just crazy about him, but Annabelle snatched him up before any of us could get him."

"Gwen, you're exaggerating," Reginald said. "But don't stop, please."

Reginald and Jane shook hands.

"I'm glad to meet you," Jane said.

"I'm glad to meet you too," Reginald said. He turned to Gwen. "They did a good job with Amanda, don't you agree? I hope you approve of the dress I selected. It was one she often wore to church. She looks truly dignified. I was here last night making sure everything was in order. I think she'd be pleased."

"Oh, yes," Gwen said. "It was very important to Mother to look dignified. Very important."

"Well," Reginald said. "May I drive you ladies back to your hotel? It's on my way, and it would be my pleasure."

"Thank you, Reginald. You're sweet, but I've rented a car. We're going to go over to Amanda's to take care of a few things.

My boys will be here in the morning, and I'd like to have everything done by then. But thank you."

"Well, if there's anything I can do, please don't hesitate to ask." Gwen smiled.

"I won't. I promise."

"I hope you'll find a little time for us to have a drink together before you go back. We could have lunch at the club."

"Yes," Gwen said. "I'd love to see Annabelle."

Reginald flushed and cleared his throat.

"We'll talk about it after you settle in a bit," he said. "It sounds perfect."

He kissed Gwen's cheek and shook hands with Jane.

"Well, if there's nothing more I can do, I'll be off," he said. "It's a shame Amanda had to leave us just before Christmas."

"Yes," Gwen said. "Mother did so hate to inconvenience anyone. She set such store in making people comfortable."

"Indeed," Reginald said. He bowed his head. "She was a true lady."

"Thank you, Reginald," Gwen said. "That means a lot to me."

As soon as he was out of the room, Jane turned to Gwen and said, "*You handsome devil?* What was that all about? And he couldn't have been any more obvious about his intentions if he'd knocked you to the ground and mounted you."

"I know. He was always like that. And I can't help myself when I'm down here," Gwen said. She shook her head and looked into the coffin one last time. "Dignified. She looks dead. She looks like a dead old woman, and she would've hated it. Let's go. I've had enough for today."

"I'm ready," Jane said.

Gwen took Jane's elbow and steered her toward the exit.

"I wonder if Amanda can hear us," Gwen said. "What do you think?"

"I think if she had heard you call her a dead old woman she would have risen from the coffin," Jane said.

Gwen gripped Jane's arm and quickly led her past the front desk. Amanda would have found their laughter unseemly in front of strangers.

Even though it was no longer the expansive home of her childhood, Gwen let herself into Amanda's one-bedroom apartment as carefully and quietly as when she was a teenager coming home from a date. Back then she was always late and always sure that she could make it through the kitchen door without getting caught. "*Gwen-do-lyn?*" Amanda's voice would bounce down the stairs, the syllables accented in a way that made it sound as if she were really calling three people. "Is that you? Lock up good and tight now, you hear? And stop in for a goodnight kiss." Gwen knew it wasn't a goodnight kiss Amanda really wanted. She really wanted to get close enough to Gwen to see if the pungent odor of sex was on her. Gwen would bend over to kiss her mother's cheek, and she would latch on to her arm with an iron hold. "Hmm. So you went to the drive-in with the Cavanaugh boy. Did he try to get fresh with you?" After reassuring her that Jake Cavanaugh had been a perfect gentleman, Gwen would go down the hall to her room, undress, shower quickly, and then brush her teeth and gargle to eliminate all traces of the taste Jake Cavanaugh had left in her mouth.

But this was Amanda's apartment now. Gwen sniffed. Lilies of the valley. Cream sachet. Amanda had never used anything else. Gwen stood poised on the threshold, afraid to enter the apartment.

"Aren't you going to go in?" Jane said.

"Amanda hated for anyone to go through her things. She just hated it," Gwen said.

"I don't think there's a choice here."

"I know. It just doesn't feel right."

"It would be worse if a stranger did it. Go on now, Gwen. Go inside."

Gwen nodded and stepped into the foyer.

Time was I used to have a parlor for greeting my guests. Now I have a tiny little space not even big enough to hold the broken hearts of all the beaus I had in my day. Not even half of them. It's a real shame. Not the broken hearts, of course. That's a tribute. But these living quarters just lack elegance. I'm sorriest to see elegance go. We need more of it in our lives, not less.

"Mother?" Gwen said.

She grabbed Jane's hand.

"I swear I heard her voice," Gwen said. She sniffed the air again. "Do you smell that? It's that cream sachet she always used. She swore it lasted longer than cologne."

"It smells sweet," Jane said. "Too sweet."

Gwen set her purse down on the hall stand and looked at herself in the mirror.

You could use a haircut, Gwendolyn. At least have it shaped a little bit. That style doesn't suit you very well. Oh, it did a few years ago, but you've outgrown it, dear. Why don't you let me make an appointment with Armando. He's gay. I'll never understand why they refer to themselves that way, but they do know how to cut hair. Let him put a little rinse in for you. Those people have a wonderful sense of color.

Gwen wondered where all the anger she had felt toward Amanda was now that she was gone. She had moved between the borders of love and rage with Amanda all their lives. It had left her weary from the disparities, and puzzled by the similarities.

In the kitchen she opened cupboards and stared at their contents. When she opened the cupboard over the broom closet, she gasped. "She alphabetized her spices. Look at this. It's unbelievable. You have to see this. Allspice, arrowroot, brandy extract, butter flakes, cardamom, cayenne pepper." She shook each bottle of cayenne pepper. There were three bottles in all. Two were still sealed. "Three jars of cayenne pepper? She didn't even eat spicy foods. This is bizarre. I wonder what she did with all this pepper."

"She put the cayenne pepper in her socks when she was cold."

"What?"

"She told me about it before Caroline first left for New Paltz. She sent some things for Caroline. Little things like notepaper and bath oil. The jar of cayenne pepper confused us. When Caroline phoned to thank her, she asked about the cayenne pepper. I'm sure I told you. She was worried about Caroline going up to New Paltz and said that cayenne pepper was a natural remedy for cold feet. Just a bit in your socks keeps your feet warm. Caroline says it works."

"Where could she have heard about it?" Gwen said.

"Why does it matter?"

"I don't know. It just seems as if there were whole chunks of her life that I wasn't part of. It bothers me. Why didn't she ever tell me about the cayenne pepper?"

Jane stepped back to get a better view of the remaining contents of the spice cabinet. There were two sacks of yellow cornmeal on the top shelf.

"She made great hush puppies," Jane said. "And grits. It was the only time I ever ate grits."

Gwen pressed her temples with her fingers and said, "Why, Jane? Why didn't she tell me?"

"You're making too much of this, Gwen. It's not such a big deal. Did you tell her everything? Do you tell *anyone* everything?"

"But she told you. She even sent you some."

Jane spun around and slammed her palm flat against the Formica counter. Gwen stepped back and clutched the jars of cayenne pepper to her chest.

"Damn it, Gwen. You would've laughed at her," Jane said.

Her words jolted Gwen. The jars dropped to the floor. Only one broke and spread its fine red powder across the floor. With the tip of her booted foot, she tentatively moved through the spilled pepper as if it were toxic.

"You can't undo what's been done," Jane said. "She loved you, Gwen. It's not that she didn't love you, but she knew who you were. You would've laughed. You would've told her she was crazy. I would've done the same thing to my mother, but I wouldn't have done it to yours. She knew that, so she told me. It's just the way it is. It can't be undone now."

Gwen fell to her knees and scooped up the powder into her cupped hand. She sneezed as she did it and turned her head to keep from scattering what she had salvaged. Without looking at Jane, Gwen stood and forced off one boot by using her other foot. Then she repeated the same maneuver to remove her other boot. She rubbed one stockinged foot against the other and was satisfied. Careful not to spill any more of the pepper, she opened her hand and emptied its contents into the boots.

"Do you think it's enough?" she said.

"I don't know," Jane whispered.

"You think I'm crazy?"

"I know you're crazy."

Jane opened one of the jars and poured some more pepper into each of Gwen's boots.

"Why take any chances?" Jane said.

Gwen nodded and pulled on her boots. She stood still, waiting for something to happen, anything, some sign that Amanda forgave her. She walked back and forth the length of the small kitchen, but her feet felt the same.

"Maybe I didn't put enough in," she said.

"Why are you doing this?" Jane said.

"I want to tell her that I'm sorry." She quickened her pace in the small area and was almost running now. "I should've been allowed to do that. I want her to give me a sign that she forgives me. Can you understand that?"

"I don't have to understand."

Gwen stopped running and leaned against the counter. When she tried to speak, she could barely catch her breath.

"I don't feel anything," she said.

They both stared at Gwen's boots as if they expected them to glow from the heat concealed within. Finally, Gwen tugged at one boot, and Jane pulled with her. When they were done, they both stared down at Gwen's feet, now flecked with pepper that stuck to her stockings in an uneven pattern.

"I probably didn't use enough," Gwen said. Her voice quivered with disappointment. "I guess I did something wrong."

"I guess," Jane said. She opened the broom closet and took out the dustpan and broom. "I'll sweep everything up."

"No, don't. Please, leave it."

Jane shrugged and stepped over the mess.

"You're right," she said. "I would've told her she was crazy. I would've challenged her sources and ridiculed her for always believing the nonsense she heard."

"And what would she have done?"

"She probably would've tried to change the subject. You know how she had a knack for steering things in a different direction. I hated it when she did that. I always wanted the confrontation, but she avoided it. She endured it, so both of us could feel bad. I'd feel guilty, and she'd be hurt." Gwen shivered, and then laughed. "Well, she got me again."

She took the broom from Jane and with great tenderness began to sweep the pepper into a small pile as if the red powder were her mother's ashes, rather than the result of her own impulsive behavior.

You have your mind on too many things at once, Gwendolyn. You're always running away from what you should be running toward. It doesn't do to be afraid of things in this life. If something is going to catch up with you, it doesn't matter how fast you run. Can't always sweep the mess under the carpet. Just take hold of that broom and fix your mess. You made it. You fix it. Do you hear me? Is whatever you're looking at out that window more interesting than what your own mother has to say?

"No, Mother, it isn't more interesting," Gwen said aloud. "I'm listening. I was *always* listening."

Jane bent down to hold the dustpan, but Gwen shook her head. She took the dustpan from Jane's hand and cleaned up her own mess. The way her mother had taught her to do.

The red light on the phone in their hotel room was blinking when they got in. "Daniel phoned," the clerk said. "You may reach him at home." Gwen thanked her and leaned back against the cushions. She could hear the water running in the bathroom. Jane was preparing a bath for herself. "Are you sure you won't let me fill the tub for you?" Jane had asked. But Gwen had insisted that Jane go first. "I need to unwind a little, and I want to phone Daniel and the boys." Jane ordered some tea and sandwiches from room service and waited until after everything arrived. She poured tea for Gwen and placed the cup and saucer on the night table. "Have something," Jane insisted. And Gwen promised she would.

They could have stayed at Amanda's apartment, but Gwen could not bear the thought of being there without Amanda. Tomorrow she would stay at Amanda's with Daniel. Matt and Ethan would stay at the hotel. After the funeral, Daniel would stay on for a day and then fly back to spend Christmas with Kate and his new granddaughter.

She picked up the phone and placed it on her stomach. It was only three o'clock, but it felt like the middle of the night. She barely had the energy to lift the receiver. The funeral was the day after tomorrow. Wednesday. Reginald would take care of all the details. He had told her so over the phone. The memorial service was scheduled for eleven-thirty. Amanda would have considered anything earlier indecent.

Reginald had promised that "the good ladies from the church will take care of everything. They will be preparing a little something for us to have after the burial." There would be people to thank whose names she could not even remember. *Take care.* It was what she always told her boys when she kissed them goodbye. Her parting words, given like some talisman against potential danger. *Take care.* Now she wondered why she always whispered the words instead of shouting them.

"I must've dozed off," Gwen said.

Jane rubbed her wet hair and then rolled the table over to the bed. "Egg salad on rye toast." She moved the plate close to Gwen. "Eat something. I cleaned the tub. I'll run the water for you when you're ready. Do you want some more tea?"

She opened a napkin and placed it across Gwen's lap. Then she filled her cup with hot tea and added sugar and milk.

"Thank you," Gwen said. "Thank you for taking care of me."

Jane sat down on the bed and tucked her legs beneath herself. With her fingers, she picked up some of the egg salad that had fallen onto the plate and dropped it into her mouth.

"You're welcome," she said. "Mmm, that's good."

"Thank you," Gwen said again.

Jane tilted her head to the side to get a better look at Gwen.

"You don't have to thank me for anything," Jane said.

"Oh, but I do. I have to. I don't know what I would've done without you."

"Or I without you," Jane said.

They gossiped then about the locals, people Jane would meet in the next two days. Gwen reminisced about her childhood and the Amanda she remembered. Jane listened, saying little or nothing more than an occasional exclamation of surprise or pleasure.

Once she squealed, "You didn't!" And Gwen reassured her that, yes, in fact, she had. But it was when Gwen told her about the freak shows that traveled to these parts every spring that Jane grew very still. Gwen drew her into a recollection of the Siamese twins who had seemed more sorrowful than anyone she had ever seen. She told Jane how Amanda had pulled her past their stall and advised her not to look. "Horrid thing to see! An outlandish mutation!" And Gwen had averted her eyes, ashamed, and afraid to do otherwise.

In the quiet of the dim room, Gwen took Jane back to that afternoon to help her see what should have been different. In a day's time, they would watch as Amanda's body was placed in the earth. It was likely those poor Siamese twins had known truths it took others a lifetime to determine. The twins had known that primeval urges may be muted with careful schooling and dressed in finery to conceal their baseness, but they were always present, waiting in readiness for such oddities as the traveling freak shows. The Siamese Twins, the Giantess, the Bearded Lady, the Living Skeleton, and the Fat Lady were all evidence of how close to the surface everyone existed, how great people's fears really were once they saw that the impossible could happen to anyone. The good folks avoided the eyes of the Siamese twins and stared instead at the place where they were joined. But Gwen still wished she had not listened to Amanda and turned away. She wished she had been smart enough to look into the eyes of the two girls whose physical anomaly and nothing more was touted as their only uniqueness. Gwen should have smiled at them. But Gwen had only been a child, and she had been afraid.

Amanda's intent had been to protect Gwen. Jane felt certain of that. But Gwen was less certain now. She believed the fused girls exposed Amanda's worst fears, that which could happen *anyway*. There was no one answer, no one explanation for what had compelled Amanda to take Gwen to a freak show in the first place. But Jane finally told Gwen it was all right to forgive herself for having looked away, and Gwen finally did.

Chapter Seventeen

The funeral home was overheated, and Jane fanned herself as she stood beside Gwen. "Don't leave me even for a minute," Gwen whispered. Jane was grateful to have an excuse not to mingle, since she felt conspicuous among so many strangers, even though everyone had been extremely kind, especially Amanda's friends. And there were so many of them. Even Gwen seemed startled at the number of people who had been part of Amanda's circle. They arrived in twos and threes, wearing almost identical black dresses and tasteful veiled hats. Jane recognized some of the women from the stories Gwen had told. These good women had already stopped by Amanda's place and stocked the refrigerator with casseroles and plastic containers of potato and macaroni salad. They modestly assured Gwen that they had made all the necessary preparations for "after the cemetery" and chorused, "Don't worry about anything, dear." She thanked them and moved them along the reception line so gently and graciously that Jane suspected many of them would have liked to return for a second, even a third, encounter with Gwen.

Jane merely smiled and shook hands while Gwen made the introductions. "This is my friend Jane Hoffman," Gwen said over and over. Saying it seemed to calm her. Daniel sat sideways between Matt and Ethan on a settee that was clearly meant for one. It made all three of them look boyish, almost foolish, if not for their somber expressions. Now and then, Gwen would turn and point to them, and they would all rise and nod in unison, their timing off just a bit, as if some amateur puppeteer were guiding their movements. Daniel shook hands with the men and practically bowed to the women. He looked ill at ease in his role, which surprised Jane, until she remembered that what she knew about Daniel was mostly through Gwen.

But Gwen seized her part as "Amanda's girl" with grace and confidence. She offered each person a brief phrase that confirmed recognition. "Yes," she said, "Mother told me what a great help you were when she first moved," or "I know. Mother told me you played cards together. She enjoyed that very much." They each went away satisfied, if not slightly stunned that *this* was Mandy's daughter. Jane felt sure the people who had never met Gwen before would have been unable to describe what they expected her to be like. They just staggered away, amazed that this sober, decorous woman was the daughter of the friend who had introduced them to Singapore Slings and brought them mementos from New York that had to be hidden from their grandchildren. Gwen was astounded to learn her mother had purchased novelty pens that paraded topless women and hologram postcards of the

Statue of Liberty in compromising positions. Only rarely had there been glimpses of the lively and spirited woman that these strangers spoke so warmly about. Gwen longed to have known her, sadly wondering why she had struggled to maintain such duplicity.

As Jane observed these small dramas, she saw that Daniel was doing the same. When Reginald arrived with Annabelle, it was the first time Jane actually saw Daniel smile, and she realized that he probably knew about the incident in the funeral parlor. Annabelle was a very large woman. The black saronglike skirt looked as if it had required yards of fabric to wrap around her ample hips and to stay securely tied at one side. Jane was certain that if she pulled at the bow, she could unravel the entire skirt and release the thin Annabelle of a vanished time. Poor Annabelle looked so self-conscious and unhappy that Jane, who had never met her before, wanted to console her.

Jane watched as Gwen transformed Annabelle into the high school cheerleader who had tantalized the boys with glimpses of the cotton crotch of her panties. "Annabelle," Gwen murmured against her damp and bloated cheek. "Reginald told me you have five children. Five! My goodness, and a grandchild already! Don't you look too young to be a grandma! You still have the loveliest skin. I'm so glad you came. Mother always talked about you." Gwen's words were as prudently culled with Annabelle as they had been with Amanda's friends. There was no deceit intended, merely a desire to allay any hysteria that might create a scene or shatter her own composure. Gwen must have known that Annabelle's excited state had little to do with Amanda. Annabelle clung to Gwen with such fervor that no one would ever have guessed they had barely acknowledged each other all through school. Gwen patted her back and offered words that were unintelligible to Jane, yet obvious in their effect. Reginald cleared his throat, but they ignored him. Yet, whatever confidences were being exchanged between Gwen and Annabelle were apparently disturbing to Reginald.

Jane wanted to tell Reginald that what was happening between his wife and Gwen had nothing to do with him, but he would never have believed that. He would never understand how difficult it had been for Annabelle to come. But Gwen knew, and Jane understood it perfectly well. Jane suspected that Annabelle might have tried to tell Reginald how nervous she felt about seeing Gwen again after all these years. *She was always so glamorous. What will she think when she sees what I've become?* Jane could hear the distress behind the words. The useless appeal for understanding. *What's this foolishness now, Annabelle? You look just fine.* Reginald would have said all this without even turning to look at his wife. And the heartfelt sigh she uttered as she took one last miserable look in the mirror would go completely unnoticed.

Jane placed herself in front of Gwen and Annabelle and made herself a human shield. She merely wanted to give Gwen and Annabelle a few more moments together. A little more time to remember who they had been before they made the wrong choices. But when the funeral director finally entered the room and asked everyone except the immediate family to please move into the chapel, Reginald walked around Jane and pried Annabelle away from Gwen. "Go along now," Gwen said to Annabelle. "It'll be all right."

And when at last it was time to kiss Gwen once more before entering the chapel, Jane felt a wrenching sense of loss and loneliness that was suddenly about her own mother's death. Jane reached up to circle Gwen's neck with her arms and whispered, "I miss my mother." Gwen kissed her hair and said, "I know. Oh, I know. I really know." They held on to each other while Daniel, Matt, and Ethan looked on, not in bewilderment, but like three boys who had still not been picked for any team and could not understand why.

Gwen finally straightened up and kissed Jane's cheek.

"I'm all right," Gwen said.

"Sure?" Jane said.

"Sure."

Gwen turned to Daniel and fussed with his tie. She patted his chest.

"Take care of Jane," she said.

"I will," he said.

His tone was so formal that they all smiled. Jane kissed each of the boys and took the arm Daniel held out for her. They walked into the chapel, moved slowly past the coffin, and took their seats. A moment before Gwen was about to enter the chapel with Matt and Ethan, Annabelle leaned forward and patted Jane's shoulder. "It's Jane, right?" Annabelle whispered against Jane's ear. Before she could turn around, Annabelle said, "Thank you." Jane grabbed her hand before she could take it away and squeezed. They sat that way throughout the service. Annabelle perched on the edge of her chair with her hand on Jane's shoulder, and Jane with her arm bent awkwardly back, both women in positions that only seemed uncomfortable to others.

⌒

Jane would never forget the sight of Gwen in her black sheath dress as she ate tuna surprise off a paper plate. She even ate the canned onion rings that had been crushed and spread over the top. Jane also noticed how Gwen sipped coffee after each mouthful and swallowed slowly and methodically and made sure that her cup was always full.

Her suitcase waited by the door. Daniel caught her attention and pointed to his watch. Jane nodded and said goodbye to Matt and Ethan and shook hands with people whose names she no longer remembered. Gwen expertly maneuvered her away from the crowd and into the hallway.

"If I taste one more tuna casserole, you'll be at my funeral next," Gwen said.

"You're unbelievable," Jane said. "Amanda would've been proud of you."

"For once, huh?"

"That's not true. She was very proud of you, Gwen."

"You really think so?" Gwen blushed. "I'm being silly, right? It's just that all morning I kept asking myself if she would have approved of the way I was handling things."

"She would've approved."

"She never told me," Gwen said. "Never."

"She should have told you," Jane said. "It was wrong not to."

Then Daniel stuck his head out the door and cleared his throat.

"I'm sorry," he said. "We have to leave, or we'll miss your flight."

"I'm ready," Jane said. "My bag is just inside the door."

"I'll get it," Daniel said.

"Thanks," Jane said.

"Call me as soon as you get in," Gwen said. "I wish you could stay."

"I do too, but I have to get back to Caroline."

"You'll handle it, Jane. Trust your heart, not your head."

"That's the same advice you've been giving me for twenty years," Jane said. "I'm trying to. I really am. I want to do what's best for her," Jane said. "And for the baby."

"Yes, Grandma."

"I hope it's a girl."

"I do too," Gwen said. "We need another girl."

"I love you," Jane said. "I should tell you more often."

"You tell me all the time," Gwen said.

Then Gwen rubbed herself against Jane like some lackluster piece of tarnished silver that would be burnished to a high sheen merely by making contact with her. And because it was through each other that they mattered, Jane rubbed back.

Daniel told her that his father had been a gambler.

"I never knew that," Jane said.

"He wasn't a big-time gambler. The ponies now and again. Every so often, he lost way more than he could afford, but he always managed to recover. I knew he was in trouble if he wore his coat inside out."

Jane opened her window to let the cool breeze of dusk dissipate the strong smell of plastic that was always present in rental cars. She felt slightly nauseated and rummaged in her purse for a mint.

"Inside out?" she said.

She popped a mint into her mouth and held the roll out to Daniel. He shook his head, then changed his mind and broke one off with his thumb. Jane noticed his fingers were almost square at the top.

"He was superstitious. Most gamblers are. There was some old fairy tale that said turning clothes acted as a change of identity. It was a way of misleading any evil spirits that might be at play. He thought that if he turned his coat, it could break a run of bad luck. Sometimes he'd wear his coat inside out for weeks. My mother never said a word about it."

"It's funny the things we remember about our parents. It makes you wonder what our children will remember about us."

Daniel clenched the steering wheel, and Jane regretted her ill-chosen response. She knew that Daniel's children were angry at him. It had been careless of her to remind him.

"Do you ever wear your clothes inside out?" she said.

"I'm not superstitious."

"Oh," Jane said. "I'm sorry."

He gave her a sidelong glance and shook his head slightly.

"I know you disapprove of my relationship with Gwen," he said.

"That's not true. How can I disapprove of something that makes Gwen so happy? In any event, these days I'm not the best person to judge relationships."

"I left my wife, you know."

"Oh?" Jane said.

"Look, I know Gwen tells you everything." He saw her begin to protest and waved his hand. "Don't even try to pretend it isn't true. I don't know what it is with women, but you can't seem to live without each other. I've seen Gwen come back from spending a day with you and then call you at night to talk some more. It's remarkable. It's hard not to be jealous of that."

Jane laughed and patted Daniel's arm.

"You're right," she said. "You should be jealous. It must be hard to understand."

"Not really. I read this whole scientific explanation for the difference between men and women. It has something to do with a smaller number of fibers that connect the two sides of the male brain. The power to verbally express feelings is on the left side and emotions are on the right side. The flow is restricted because of the fewer fibers, so it's harder for the information to get to the verbal side."

Jane was speechless for a moment, and then she couldn't stop laughing. "No doubt it was the discovery of a male scientist," she said, still gasping for breath.

"It's all right," he said. "You know, Gwen laughed also. She thinks that all male emotions are between our legs, and that any information goes directly *there*."

He reddened, endearing himself to Jane. But she sensed that he expected her to vindicate him in some way, and she didn't know what she could say that wouldn't seem patronizing.

"I'm sure you agree with Gwen," he said. "About men."

"Well, it's one theory."

"I guess it's partly true. I seem to have made such a mess of things." He hesitated and looked at her briefly. "Do you mind if I talk?"

"No. I don't mind," she said.

Daniel was quiet. For a moment she thought he might have

changed his mind. She knew so little about Daniel. His idiosyn-
crasies were unfamiliar. She saw that he was thinking, trying to
draft his words into some form she would be able to comprehend.
When he finally spoke, it was in slow and measured phrases that
made her ache for his pain.

"I would have said I was a happy man. I loved my wife and
my children. I had a good job. I had no right to want more, and I
didn't. I went to Gwen that first day because I felt as if I had misplaced something, *something important,* and she was the only one
who could help me find it."

Jane was contained by Daniel's confession. He took one hand
off the wheel just as Jane reached for him. Except for a perfunctory kiss, she had never felt his flesh. His skin was smooth and
well cared for. His touch full of heat and moist with perspiration.
She felt powerful. All she had to do now was part her lips and
speak as if through her mercy alone indulgence were possible. He
withdrew his hand and placed it back on the wheel.

"Did she help you find it?" Jane said. "What you thought you
had misplaced?"

"Yes," Daniel said. "She did."

Jane did not need to ask Daniel what it was that he had misplaced. It didn't matter. She knew his confession was about that
which could not be predicted, the unknown, the unforeseen that
Amanda had tried to shield Gwen from that afternoon long ago at
the sideshow. But love was a sweet and unavoidable trap that one
could not easily avoid simply by looking the other way.

"When Caroline wasn't even two," she began, "I fell down a
flight of stairs with her in my arms. I was visiting a friend who
lived in a walk-up. The stairs had just been washed. There was a

strong odor of antiseptic that still makes my heart pound whenever I smell pine. I remember thinking that the stairs must be slippery, and I'd better be careful. I lost my step and went flying. I'd had that dream a thousand times. Even before Caroline was born I used to dream that I was falling with her in my arms, and then it was actually happening. I never let go of her, but I fell on top of her and broke her leg. I was unharmed except for a few bruises, but she had a cast that would stay on for quite some time. I called Gwen from the hospital, and she came immediately. I was so hysterical they had to give me a tranquilizer. Gwen carried Caroline to the car, and I followed behind, weeping and damning myself for the accident. Poor little Caroline fell asleep almost instantly, but I felt I would never sleep again. I was afraid of my own dreams. Gwen let me carry on until we reached home. Then she said, 'Blame yourself if you like. Blame yourself for every twist of fate, every corner that you can't see around. Take full responsibility for the unknown. Pretend you know everything there is to know.'" She clapped her hands together. "Bless me. It sure put an end to my tears."

Daniel reached across and patted Jane's knee in a clearly paternal way. She placed her hand over his and patted back. They stayed that way for only a moment. Any longer would have made them both self-conscious, regardless of the intent.

"I'm sorry about Arnold," he said. "It was a lousy thing to do."

"Yes, it was. Thank you. Thank you for saying something. I appreciate it."

Daniel nodded and exited for the airport. He looked sad, and that made Jane sad as well. Daniel had expected forgiveness, but sometimes there was none to be had. He could not be forgiven for the heartache he had brought to Sandra. Nor could he be forgiven for the disappointment that would inspire his children forever. He knew it for certain now, and Jane had made it plain. Instead of forgiveness, she offered tolerance. Not the long-suffering resignation of the wounded, but tolerance for pledges left to chance and oaths that should never have been sworn.

Chapter Eighteen

As her marriage to Theodore began to falter, Gwen's world had shifted between the jagged edges of his rancor and the amorphousness of new motherhood. One morning when Theodore had not yet returned home, she took Matt and boarded a bus to New Jersey. She knew she was looking for answers where there were none to be had. With no real destination in mind, she hoped that somewhere over the George Washington Bridge she might at least temporarily elude Theodore's scorn.

Shortly after she settled into her seat, a young man passed her in the narrow aisle and then returned to sit beside her. He wore sandals and the brown robe of a monk with a rope belt that wrapped around his waist three times. He was extremely thin and pale. Almost immediately, he introduced himself as Christopher and explained that he had run away from home and lived among "true brothers and sisters" until his parents had hired a detective and found him. Christopher was a Catholic from Omaha. Their family pastor, Father Dooley, had arranged for Christopher to stay in the monastery while he was being "deprogrammed."

Christopher laughed into his wide sleeve as he told Gwen that it "makes me seem as if I'm having all my channels erased." He told her that at night, he mouthed what he could remember of his previous life over and over, so that in the morning he woke feeling as if his entire memory had not been canceled. Throughout their conversation, Matt slept against Gwen in a makeshift halter of her own design. She had bought a length of gauzy cloth and improvised a contraption that would free her arms. She liked him against her hip, and he looked sweet wrapped inside the vermilion-colored nest. He had started to stir just as Christopher first revealed that every individual was responsible for his own salvation and then condemned the two extremes man was likely to choose. "Neither a profitless life of indulgence and sensual pleasure nor an equally profitless one of self-mortification will bring insight, knowledge, tranquillity, or ultimate enlightenment. Choose the Middle Path," he urged. The fervor behind his words drew warm rushes of lust that made Gwen want to push the young man to the ground and reach beneath his robe. Instead, she dipped her hand into the depths of Matt's nest, pushed aside her blouse, and helped him latch on securely. He had woken and immediately begun to graze. He rubbed against her breast with his whole face, opened his mouth, and searched for her nipple. With one hand she positioned him, and from behind his fabric screen, he smiled. Gwen smiled back at him and turned back to Christopher. He was *so* young.

"Let me tell you about the truth of pain," he said. "Birth is pain, old age is pain, death is pain, union with the unpleasant is pain, separation from the pleasant is pain, and not gaining what one wishes is pain. The Middle Path is the only answer." She had gulped air and tried not to laugh when he explained that suffering was a result of desire and that only through enlightenment could it be ended. Had he run away to forget the indifference of the girls in his high school class? She turned away from his bad skin and his jagged fingernails. His shaved head gave him the appearance of a large infant, but she found the effect poignant. So much so, in fact, that she was tempted to draw him to her and offer him the nourishment he had so clearly missed in his life. While Matt rested, she reached in and turned him so that he would be able to continue nursing from the other side. As she repositioned Matt, her breast was briefly exposed. The nipple, elongated and hard from Matt's attention, was the color of a cranberry. Christopher's attention was riveted. He had stopped speaking, had almost seemed to stop breathing. Gwen didn't hurry to conceal herself. She wanted him to see that if suffering was the result of desire, enlightenment was a poor substitute for even the most fleeting pleasures.

"I urge you," he finally managed to say in a hoarse whisper, "choose the Middle Path." Gwen smiled indulgently and pulled her blouse closed, savoring the unanticipated flutter caused by publicly touching herself. There was no purpose in demonstrating her knowledge of pain to him. Instead, she thanked him and pretended to sleep.

At the Fort Lee stop, Christopher nudged her to say goodbye. "I didn't know there was a monastery here," Gwen said.

"Oh, there isn't," he said. "I live near Pawling now, but I love Palisades Amusement Park. I was allowed to visit a friend in Fort Lee for the day, but I'm going to the amusement park instead. I love the rides, and they have the best hot dogs. If I don't spill on my robe, no one will ever know." Gwen wished him luck. At the next stop, she gathered her things and held on tightly to Matt. When the bus pulled away, she crossed over to the other side to wait for the next bus home.

It was clear that Theodore had not yet been home. She placed Matt in his crib and covered him with the blanket. He sucked his tiny fist and whimpered. Soon it would be time for him to eat again. She hurried to bathe and fix herself some food. In her haste, she had forgotten to bring along something to eat for herself. She ate oatmeal with honey and cut-up dates. When she found she was still hungry, she stood over the sink and peeled a mango, splitting the flesh of the fruit as she pulled off its skin. She thought she would never be full. Strands of mango stuck between her teeth, and she gnawed at the pit. She felt ill and turned at the sound of Theodore's voice. In one hand she held the remnants of her scavenging, and in the other she clutched her belly. *You wouldn't even notice if we disappeared,* she did not say.

"Did you have a good day?" Theodore asked.

"You have led a profitless life of indulgence and sensual pleasure," she said in answer.

He laughed and reached for her. Matt cried. "Don't go to him yet," Theodore said. "Me first." He tugged at her clothes. She stepped out of them the way she had as a child while her mother undressed her. Gwen saw herself, holding on to her mother's shoulder, passive, indifferent to her mother's words of encouragement, and interested only in the cup of cocoa that would be hers once she was ready for bed. Her own weariness and hunger more important than anything else. Her knowledge of pain minimal and uncomplicated. Her desires few. *Insight, knowledge, tranquillity, and enlightenment.*

"What did you do today?" Theodore said against her ear.

"I learned about the Middle Path," she said.

He wasn't listening anyway. The only suffering he cared about was his own, and he was eager for relief. She tasted the flavor of unfamiliar soap on his skin. Something fragrant and expensive. She thought perhaps it might be almond, but couldn't be sure. *Why don't you love me anymore?* she did not say. And when he brought her to the very edge of her will, she closed her eyes and thought about the young boy and his scarred skin. At least, she told herself, when Theodore reached his own extreme, he would always be alone. This hardly brought her any satisfaction, because it seemed not to matter to Theodore that their union brought her no pleasure anymore. Her insensibility aroused him even more. When his breathing quickened, it was his own name he shouted with self-congratulatory fervor. "Good man, Theodore," he said. "Good man."

Gwen thought about Christopher in his dark brown robe, eating hot dogs and going on the rides, unconcerned about the stares of strangers who pulled their children a little closer as he passed. Matt cried again. This time the cries were shrill and unrelenting. Gwen went to him, calling to him as she approached, letting him know his hunger would soon be satisfied, his loneliness relieved, his every need met, for now, by what her body and heart could offer. It was the first comfort she had known all day.

"Why didn't you leave him?" Daniel said.

They sat on the floor of Amanda's living room surrounded by

the remnants of her life. There were boxes of old letters and greeting cards. She had saved every drawing Matt and Ethan had ever sent, every birthday card, every Mother's Day card. *How much do I love you, Grandma?* When the card was opened, it offered a pair of long paper arms that extended from a smiling boy. *This much!* Matt had scrawled his name with a backward *a* and a large heart. There was also a series of squiggles that must have been Ethan's attempt at a signature. Gwen held the card aside to show the boys.

"I didn't think it was a choice," she said. "I had no friends. I had no one to talk to. My parents never asked me if I was happy. I thought it was me. I was pregnant that first year, and I was so pleased. At last, my life would have meaning. After Matt was born, I thought things would get better. Of course, they didn't. I think that first year after Matt was born was the loneliest year of my life. I remember long periods of darkness. It was such a cold winter. I spent most of it under a quilt with Matt. I didn't know anyone else with a baby. All the girls my age were in college or out working. When spring came, I put Matt in the stroller and went over to Theodore's office to surprise him. He told me never to do that again, especially with the baby. Theodore only wanted me to be present at university functions. You know, when it was important to have a wife on his arm. 'Bring pictures of the baby,' he said. 'Don't talk about breast-feeding or teething. Just smile a lot and agree with everything I say.' The other wives ignored me, so I ignored them back."

Daniel pulled her down so that her head was in his lap. He pushed the hair out of her face and bent over to kiss her forehead.

"I'm sorry I wasn't there to take care of you," he said.

"Where were you then?" she said. "What were you doing twenty-two years ago?"

"Twenty-two years ago? Let me think a minute. I was starting my first job as a principal in Freeport. I think Sandy must've been pregnant with Rosie. We had just bought a house. Kate and Sam were in school already. It was a good time in my life."

She reached up and caressed his cheek. He had not shaved, and the stubble was rough under her hand. He held her hand and kissed her open palm.

"You were a good husband and father. I'm sure of it," she said.

"I thought I was, but I'm not so sure anymore. I always wanted a family. I never wondered if Sandy was happy or not. I just assumed she had everything she wanted. I'm sorry about that now."

She sat up and reached over to kiss him. Her tongue probed the inside of his mouth deliberately. At last year's school fair, she had accepted the pink confection a student shyly offered. Gwen had been eager for the sweetness, had pulled off large pieces of spun sugar and held them in her mouth until her teeth ached. When her lips were coated, she covered her mouth with one sticky hand and ran her tongue in circles to pry loose any stray pieces of hardened candy. Soon there was nothing left except a paper cone that had more weight than the sugared air she had hungrily consumed. She devoured Daniel now with the same need, pulled at his flesh as if it were possible to take pieces of him with her, just in case later her appetite flared and he was gone.

At the foot of Amanda's bed was the hope chest her own mother had passed down the year Amanda had her coming-out party. The dark mahogany was ornately chiseled into delicate curlicues that wound around the feet of tiny cherubs. Amanda had refused to give Gwen the hope chest when she married Theodore. "I'll give it to you when I'm satisfied that it will last," she said. Gwen had pretended not to care, but she was hurt that Amanda was so obvious in her dislike of Theodore. "I never saw a man so full of himself," Amanda announced, "and with so little reason to be." Gwen soon stopped trying to defend Theodore. The words would have stuck in her throat, and Amanda knew the truth anyway.

After Ethan was born, Gwen struggled for a few more wretched months to keep her family together before Theodore made the decision for them. She knew better than to appeal to Amanda. She was unremittingly mulish about independence and "forging one's own way." But sometimes the loneliness was so intense that Gwen wondered if Amanda would relent if she knew how terribly unhappy her only living child really was. Still, the thought of risking Amanda's ridicule was too much, and Gwen folded herself into a ball with her babies at her side and waited for salvation.

A short time after Theodore was gone for good, Amanda sent for Gwen and the children. "Just for a visit," Amanda said. "I don't want you to get the wrong idea." Gwen assured her that it wasn't likely. After the children were put to bed in the spare room, Amanda invited Gwen to her dressing room. "We'll have some cocoa and chat." Gwen arrived, dressed in a robe and with wet hair. Amanda's displeasure was immediate. She didn't approve of such casualness. "You might as well sit," Amanda said. She handed Gwen a monogrammed towel. "Dry your hair. It's unwise to keep your head wet for too long." Gwen took the towel and held it in her lap. She was too weary to even lift her arms. Amanda took the towel and rubbed Gwen's hair, harshly at first, but then with even, light movements. Gwen could not remember the last time her mother had touched her.

When Amanda was done, she draped the towel across the back

of the chair and reached for her own tortoiseshell comb. "Lean forward a bit," she instructed. She tugged at the knots until Gwen's hair was untangled and hung damply around her shoulders. "Am I hurting you?" Amanda said. And Gwen, who could not have been any more amazed by the question than if her mother had suddenly grown wings and flown around the room, shook her head no. "I know you think I'm a hard woman," Amanda said, "and I'm not denying the obvious. I can be difficult. But there's a lot you don't know about me, Gwendolyn." She put the comb down and pointed at the hope chest. "Come sit next to me. I want to show you some things." Gwen watched as Amanda lifted the heavy lid and took out piece after piece of silk and satin, each more exquisite than the one before it. There was a pale peach bed jacket trimmed in handmade lace. A peignoir set, once white and now yellowed with age, still had its price tag attached to the sleeve. There were dozens of pairs of underpants and camisoles. As she took each item from the chest, Amanda placed it in Gwen's lap and then patted the pile of things and said, "I had such dreams once." Gwen nodded and said, "I understand." Amanda raised one eyebrow and smiled. "Yes. I'm sure you do." The next morning at breakfast Amanda asked Gwen if she'd like the hope chest and its contents now that she had a "real future to look forward to." But Gwen said no. She didn't see the point. "Well, it's yours when I die," Amanda said. "Or before if you change your mind. Whichever comes first."

Gwen had not changed her mind, and now Amanda was gone. Gwen lifted the embroidered cover from the hope chest and ran her hand over the wood. Her mother had married a man who never entered her bedroom unless it was the right day of the week.

A man who scarcely knew what she did with her time or cared to ask. She had lost a son to a senseless accident and had watched a daughter run off with a stranger who treated her with disregard and neglected their children. Gwen would now have the chest shipped to her own home with a few other small items. Everything else was going into storage. Matt and Ethan could choose what they wanted when they were ready. She would place the chest at the foot of her bed, polish the wood with lemon-scented oil and an old undershirt from one of the boys, and from time to time examine the pieces that were Amanda's failed dreams and wonder at the life she had built in spite of them.

For several years after Theodore left, Gwen attempted to create a world for herself and her children that would inhibit further injury. She created an environment much like the paper rooms the Japanese had designed to protect themselves from the devastation of earthquakes. There was nothing breakable in a paper room. Nothing that could either shatter or splinter. If the walls came down, the people could emerge unscathed. This was Gwen's goal. To surface intact from the ruins and create a sanctuary from the madness that had been her life with Theodore.

They saw only the people necessary to their lives. She took the children to the park and watched them play, but she sat apart from the other mothers, afraid of what they might ask of her, almost fainthearted at the thought of a conversation. Occasionally, she could bear the loneliness no more and coupled with someone she met at school or work only to create a diversion from satisfying herself. But, really, it was no different to her. She could hardly bear to be away from her children. Her fears were terrible ones, but they were not only about the harm that might come to Matt and Ethan. Her fears were about being forgotten. She envisioned coming home to find her personal effects in the hallway and the locks changed. There would be a note from Mrs. Lombardi that read, *The children and I agree there is no room for you in our lives. We wish you the very best of luck with your future. Please don't bother to phone or write. It's better for all of us this way.*

She would be left not just alone, but without purpose, with nothing to fill the hollow that was the aftermath of Theodore's lengthy siege. At dinner, she questioned the children about everything they had done during the day. She wanted to know everything Mrs. Lombardi had said, and what they had answered. "Did she say anything about Mommy?" Gwen asked. The children shook their heads and became quiet. At night, she whispered to them in their sleep, "You love Mommy best. You love Mommy best." She ran her hands over their bodies, memorizing every detail of their bone structure, examining their perfect skin, and stroking their shiny hair. She didn't know what she was looking for, but she couldn't stop.

One winter morning she fixed pancakes as the boys played quietly in the living room. She glanced up every few seconds to make sure they were still there. Her thoughts wandered briefly, and then she turned to listen to Matt's voice. He was explaining something to Ethan. They had little plastic figures assembled on the rug. "No," Matt said. "The children stay with the mommy *all* the time. They can't go anywhere much because the mommy needs them. They have to stay with her and take care of her. Forever. For always. Understand?"

Ethan was busy tugging at his diaper. He had just learned how to undo the tabs at the sides, and he was very proud. Still, he nodded and offered Matt a wet pacifier. *What have I done?* Gwen covered her ears so she wouldn't hear herself shriek. But her mouth was closed. There was no sound. Her body shook, and she sat on the floor and hugged her knees. "Mommy?" Matt's concerned little face hovered in front of hers. He was holding Ethan's soiled diaper in his hand. "Ethan pooped. I don't know what to do." She smiled at him and reached out to hug him. Not ferociously, the way she had been these last months, but reassuringly. "I know what to do," she said. "I'll take care of it." And she had. Things got better. Their lives slowly took on a routine that was no longer thwarted by unseen dangers.

Jane was the first to catch her out of the paper room. Gwen had dared to step out just far enough to still be able to race back to safety when Jane blocked the path and made it impossible to return. Gwen should have seen her love for Jane as a caveat. It had been too easy to open the gates for her. She had sailed right through Gwen's impressive fortress and put down camp with all the trust that Gwen lacked. Jane simply refused to stop coming over. It was only weeks into their relationship that Caroline was born. When Jane called Gwen to tell her she was having contractions, she was there before Arnold. Carefully, she helped Jane shave her legs, because she was too big to bend. And when Arnold arrived and told Gwen she was free to leave, Gwen said no, she'd follow them to the hospital. Mrs. Lombardi was with the boys. All night, Gwen waited for Caroline to be born, sneaking in to see Jane whenever possible. "I'm her sister," Gwen said, daring anyone to believe anything different. After Arnold went home,

Jane and Gwen examined Caroline together and exclaimed over her extraordinary beauty. "We have a girl," she said. "Thank goodness." Jane couldn't disagree.

They shared meals and children and secrets long buried without wielding judgments. Gwen confessed that she blamed herself for Warren's death and admitted that it was only his occasional visitations that brought her any comfort. Jane listened, and even if she doubted such a thing was possible, she never let on. When Gwen cried, something she was loath to do in front of anyone, Jane cried more. And when Jane told Gwen that she had married Arnold because he hadn't been interested in Ellie, Gwen said it was as good a reason as any. Even after Jane said it had not held up very well, Gwen absolved her.

Gwen cut Caroline's tiny nails when Jane was too afraid to do it herself. Jane nursed Ethan through chicken pox when he and Caroline became infected almost simultaneously. Quickly, Gwen grew careless and lazy, saturated with love and goodwill. Over the years, Gwen found it easier to turn her back on the hordes of demons who had guarded her for so long. And then Daniel appeared out of nowhere. By then, she was defenseless. She had lost the resolve to fight her way back alone. She had even forgotten the words of power that would safeguard her. *I don't want to get involved. I'm not interested in a relationship.* She couldn't remember why she had ever wanted to express such foolish thoughts. Daniel had conquered the evil spirits within her and left her with the gates open and unguarded. Now her greatest fear was that she would have to be alone once again.

Tomorrow morning Daniel would leave. He had asked if she wanted him to stay longer. "You need to get back," was her answer. "Kate's expecting you. It's the baby's first Christmas. I'll be fine." There was still a great deal that had to be done, but Matt and Ethan would stay an extra few days. They still had time till their winter break was over, but Gwen had to be back at work by the third of the new year. "It was thoughtful of Amanda to die over winter break," Gwen said. Daniel was amused. "And so unlike her," he answered. After he finished packing, they went out for Reuben sandwiches and cold beers. "This will keep me up all night," Daniel predicted. But he was wrong. He fell asleep while she was in the shower. The odor of Ben-Gay assailed her the moment she stepped into the bedroom. He had rubbed himself with liniment found in Amanda's medicine cabinet. Gwen wondered why he hadn't asked her to massage his sore muscles. He had lifted boxes although she had begged him not to. Perhaps he was embarrassed by his own frailty. She pulled back the covers and lay down next to him, her back pressed against his chest. She did not want to look at him. He stirred and mumbled something unintelligible, but she thought she heard "bushed" and "sorry." Her feet wrapped around his ankles, and she moved as close to him as possible without disturbing his sleep. Daniel mumbled something else and tried to move, but she was firm. Nothing seemed as important anymore as staying close to Daniel. *I'll never let him go.* She gasped, horrified, and unwound her feet. He immediately turned and found a more comfortable position. Gently at first, then with greater insistence, she shook his shoulder. "Daniel," she said. "What am I going to do now?" He slept on. She reached over him and took Amanda's tube of liniment and sat up in bed. The scent of camphor and eucalyptus was released as she squeezed liniment into her palm and inhaled. Night after night,

Amanda had sat in this room trying to heal herself with manufactured warmth, pondering her own misfortunes.

When she moved back down beneath the covers, Daniel searched for her in his sleep. She took his hand, placed it back where she was safe from his touch, and turned away.

Chapter Nineteen

One evening, many years before, after a terrible argument with Arnold, during which she ultimately railed and then pounded his chest with clenched fists, Jane wondered how he could remain so calm. No matter what names she called him, no matter what horrible accusations she made, Arnold remained as thick and impenetrable as an ancient castle wall. But she could tell that her rage pleased him. It was evidence of her instability. Proof that she was too erratic to be responsible for herself. Finally, exhausted and humiliated, Jane said, "How could you pretend I don't exist when I'm so miserable?"

He smiled, but said nothing. Jane left the room and threw herself down on their bed, where she fell asleep immediately. She was awakened by the faint sound of rustling in the darkness. At first, she was hopeful that it was Arnold. She sat up to invite him nearer, to help him close the distance between them. Then, through the darkness, a shadow moved, and a tiny voice trembled, "Mommy?

Can I sleep with you tonight?" Jane lifted the blanket and held out her hand to Caroline.

For a while, Jane listened to Caroline's rough breathing left over from a cold she couldn't seem to lose. She coughed in her sleep, and Jane spoke soothingly to her. "It's all right, baby. Just sleep." She circled her with both arms and held her as tightly as she could without waking her. The feel of Caroline's bare flesh pressed against her own and the rhythmic bursts of warm breath on her skin evoked a sensation so immediately concentrated with need that Jane was at once both repelled and aroused.

That the feelings should have been summoned by the touch of her child made Jane feel the inescapable weightiness of her own isolation. She felt impoverished by the lack of intimacy in her life. Arnold would never even attempt to move through the unlit space they shared. She should have known better than to think he might hazard falling against a chair that was not in its usual place or stumble over a mislaid pair of shoes. He was too restrained, too cautious, to leave anything to chance. Caroline moved, forcing Jane to readjust her position. Caroline had already flattened herself against the length of Jane's body in a way that was reminiscent of photographs of full humans with vestigial bodies attached to their own. Jane had felt envy for the hosts. They would never be separated from the incomplete extensions of themselves.

Caroline would not always be there to fill the empty spaces. Jane felt the imminence of her own loss. She pressed her lips to Caroline's forehead, ran trembling hands along her sturdy frame, and luxuriated in the only love that had neither concealed motives nor assigned boundaries.

～∽∾～

On the return flight from Amanda's funeral, Jane sat next to a woman from Long Island. Roberta Miles was fifty-nine years old. "I tell everyone I'm fifty-five, but I'm telling *you* the truth," she said. Roberta had three children, all girls. Two of them were married and the youngest was gay. Selena and Samantha, the married daughters, did not seem terribly happy. "They don't tell me much," Roberta said, "but I have eyes. I can see." Selena had two children of her own. A boy and a girl. Jeffrey and Evelyn. Samantha still couldn't conceive. The doctor thought her tubes might be blocked, so she was going in for some tests.

The gay daughter, Sybil, lived with her partner in North Carolina. They were trying to adopt a child. Roberta had just spent a week with them. Edgar, Roberta's husband, refused to accept Sybil's lifestyle. "He says she's disgusting," Roberta told Jane. "I say, 'She's your daughter, Edgar. What's the choice?' You understand, don't you?" Jane nodded vigorously. For two hours, Jane found herself completely involved in Roberta's family history. Jane expressed support for Roberta's dissatisfaction with Edgar's attitude toward Sybil. It was unfair to be so inflexible. After all, Sybil was his child. Roberta patted Jane's hand and reassured *her* that things would work out. Jane offered the name of a doctor who had helped a friend's daughter conceive after everything else had failed. Roberta folded the piece of paper and tucked it into her wallet. When the meal was served, they shared their food. Jane gave Roberta her roll and two pats of extra butter. Roberta scraped the peas off her plate onto Jane's. Roberta spoke as she ate, and Jane even brushed stray bread crumbs from Roberta's sweater.

"Excuse me," Roberta said. "I shouldn't talk with my mouth full. Edgar always tells me it's a bad habit."

Roberta explained that there was no particular reason for choosing names that began with an S, other than the fact that she liked all three names. "Nowadays," Roberta said, "everyone is looking for symbolic meaning." Jane agreed. "Edgar says it's *all* my fault," Roberta admitted. Her eyes filled, and Jane wanted to cup her hands in readiness, fill them with Roberta's pain. "He says it's my doing that Sybil is a 'queer.' He says I loaded her head with strange ideas. He says it's my fault that Selena and Samantha are unhappy. According to him, it's even my fault that Samantha is barren. I hate that word. It sounds exactly like what it is. I don't think it can be all my fault."

Jane took another sip of her complimentary glass of wine and told Roberta about Arnold and Caleb, and then about Caroline and the baby. Roberta sighed, and then reached into her bag and withdrew something that resembled a small piece of black shoe leather. It was engraved with odd symbols that Jane had never seen before. "I bought it from a fortune-teller, a storefront gypsy," she said shyly and pressed it into Jane's hand. "It's made from a bat. The gypsy said bats have great potential for good. They can see in the dark, so they can find and return lost happiness. I want you to have it. I'd have to hide it from Edgar anyway." She dabbed the corners of her eyes with a crumpled tissue and sniffled. "It's amazing what desperation will make a person do," she said.

Jane said she didn't find it so amazing at all. Then she studied the foreign markings and wondered if it was possible to return what had never been yours.

Arnold was waiting for her at the end of the gate. Caroline must have given him the arrival time. She saw him scanning the crowd and considered the possibility of ducking into the first ladies' room.

"Damn. There's Arnold," she said to Roberta.

Roberta stepped closer to Jane and took her arm.

"Are you all right?" she said.

"Yes, I'm fine," Jane said.

Arnold had already spotted her and was waving madly. She didn't wave back.

"I see my daughter," Roberta said. "Selena!" She forced Jane to stop. "I'm so glad we met."

"I am too," Jane said. But her mind was already elsewhere. "Good luck with everything."

"I'll call you."

"Yes, of course."

They hugged quickly. People jostled them in their hurry to get by.

"I guess we're in a bad spot," Roberta said.

Arnold had walked as far as the security gate would allow and was calling to her. Jane didn't turn around. Roberta hugged her again, and they continued walking. When they stepped across to the other side, it was as if they were entering another dimension, as if they knew that from that point on, neither one of them would recognize the other. Roberta disappeared almost immediately into the throng of people. Jane searched for Roberta's tan coat and streaked blond hair, but she was gone. Jane rummaged in her purse for Roberta's phone number. She felt desperate to find it.

"Who was that?" Arnold said.

He reached for her tote bag and took her elbow in one move.

"What are you doing here?" she said.

"Isn't it obvious?"

"Not to me. I told Caroline I would take a taxi. In fact, I told her I preferred to take one."

"Who was that woman? Someone you befriended on the plane?"

His tone was so sharply derisive, so filled with disdain for her, that she couldn't move. He shook her elbow to urge her along.

"What is it?" he said. "Did you forget something?" He shook her again. "What's wrong with you?"

"Stop shaking me," she said.

"I'm not shaking you. You just can't stop here in the middle of all these people."

Impulsively, she touched his smooth cheek and noted that he must have shaved before coming to the airport. His eyes flickered at this gesture, yet he remained wary. But Jane only touched him to see if he was real, not some life-size replica of a man she had once hoped to know. But it was Arnold. She sighed and walked away, not even bothering to see if he was following.

"Please, Jane," he said.

He caught up to her and took her arm. She stopped and faced him.

"Why did you marry me?" she said.

"What?"

"I want to know why you married me."

"That's a ridiculous question," he said.

"Then give me a ridiculous answer."

Arnold stepped back from her, looking over his shoulder as

if there were someone who might rescue him. Jane grabbed the sleeve of his coat and held on.

"Tell me," she said. "I need to know."

"Well, I was attracted to you. I thought you loved me...and I felt we...I wanted to be with you. I don't get what the point of all this is, Jane. It seems rather ludicrous now to be asking that question."

"Yes, it does," she said. "You're quite right."

One night shortly before she found him with the woman, Jane had been awakened to find him sitting up in bed, whimpering. In a voice she barely recognized, he said, "I wet myself." He had gripped the soiled bedding. "It doesn't matter," she said. She tried to ease his distress, but he drew away sharply. "Tell me why you're crying," she said. "I can't," he answered. He waited while she stripped the bed and put on clean sheets. All the time, she kept saying, "It's all right. It was probably a dream." As soon as she was done, he got under the blanket and pulled it around himself. She sat down next to him and repeated, "It was just a dream." He was already half asleep, but he opened his eyes and said, "But I don't dream." After a while, she got up, picked up the discarded bedclothes and his underwear, and went down to the laundry room. They would never be all right. Even if Arnold did dream, he could never tell her what could have frightened him so that it caused him to wet himself and cry. He would never understand that dreams were to be sought and then considered.

She tugged gently at his arm, so that he would be forced to look at her. "Tell me what you dreamed about that night."

"I don't remember," he said.

Arnold's denial was as emphatic as his refusal to admit his spiritual privation. Jane knew the dream was still present. Still, she wondered how anything could have survived this long, concealed as it were by doubt and neglect.

"The woman I met on the plane," Jane said. "The one you asked about. Her name is Roberta. She told me everything about herself. I know more about her than I do about you. Don't you find that terribly sad?"

Arnold tried to leave, but she held on.

"Tell me," she said. "You *have* to tell me."

"Let go of my arm," he said. He shook her loose. "You're making a big mistake, Jane."

"Why did you come here tonight?" she said.

"I don't want a divorce," he said. "I want it to be like it was before."

"Well, of course you do," she said.

Jane reached into her pocket and withdrew Roberta's gift. Then she pressed it into Arnold's hand and held it fast, so he could not resist.

"Here," she said. "I want you to have this."

If only he had told about his dream and how much it had terrified him, Jane might even have thought to love him again. But Arnold refused to change. He preferred to close his eyes, to sleep night after night and keep them tightly shut against anything that might divulge either his fears or his longings. And so Jane believed that his sleep would forever be without either color or sound, and his waking would be the same.

Caroline opened the door before Jane could use her key. As soon as she saw Caroline, it was evident that something had changed.

The curve of her belly was almost negligible, but it already had enough force to demand devotion. Caroline had begun to walk differently. Her hips were pulled forward, and her steps were more prudent. One hand rested on the slight swelling. Her fingers were spread apart to cover the small area.

"I'm glad to see you," Caroline said.

"And I'm glad to see there's more of you," Jane said.

"Really? You think so? I thought so too, but I wasn't sure." Caroline tilted her head to one side, listening for footsteps. "You must be exhausted. Where's Daddy?"

She reached for the suitcase, but Jane pushed her hand away.

"Don't," Jane said. "It's heavy."

"Nonsense. Are you angry that I gave Daddy the flight information? He insisted."

"I have no doubt," Jane said. "And no, I'm not angry, but I came home in a taxi."

"You fought."

"We disagreed…about everything." Jane looked around the house. "All right, we fought. Where's Raymond? It's so quiet."

"Come sit down with me," Caroline said. "I get tired so quickly."

"That's normal." Jane followed Caroline over to the couch and sat close to her. "So, where's Raymond?"

"Tell me about the funeral. Is Gwen all right? I spoke to her earlier, and to Matt and Ethan. They all seemed well."

"They are. Now are you going to tell me where Raymond is?"

Caroline gazed down at her belly quite fondly. Jane took her daughter's hand and waited for her to speak. Caroline sighed again and looked up, smiling rather sheepishly, but not without appeal.

"I sent Ray home," Caroline said.

"Home? To New Paltz?"

"Home to Arizona."

"And are you going to tell me why?" Jane said.

"It's Christmas tomorrow, and we don't do Christmas," Caroline said. "I thought he should be with his family."

"That was thoughtful of you."

"And I don't want to marry him."

Jane did not hesitate for a moment. She would always be proud of herself for that. The right thing came easily because she didn't think about it.

"All right," Jane said. "It seems like a rational choice."

"Really?" Caroline looked amazed. "I'm so happy, Mom. I thought you'd go crazy. I tried to talk to Dad about it, but he... well, he didn't quite share your enthusiasm."

"What about Ray? What about his plans?"

"He resisted at first. But I made him see that marriage would only make everything harder for us and for the baby. I love him, but I don't want to get married now. I think he's relieved. I want to finish the semester. I'm not due until May. With a little luck, I might make it through," Caroline said. "Everyone says the first one is always late. Then I want to come home. I'll apply to some schools around here. I'll just take a class or two at night. Of course, I'll only do it if you think it's possible."

"I think it's very possible."

Caroline rested her head on Jane's shoulder.

"I think I felt something," Caroline said.

Jane thought it was probably too soon, but she didn't say so. She stroked her daughter's cheek and wondered at her courage.

"Do you want to touch?" Caroline said.

Jane placed both hands, palms down, fingers spread apart, over the scarcely noticeable mound. Then Caroline placed her hands over Jane's, palms down, fingers spread apart, and pressed ever so gently.

Chapter Twenty

Gwen checked the answering machine as soon as they arrived home. Daniel had left a message that he would be there before eleven. He would drive down straight from Kate's. He could do the drive from Somers in about one hour. "Do you mind that I won't be at the airport?" he had asked when they spoke the night before. She knew it was impossible to compete with an infant granddaughter and had told him so. "I'll do anything to see Elena, even if it means I have to endure disparaging remarks about my character," Daniel had said. Gwen had made him promise to wear his seat belt and to stay within the speed limit. The roads were icy, and she worried about him driving at night.

Jane had seen to it that the refrigerator was well stocked. Matt and Ethan had already made sandwiches with the sliced meat and cheese she had supplied. Their heads were bent low toward each other as they ate, but they stopped talking as soon as Gwen entered.

"Aren't you going to eat?" Matt said.

She lifted a slice of Swiss cheese off the waxed paper and bit into it.

"I'm not very hungry," she said.

"Did you speak to Daniel?" Ethan said.

"He's not back from his visit with his granddaughter."

"Have you seen her yet?" Matt said.

"Only in the pictures Daniel brought. She's very pretty."

The boys exchanged looks, but they said nothing. The cheese stuck in Gwen's throat.

"Will you ever see her?" Ethan said.

"Ethan," Matt warned.

"No," Gwen said, "it's all right. You'll be off again in a few days, and we might as well settle whatever is bothering you both. Yes, I hope to meet Daniel's family, especially his granddaughter."

"I'm sure they'll be *thrilled* to meet you," Ethan said.

"Is this leading to something, Ethan?" she said.

Neither boy said anything, but she knew there was more.

"Why now all of a sudden?" she said. "Did something change?"

She saw Matt shake his head at Ethan.

"We just wondered if you had as much access to his new apartment as he does to this one," Ethan said.

"I didn't know that I was expected to consult you about my private life," Gwen said.

"We have a right to know," Ethan said. "He practically lives here."

"He's around a lot, Mom," Matt said.

She wanted to tell them that Daniel was *around* more than their father had ever been. She wanted to tell them that she spent more time talking to Daniel about being a parent and meeting their needs than she had ever done with Theodore. But none of that was possible because Theodore was their father and Daniel was not.

"I didn't think it was necessary to make you privy to my living arrangements," she said. "What Daniel and I do is none of your concern. It seems to me that's all you need to know."

"Do you have the key to his apartment?" Matt said.

Matt, the eternal pragmatist. The seeker of balance and justice. *If you scream at me, I can scream at you.* He was six years old the first time he said that to her. Even when she had explained the difference to him, he would have no part of her logic.

"I don't want a key to his apartment," she said.

"But did he offer you one?" Matt said.

"I don't think this conversation is necessary. I'm flattered that you're so concerned about me. This *is* about your concern for me, isn't it?"

"We really like Daniel, Mom," Matt said. "You know we do, but it just seems that he has more access to your life than you do to his."

"I've allowed him the access that he has to my life."

"You've been his *mistress!*" Ethan shouted.

She had been resealing the packages of meat and cheese while speaking. Her hands shook as they struggled to follow the arbitrary creases of the original folds, with awkward results.

"I never seem able to get it right," she whispered.

Matt and Ethan watched her hands fold and refold the stiff paper. They were little boys again, waiting for her to finish another origami creation. Their admiration was inexhaustible. She put her hands over theirs and folded with them until they believed the yellow crane or the red swan was their invention. Then they would take the fragile paper menagerie and give life with their words and movements. One day, Matt had sadly confessed that he had tried and failed to make his own paper bird. *We can't really make them without you.* She had scooped him up and covered his face with kisses. *Maybe so, but they can't live without you and neither can I!* Her assurances were a pledge that made him whole again.

"Mom," Matt said. "We didn't mean to upset you."

Their feet touched the floor now. They were no longer swinging chubby legs beneath the table. Their breath didn't smell of pretzels and apple juice. The arms that had once eagerly reached for her were now rigid and motionless, as unyielding as their judgment of her.

"What do you want from me?" she said. "I need to know."

"We just want to protect you," Matt said.

Ethan stared down at his plate and refused to look at her.

"I love Daniel," she said. "It's neither an excuse nor an apology. It's regrettable when people get hurt, and people always do. I suspect that someday you'll find yourselves in the unfortunate position of being responsible for someone's pain, and I'll bet you'll be grateful it isn't you who's been hurt that time. Sorry as you may be, you'll be glad to have survived."

"People were talking at Grandma's house," Matt said. "We heard them. They said Daniel would be after your money now."

Gwen laughed and reached over to grab Matt's hand.

"Not my sumptuous body?" she said. "How disappointing."

"It was Mr. Fisher," Ethan said. His voice was almost toneless. "He told his wife that you were Daniel's mistress, and he was just there to find out how much Grandma had left for you."

"My dear sons, listen to me carefully. Mr. Reginald Fisher is the sort you have to watch out for. The kind who says, 'Let me be honest with you,' and then never tells the truth."

"What is the truth, Mom?" Matt said.

"The truth about what? The truth about Daniel? The truth about your father? The truth about me? Which do you want? I'll give you one reality today only to have you discover it's fiction tomorrow. Find your own answers, my dear. I'm still grappling with mine."

The intercom buzzer rang, and Gwen went to answer it.

"Yes, William.... Of course, send him up." She looked at her boys. "Daniel's on his way up."

She went back to the table and took Ethan's face in her hands. He didn't resist, but he didn't relent either. She felt the growth of hair along his chin, and noted the bones that were no longer hidden by soft flesh. She lightly kissed each cheek before he could pull away.

"My baby," she said. "I love you so." She looked over the top of his head at Matt. "Let me grow up," she said. "Please."

There was a knock at the door.

"All right?" she asked.

"All right," Matt said.

Ethan stood and said, "I didn't mean to hurt you."

"I know," Gwen said.

She hurried to Daniel. She unwrapped his scarf, unbuttoned his coat, and put her hands inside as if she had been the one to come in from the cold. His mouth was warm against hers.

"Hello to *you*," he said.

"I'm glad to see you," she said. "I missed you." She kissed him again. "Go on inside. I'll just hang up your coat."

When she came back, he was sitting on the arm of the couch talking to Matt and Ethan.

"How was your holiday?" she said.

"I don't think it was much better than yours," Daniel said.

"Oh, no! That bad?"

"I'm afraid so." Daniel looked toward Matt and Ethan and smiled. "Lousy Christmas. I didn't even get anything for you guys." He took two envelopes from inside his jacket pocket. "This is just a little something."

"It's not necessary," Ethan said.

"Really," Matt said.

"I know. Take it anyway," Daniel said.

"Coffee?" Gwen said.

"Sounds good," Daniel said.

"I think I'll hit the sack," Matt said. "I'm wiped out. Thanks, Daniel."

"Yeah," Ethan said. "Thanks."

They each kissed Gwen's cheek and shook hands with Daniel.

She knew what they hoped for as they left her with Daniel. They hoped she would come to them, pull their blankets around their grown bodies, and hear their final undisclosed fears. Countless times she had taken their worries and fears and made them her own, so they could be free. They wanted her to choose again. And then they would want her to choose some more. She waited until she heard their doors close, and faltered only slightly as she imagined them children once again, blankets pulled high up over their heads because of what they thought was hidden in the dark. *Come lie down with me, Mommy. Just stay with me until I fall asleep.* Their voices seemed distant now, in some outlying region of a place she had already been and left.

"How's Kate?" Gwen said.

She leaned against him as she refilled his cup. He put his arm around her waist and pulled her onto his lap.

"Careful," she said. "I'll burn you."

He took the pot from her hand and set it on the table.

"Burn me," he said. "Please."

He looked tired. His eyes were bloodshot, and he smelled as if he had been drinking.

"You've been drinking," she said.

"That's right. Kate drove me to it."

He rubbed his face across the front of her blouse, and she felt powerless to object although she murmured, "The boys are inside."

"I know. I know."

"What did she do to you?"

"Well, she asked Sandy to come over."

Her reaction was reflexive, but he held her fast.

"I didn't invite her. Kate did."

She laid her head on his shoulder and told herself she had no right to object. *Mistress.* She silently formed the word against the cloth of his shirt as if she spoke some curious sign language.

"Did you say something?" Daniel said.

"No. Nothing," she said. "Go on."

"It was as awful as it could be. Kate started to cry the minute I got there. I tried to leave, but Sandy insisted she would leave. Then Rob suggested that we be *civilized,* and I wanted to ask him if that meant we would take turns killing each other. Lord, Gwen, when will this be over? Kate threw herself at me in the kitchen and told me that I'd destroyed all their lives. Can you imagine having that much power?"

"Oh, yes. I can." She did not want to hear the gruesome details of his evening, but knew they had to be told. "Tell me more."

"Well, I was sorry to see her in so much distress, but the histrionics assuaged my guilt. That and two shots of whiskey. I wanted to ask her why it was all right for her to change, but I was expected to stay the same. Instead, I listened to this young woman, who used to think I was the most wonderful man in the world, berate me for everything I've ever done to her."

"Where was Rob?"

"In the other room with Sandy."

"And how was Sandy?"

"Impressively sane."

They sat quietly for a moment, rubbing each other's back.

"I'm sorry, Daniel. I should have sent you home that first time. I should never have opened the door. I'm sorry."

He pushed her away, so he could see her.

"I want you to marry me," he said. "I want us to have a baby together. Elena was so sweet, so indifferent to everyone's problems. She just wanted to be held and kissed and loved. I can do that. Let's have a baby, Gwen. Let's start all over."

He was so earnest that her disbelief seemed frivolous. She was enticed by his innocence, purged of doubts and misgivings. He was unbuttoning her blouse, reaching inside to persuade her that he was right.

"Just say yes," he said.

"Daniel..." she said.

"Just say yes. Just let me pretend for tonight. Let's be twenty and starting a new life together. Let's make a baby. Just say yes."

Matt and Ethan were inside. They would know if Daniel stayed. She was sure they were waiting to hear him leave. Daniel's hands moved up her throat, behind her head, lifted her hair away from its roots, and forced her to give her consent.

"Say yes," he said, and moved her lips with his.

"Yes," she said.

She tried not to think about how much pain they would be in tomorrow.

Every summer until Gwen's brother, Warren, died, the family vacationed at Virginia Beach. They rented the same house each year and cultivated summer friendships with neighboring renters. It never seemed odd that these relationships were restricted to the one week that Amanda did not consider it common to run barefoot from morning to night.

Hildy Butler was Gwen's best summer friend. Her family was from Jacksonville, Florida, and they raised bees. Hildy knew how to make sand castles that brought admiring crowds and once even a local reporter, who interviewed her and took a picture of her pointing to one of her most elaborate creations.

At Gwen's urging, the summer always began with the recounting of how Hildy overcame her allergy to bee stings. Gwen loved the story. She always wiggled her bottom in the sand until she was in deep enough so that the sand poured over onto her legs. Then she would lean back, shield her eyes from the sun, and say, "Go on, Hildy. Tell me what happened." Hildy said that when she was two years old she got stung on the foot. "I swelled up pretty bad," she said. "My nose and ears and lips all blew up. The doctor came and said I needed shots. Wouldn't do to have a beekeeper's daughter with an allergy to bee stings. So they shot me up for months. Even after that, the doctor said I'd be needing a shot or a bee sting every few weeks for years to come. Mama would go outside and catch a bee. In her hands, just like this." Hildy pressed her hands together the way they did when they caught fireflies. "She'd take hold of my arm and roll my sleeve up. My dad would get the bee real angry and then stick it on my arm. We'd all count to ten together, and then Dad would pull the stinger out. It worked. Now, when I get stung by a bee, nothing happens to me." Hildy would make a buzzing noise and pretend to be a bee. "I sure hope you ain't allergic," she'd shout.

Gwen wondered what had happened to Hildy. They had finally heard from some other summer people that Hildy's dad was very sick, and they wouldn't be coming for the summer. Eventually, Amanda spoke with Hildy's mother, but Hildy never wanted to come to the phone.

The final summer at the beach house was lonely. Gwen spent it walking along the seaside and throwing rocks at the gulls. Nothing was the same without Hildy's raucous laughter and electrifying stories. But no matter how many stories Hildy told, none of them stayed with Gwen the way the story of the bee sting did. It was miraculous to her that Hildy had actually been fortified to defend herself against something dangerous. When Gwen was older and understood that Hildy had only been given what was necessary to develop an immunity to bee stings, Gwen decided she liked her version better. If she had told the story, it would be possible to hold out your arm and be safeguarded against disappointment and loneliness, against all hurts that had no easy cures. That summer without Hildy, Gwen had wished that there were some way to be defended against the pain she felt. She held her bare arms out under the sun and got nothing in return but burned skin and Amanda's home remedy of vinegar and harsh words.

Gwen remembered the way Hildy had once held a bee in the palm of her hand and said, "Ain't nothing to be scared of if you can't get hurt." Gwen still did not understand how it was possible to be really sure that you would not get hurt, that you would hold out your arm only to find that what you thought was true was not so after all. Gwen would have liked the chance to tell Hildy that she was very brave to have held out her arm time and time again. No matter what, she was very brave.

Chapter Twenty-one

Ernesto owned the Friendly Island Coffee Shop on Amsterdam Avenue, where Gwen stopped in every morning for a cup of fragrant espresso. They had been friends for better than ten years now, although they never saw each other outside of the coffee shop. They knew about each other's lives, shared photographs of their families and stories of their children's achievements and disappointments. But their friendship never went beyond the perimeter of the coffee shop.

Gwen had known from the start that Ernesto knew things. He meted out bits of his wisdom in the early hours of the morning while she sipped coffee and ate her toasted English muffin with the homemade guava jelly his wife made. On some mornings Gwen would come in to find him frying plantains or preparing cornmeal sticks. He always seemed to know when she needed something extra to fill her up. Often he would turn around from the stove before she even said hello and say, "Sit, my friend." Then he would fill her cup and take a piece of plantain from between the sheets of brown paper he used to absorb the oil. After carefully sprinkling the fried fruit with just a touch of salt, he would hold it out and crinkle his brown eyes that were already so small and heavily lidded he often looked as if he were sleeping. Ernesto's face was not particularly handsome, but Gwen loved his dark leathery skin and the shock of bushy black eyebrows that seemed too high on his forehead. "Eat," he said. The fried plantain was sweet and salty, and Gwen was always ravenous for it after the first bite. She never tried to duplicate the dish at home because she knew it would never taste the same. Ernesto's cast-iron skillet was aged, and she could never have sliced the fruit as thin as he did.

On the first day back to work after the winter break, Gwen left the house earlier than usual. Matt and Ethan were still asleep when she left. They had another two weeks before they were due back at school. She scrawled them a quick note, reminding them they had appointments with the dentist that afternoon.

It was a very dark and wet morning, but she was warmed by the thought of Ernesto and the coffee that would be waiting for her. Although they had not spoken or seen each other since the last day of school, Gwen knew that Ernesto would have sensed her despair. He would be ready with food and kind words. As she drove the familiar route into the city, she wondered if Ernesto was as good to his wife as he was to her.

It had turned unusually warm. Instead of snow, there had been constant rain. Thunder and lightning accompanied the steady downpour, and she was grateful to reach the coffee shop. Ernesto was frying plantains at the stove. By her seat at the counter, an empty stoneware mug was waiting to be filled. Ernesto didn't even turn around when she walked in, but he reached for the coffeepot. He knew she was there.

"Chango is playing the drums," Ernesto said. "It's a day to punish the lizards."

Ernesto's mother had been a spiritualist, and although his wife raised their children Catholic, he had never forgotten what his mother had taught him. A framed picture of her was near the cash register. Several statues of saints surrounded the makeshift altar. Every Friday he placed fresh flowers at the base of his mother's picture. Gwen knew that Ernesto visited the neighborhood Pentecostal church in spite of his wife's protests. She objected to his indulgence of superstition and charms. He had told Gwen all this with just the edge of anger in his voice, but she knew he felt his wife's objections were an insult to his mother. It was Gwen whom he trusted with tales of the possessions he had witnessed and of church members who had spoken in tongues. His own dearly beloved mother had practiced *espiritismo* and had been greatly sought after for her spiritual gifts. She had been especially known for her unerring readings. Ernesto told Gwen it had not been unusual to see his mother fall into a trance. When he spoke of his mother, he always lowered his eyes and whispered. Gwen always did the same.

"Good morning, Ernesto," Gwen said. "I suspected Chango was responsible for all the rain."

Ernesto had often entertained her with stories. He had told her that disciples of the Yoruba faith believed their newly departed entered the heavens, but in the first downpour would be returned to the river, where the spirit embodied a stone. The *babalocha*, high priest, would then lead a procession of family and friends to the river, where the stone was found and brought home. There the stone was treated as if it were alive. It was fed at mealtimes, and it was not unusual to see someone engaged with it in an animated monologue. Chango, a well-loved saint, had first lived and died as an ordinary man. When his tribe was threatened by an invading army, Chango's stone miraculously took the form of a fierce warrior who saved his people. His followers carried a smooth circular stone believed to be part of their god, also known as the King of Impossible Things. This title alone made him Gwen's favorite.

Once, Chango, a lover of wine and women, had sent his messenger, a lizard, to deliver a ring to a resistant woman, hoping the gift would sway her. The obedient lizard placed the ring in his mouth. Along the way, the ring became lodged in his throat. When Chango visited the woman, she knew nothing of the ring. An enraged Chango confronted the lizard, but he was unable to defend himself. The ring was still caught in his throat. In his fury, Chango struck him with lightning. Ernesto had explained that thunder and lightning meant Chango was playing the drums and still punishing the lizard.

Gwen watched as Ernesto filled her cup. As she drank, he held out a piece of plantain.

"Hmm, good," she said. "It needs a little more salt."

Ernesto flattened the plantains between the brown paper with the back of a spoon. She watched the grease spread and wiped the oil from her own lips.

"You have much to tell me," he said. "I see it in your troubled eyes."

"My mother passed on," Gwen said.

Ernesto nodded. He had never met Amanda, but Gwen had

told him many stories about her childhood and the woman who had dominated those years.

"I'm sorry," he said.

"It's all right."

"And the man?"

Ernesto always referred to Daniel in this way. It was never *your man,* but *the man.* Gwen thought it was a rather puritanical reaction from a man who used live chickens in some of his religious rituals, but she didn't argue. She knew he would not allow himself to call Daniel *your man* because he was married to another woman.

"*The man* left his wife," she said.

Ernesto took a long swallow of coffee and set the cup back on the counter with a thud.

"I'll fix you a muffin," he said.

"That would be good."

She watched as he tore apart an English muffin with his fingers. People had started to drift in. They greeted Ernesto in Spanish and smiled at Gwen. Ernesto did not speak to her as he waited for the muffin to toast. When it was done, he spread it lavishly with jelly and then placed the plate in front of her. As she reached toward the plate, he placed his hand over hers.

"How are the children?" he said.

"They're fine."

"Señora Hoffman?"

Jane was the only one Gwen had ever brought to meet Ernesto. She thought he was spooky and was always reluctant to come along. Sensing this, Ernesto played into her notion of him, much to his own and Gwen's delight.

"Her husband was unfaithful, and her daughter is pregnant."

He sighed deeply.

"So everyone is unhappy," he said.

"Everyone is troubled."

"Ah, there is hope in that statement."

"Some," she agreed.

"Come back Saturday afternoon. Bring your sons."

She was surprised by this request. He had never extended a formal invitation before, certainly not one that included Matt and Ethan.

"And bring Señora Hoffman and her daughter."

Gwen laughed now. Jane would be reluctant.

"I don't know," she said.

"You don't believe in me."

"I want to."

"Wanting to is sometimes good enough," he said.

"All right," she said. "We'll come."

He pointed at the muffin.

"Eat."

"How is your family?" she said.

"My wife tells me she doesn't have to wait for me to die. It already feels like she's talking to a stone." He shrugged with exaggeration. "What can I do?"

It took Gwen a moment to make the connection between his comment and the Yoruba beliefs. Then she laughed, and Ernesto looked pleased.

"I'm not going," Jane said. "He scares me."

"He does it on purpose. C'mon, Jane, he invited all of us. The kids too."

Gwen had stopped over at Jane's house on the way home from

work to extend Ernesto's invitation. Jane sorted through a stack of mail, pretending to be deeply absorbed in looking for something.

"The kids too?" Jane shouted. "Are you crazy?"

"Keep your voice down," Gwen said. "I just want you to come with me. I don't want to be rude. Ernesto is very sensitive."

"Sensitive?" Jane said. "That man is spooky. Anyway, I'm busy Saturday."

"With what?"

Jane shifted the pile of mail for the third time.

"I swear I'm going to throw all those envelopes on the floor in a minute if you don't stop fussing with them," Gwen said. "You have to go with me. He invited us."

"I don't care."

"Please, Jane. It won't take long."

"I told you. I'm busy."

"You're lying. I know you are," Gwen said. "Forget it. I'll go without you."

"I hate it when you do that. I really do. And I hate that voodoo stuff you get so involved in all the time."

"It's not voodoo. What makes you think that the person has to be wearing a prayer shawl and a skullcap for the rituals to be legitimate?"

Jane narrowed her eyes and leaned all the way over to Gwen.

"Is that an anti-Semitic remark?" Jane asked.

"Yes," Gwen said.

"I thought so."

"Will you come?"

"I'm not eating any of those awful fried bananas again."

"You're just so cosmopolitan," Gwen said. She kissed Jane's cheek. "I love you."

"You should," Jane said.

"So he's a spiritualist?" Matt said.

"No," Gwen said. She turned around to look at the children. Jane was driving. It was raining again. Heavy sheets of water mixed with ice, creating a high sheen on the roads. "His mother was a spiritualist. Ernesto is just spiritual."

"Big difference," Jane said.

"I think it'll be fun," Caroline said.

"Don't eat anything he gives you," Jane said.

"Jane!" Gwen said. "Will you stop it?"

"I mean it," Jane said. "I don't trust that man."

Matt leaned forward and put his arms around Jane's neck.

"Don't worry, Jane," he said. "Ethan and I will protect you."

She laughed. "Don't make fun of me, Matt. I used to bathe you."

"Do you know how many women wish they could make that same statement?" Matt said.

Ethan howled. Caroline pulled Matt back and covered his face with kisses.

"Please, please," she said. "Let me be one of them."

"All right," Gwen said. "I expect you all to behave." She looked pointedly at Jane. "That includes you."

"I won't say a word," Jane said. She took one hand off the wheel and made an X across her chest with her finger. "Cross my heart and hope to die."

"You will if you embarrass me," Gwen said.

When they all crowded in through the front door, Ernesto was playing dominoes with a group of men at the back of the coffee shop. One of the men said something to him in Spanish, and he looked up, waved, and came toward them immediately with open arms.

"Señora Hoffman," Ernesto said. "I'm so glad you're joining us. I haven't seen you in a very long time." He turned to Caroline. "And Señorita. Gwen talks about you all the time. And these boys, men I should say." He held out his hand. "I am very impressed."

They were all still huddled in the doorway of the coffee shop.

"Please, come in. Sit down. I offer you some refreshments."

Jane poked Gwen in the back. Gwen glared at her. They all followed Ernesto to a table that had obviously been set in their honor.

"I know Gwen does not need any convincing to try my plantains."

"That's right, Ernesto." She smiled fondly at him. "You went to a lot of trouble for us."

"No trouble at all," he said. "Sit. I'll bring the food."

As soon as he was out of earshot, Jane whispered to Gwen, "I'm not going to be offered as a human sacrifice, am I?"

"It's doubtful," Gwen said. "You're too old."

"I'm not," Caroline said.

"No," Gwen said. "But you're not a virgin."

Caroline giggled, and before Jane could say anything more, Ernesto was back with a pot of coffee, a platter of fried plantains, and a basket of steaming cornmeal sticks. A pretty girl, about Ethan's age, brought little dishes of jelly and butter. She smiled shyly at them and hurried off. Matt and Ethan elbowed each other and winked.

"My daughter," Ernesto said, catching their gaze. "Josefina. She's eighteen and knows everything better than her parents."

"She's lovely," Gwen said. "My boys seems to concur."

Matt and Ethan laughed and agreed.

"Yes," Ernesto said. "But that is not why I asked you here today."

"Why did you ask us here?" Gwen said.

"I believe I can help you. All of you." He leaned in toward the center of the table. They all imitated his position, waiting for him to speak. "I have prepared gifts for you."

"Ernesto—" Gwen said.

He held up his hand.

"Señora Hoffman," he said. "You are first."

Jane paled and opened her eyes wide.

"Why do you look so frightened, Señora?" Ernesto said. "I'm quite harmless."

"I know," Jane said. "I'm not frightened."

"Josefina!" Ernesto shouted. "Josefina!"

His daughter appeared from the back, carrying a large carton. Matt and Ethan nearly knocked each other over as they jumped up to help her. Matt reached her first and took the carton from her arms.

"Put it down here," Ernesto said, pointing to the center of the table. "In the middle." He stood and peered into the box, drawing his bushy eyebrows together in a seemingly straight line. "Ah, yes, good." He turned to all of them and sat down again. "It is the common lot of humans to make enemies and to keep them. I believe that it is important never to express in thought, word, or deed any destructive emotions. It is best to think only thoughts that express love, truth, faith, and gratitude. We all have the power to create whatever we choose to create. We have that power now, within us." He stood again and reached into the box. Jane gasped so audibly that he stopped what he was doing. "Señora Hoffman! There are no shrunken heads in here. I assure you."

"I'm sorry," Jane said. "I don't know what happened to me. Go on. Please."

"Don't apologize," Ernesto said. He withdrew a long object wrapped in newspaper and began to open it as he spoke. "Candles have been placed in this world to provide the faithful with a tangible way to show their belief." He turned to Jane. "Does candle lighting offend your religious beliefs?"

"I don't think so," Jane said.

"Then this is for you." Ernesto pulled back all the newspaper and handed her a brown candle. "To conquer your enemies."

Jane took the candle and nodded. Ernesto unwrapped candle after candle. Orange was for Caroline. For protection. Ernesto smiled at her belly, and she blushed. Red was for Matt. It promised to attract love. He asked if he might light it immediately and looked longingly in Josefina's direction. Ethan's candle was white. It would bring peace to his life. They all waited quietly as Ernesto pulled Gwen's candle from the box. It was yellow-and-white.

"Light this candle when you wish to communicate with the deceased," Ernesto said, handing the candle to Gwen. "Make peace with your mother."

Gwen nodded, ignoring the tears that streamed down her cheeks. Ernesto reached into the box one more time and pulled out another candle. This time it was red.

"This one is also for you," he said, holding the candle out to Gwen. "For the love you deserve."

No one spoke now. They each gazed down at the candles that

would not change their lives, but would compel them to think about what really mattered most. Ernesto had a perceptive mind and a good heart to go with it.

"Now," he said. "Let's eat."

Josefina joined them for more coffee and freshly fried plantains. Gwen said Josefina's were even better than Ernesto's. He regaled them with tales Gwen had heard many times before and one or two new ones. Even Jane was captivated by his stories.

By the time they left, it was already dark. The children were quiet in the backseat, holding their candles the way they had once held their souvenirs after an outing, too tired to remember why it had been so important to have a purple stegosaurus or a giant pencil in the first place. It was still pouring, but it was warmer than it had been in the morning. An occasional burst of thunder followed by a flash of lightning was a surprise this time of year.

"It's been raining all day," Gwen said.

"Poor lizards," Jane said. "Chango must be very angry."

Gwen's temporary silence was quickly replaced by restrained laughter. Glancing in the rearview mirror, she saw that the children had all fallen asleep. Gwen reached for Jane's waiting hand and squeezed.

"God of Impossible Things," Gwen said. "For certain."

Chapter Twenty-two

"This was a good idea," Gwen said. Then she pointed to the brown candle that was on the shelf next to the cookbooks. "I see you haven't lit yours yet."

"The candle?" Jane said. "No. I'm saving it. And the dinner was really Caroline's idea. I can't take any credit for it."

"But you can take a lot of credit for her."

"Yes. That I can. One percent credit and ninety-nine percent luck."

Jane had planned a final dinner for everyone before all the children went back to school.

"I think your numbers are a bit skewed, but I get the point," Gwen said. "Caroline looks well. She seems content."

"I think so," Jane said. "I know she's frightened. So much has happened all at once. I think she still harbors some hope that Arnold and I will get back together."

"My kids still want me to reconcile with Theodore. You know, he phoned me."

"About Amanda? That was nice of him."

"Yes. It was nice of him. I think he's finally settled down. Anyway, he seems to have forgotten that my mother once threw a shoe at him."

"Really? You never told me."

"There's lots I've still never told you," Gwen said.

"Such as?" Jane said.

Their children's voices were mingled with shouts and loud cries that were hard to distinguish. Gwen came over and stood next to Jane, peering down at the top of her head.

"That gray is coming in at a steady rate," Gwen said. "Maybe it's time to try the Lucy look again."

"Never. I've decided to ease into my old age without any embellishments."

Gwen looked skeptical.

"Maybe I'll try a little less red next time," Jane said. "So what haven't you told me?"

"Do you think I'm too old to have a baby?"

Jane raised her eyebrows and stared.

"Are you pregnant?" she said.

"No. But Daniel asked me to marry him. He wants to have a baby."

"And?"

"I told him the baby was fine, but marriage was out of the question," Gwen said.

"Not funny," Jane said. "He loves you a lot, Gwen."

"I know." Gwen began to cut squares into the tray of lasagna that was cooling on the counter. "He told me the two of you had quite a conversation on the way to the airport."

"Oh, that."

"How come you didn't tell me?" Gwen said.

"How come you didn't tell me about the baby?"

"I don't know." Gwen licked her fingers. "Should I marry him?"

"Ask Ernesto," Jane said.

"Very funny. Have you heard from Caleb?"

"Actually, I did. He invited me to go Rollerblading. I told him I was too old for Rollerblading, but the perfect age for sex."

"Impressive answer from a woman who's slept with two men in her entire life," Gwen said.

"It's a start."

"What about Arnold?"

"He's angry, but I think he's trying very hard to be a good father. I'm glad about that."

"Me too," Gwen said.

Caroline's voice broke through the others and interrupted them.

"Is dinner ready yet?" she said. "We're starved."

Then the three children, who were no longer really children at all, descended on their mothers, taking up all the space with their needs and wants. And their mothers, who would always be mothers, stopped talking and listened to their children's voices, knowing they were already gone from them and that it was as it should be. But just before they sat down to eat, Jane and Gwen turned at exactly the same moment and looked at each other. And their children, too busy to notice anything but themselves, missed seeing what it was that one woman recognized in the face of another.

"It's colder than I thought," Gwen said. "Crazy weather."

They were sitting on a bench in the little park near Jane's house where their own children had once played. There were tightly bundled children climbing up the jungle gym. One little girl's green boot came off and her mother ran over to rescue it. Gwen and Jane watched the young mother secure the boot. The girl giggled and took her hand off the steel bar. Whatever the mother said made the child nod, sobered by the warning. The woman went back to check on the baby sleeping in the carriage. She adjusted the blanket, looked up at something another woman said, and put the hood of the carriage up against the chill.

Jane moved closer to Gwen on the bench.

"Do you want to go?" Gwen said.

"No. I want to watch."

"Did Caroline get back safely?"

"Yes. Arnold drove her up. I thought they needed some quality time together," Jane said. "What about the boys?"

"Safe and sound."

"And what about you?"

"I'm all right," Gwen said. "I'm actually glad they're gone. I needed to be alone."

"They do take up a lot of energy," Jane said.

They both turned to watch as a boy in a navy parka scaled the rocks. They were icy still from the last snowfall, but he was undaunted. His scarf had come undone and hung around his shoulders like a shawl. He looked like an old man, but his smooth cheeks gave him away. His mother shouted something at him, but he ignored her and kept climbing. He reached a level spot and stood, clearly delighted with himself and the view his post afforded. After a moment, he pulled off his gloves and threw them down, one at a time, and waited for his mother to approach. She didn't run, but her steps were angry and purposeful. When she reached him, she put her hands on her hips and loudly called his name. "Peter! Don't make me come up there," she said. Peter threw his scarf. "I'm coming up." She hoisted herself up the rocks until he was in arm's reach. Then he kneeled down and offered his pursed lips. She craned her neck, held on to a rock, and kissed him. He fell into her arms, and she fought to keep her balance with her free hand. When they reached the ground, Peter ran off.

An array of strollers and carriages stood about like a fleet of tanks ready to move out at a minute's notice. Bags overflowed with diapers, bottles, toys, and plastic bags of cookies and crackers. Some of the bags held books and magazines the mothers had brought in case there was no one to talk to.

"What do you think they're talking about?" Jane said.

"Sleep problems and toilet training."

"Not teething?"

Gwen looked around at the children.

"Maybe," she said.

"I can't imagine Caroline doing this," Jane said.

"We'll help her."

Jane turned to Gwen and smiled.

"Thanks for that 'we,'" Jane said.

"Look," Gwen said. "Remember the roundup?"

Several of the mothers called to their children. It was almost dark. Time to go home and fix dinner. Time to fill the tub with warm water and rubber toys. Gwen watched the children race to their mothers, fall into their waiting arms, reluctantly help gather stray toys and articles of clothing. The women hovered around the children, closed buttons, pulled up zippers, tightened scarves, wiped runny noses, and kept talking to each other. A few last minutes of not being alone.

Soon there was one lone mother and her two children in the park. The youngest slept in the stroller. His feet dangled over the sides. His mother wrapped a blanket around his legs where his pants had ridden up and exposed his bare flesh. She kept her eye on the other child, who was almost at the top of the jungle gym. She seemed to hesitate, not wanting to shout out and risk waking the sleeping child, yet concerned for the older boy's safety. She looked up at Gwen and Jane and smiled. With a furtive glance back at the stroller, she walked over to them.

"Could you keep an eye on the baby for a minute?" she said. "He gets scared if he wakes up here and no one's around. I'm afraid to leave the other one alone up there."

She looked appealingly young. Her light brown hair was pulled back in a braid from which numerous strands had escaped. Her cheeks were very red, and she rubbed her bare hands together for warmth.

"You should put on some gloves," Gwen said. "It's very cold."

"You sound just like my mother," the young woman said.

"We all sound alike." Gwen smiled and stood. "Go on. We'll keep an eye on him."

"Thanks," she said.

Jane and Gwen walked over to the stroller and stood guard over the sleeping toddler. He stirred as if he immediately sensed his mother's absence. Gwen bent down and touched the blanket, murmured a few words, and he slept again, undisturbed and peaceful. The young woman helped the older boy off the metal bars and clapped when he reached the ground. She looked over at Gwen and Jane and waved. They waved back and Gwen laid her head against her hands to show that the baby was still sleeping. The mother held her child by the hand and walked back slowly. Gwen was touched that she felt no need to rush. As soon as they were close enough, the young mother placed her finger against her lips and pointed to the sleeping child so the older boy would be quiet.

"I really appreciate it," she said. "He didn't sleep much last night. He's cutting a new tooth." She gathered her things and instructed the boy to get his tricycle. "Oh, this is Timmy," she said. She held on to the sleeve of his jacket. "Say hello to the ladies, Timmy."

"Hello," Timmy said.

"Hello," Gwen said. "It's nice to meet you. My name is Gwen, and this is my friend Jane."

"Hi," Jane said.

"Hi," Timmy said.

He ran off to get his bike, mounted it, and began to ride around in wide circles.

"I know I forgot something," the young woman said. "I always feel like I'm leaving something behind."

"You probably are," Gwen said.

The woman looked up and tilted her head to the side as if she thought there was something implied in the message, but then the child stirred, and she turned to him.

"Try freezing a washcloth and giving it to him to suck on," Gwen said. "It works like magic."

"A frozen banana is good too," Jane said. "Even a spoon that's been in the freezer for a while. It relieves the pain."

She blushed, stood, and patted the bag slung over the handles of the stroller.

"Thank you," she said. "I'll try it." She laughed. "I'll try anything. And thanks for watching him. It's been a long day. We sort of meet here and commiserate. It temporarily relieves *that* pain."

"I'm sure," Gwen said. "I have two boys of my own. I remember *everything*."

The young woman seemed to want to talk, but then she hesitated and just nodded emphatically. She touched Gwen's arm, lightly and swiftly. "Well, thanks again," she said. "C'mon, Timmy. Let's go home. It'll be dark in a few minutes." She waited for Timmy to reach her on his bike. "My name's Pamela." She wrinkled her nose.

She looked so very young. Too young to be a mother herself. It was clear Pamela wanted them to say more. Gwen thought to tell her a secret she could take home and conceal until after her babies and her husband slept, placated by another evening of her attentions. Gwen knew that the slightest whimper from the nursery would make Pamela bolt, impatient to reach her child. But Gwen also knew Pamela would protest if told that she hurried to her children for her own consolation. So Gwen only smiled. If she told Pamela any one of the many secrets that time would later reveal, they would not then belong to Pamela alone.

"Well, so long," Pamela said.

"Nice to have met you," Gwen said.

Pamela stared as Jane put her arm through Gwen's.

"Did the two of you come to the park together when your children were little?" she said.

"Yes," Jane said. "We even thought about starting a coven."

Pamela giggled nervously. "That was a good idea," she said. "Too bad it didn't work out."

"Who said it didn't?" Gwen said.

Pamela was momentarily startled, but she recovered quickly and fussed a bit more with the baby's blanket, tucking and pulling where none was needed.

"Try to get more sleep," Jane said. "You look tired."

Pamela's eyes filled with unshed tears, and she trembled a bit from the efforts of her restraint.

"Yes, I will. Thanks again. Well... goodbye, then," she said.

"Take care of yourself," Gwen said.

Pamela nodded, and they watched as she hurriedly left the park. Gwen knew Pamela thought they did not know what they had divulged. Gwen and Jane kept vigil while she juggled the stroller, adjusted the bag on her shoulder, and held on to the handlebar of the tricycle. Her head turned to note any oncoming traffic, and she stooped to instruct the older boy as they crossed. The little one was awake now, and he kicked off the blanket just as they were in the middle of the street. Both Gwen and Jane tensed, suspended in the final moments of the drama. Then Pamela's hand reached over and rescued the blanket before it was trapped under the stroller's wheels. She paused at the curb, lifted the tricycle over onto the sidewalk, and struggled with the stroller. Once they were all safely righted on the sidewalk, Timmy tugged at his mother's jacket. She turned to him absentmindedly as he pointed in the direction of the park. She seemed irritated by Timmy's disruption. Then she squinted and looked.

Gwen thought to wave, even to call out something that might console. *We are you.* But Jane shook her head and pointed at the darkening sky.

"There isn't enough light left," she said. "I don't think she can see us."

Still, Jane yielded when Gwen said she felt certain that Pamela had seen them, had scanned the darkness one last time for the outline of their shapes and then memorized their path by heart.

SUGGESTED QUESTIONS FOR DISCUSSION:

1. Jane resents her dying mother's refusal to downplay the pain caused by the cancer, and "still could not forgive her for not wanting to protect her own child." (page 1) Share an incident when you wish your parents had lied to you. If you're a parent, share an example of when you've lied to your child, and explain why.

2. How can calling a fountain pen "a ten-thousand-year brush" (page 11) change its essence? Are there things in your own life that you've similarly transformed from "the ordinary into the extraordinary"? (page 12)

3. After Jane kicks Arnold out of their home, she feels afraid. Is it fear of Arnold's return or of being alone? Do you believe that Arnold was only unfaithful the one time, or were there other incidents? Does it matter?

4. Why does Gwen start to read cookbooks after Theodore leaves

her? What does her "make-believe life" (page 46) give her that real life does not?

5. Even though it was nearly twenty years ago, Jane and Gwen will always remember the day they met and, as Gwen says, "the night they had fallen in love." (page 50) Who is your best friend, and do you still remember your first encounter with her or him?

6. Caroline "often likened her daughter to the manatees they had observed on a visit to a wildlife park in Florida." (page 73) If you have children, what animal(s) do they remind you of? What animal do you yourself most identify with, and why?

7. How did Jane handle breaking the news of her and Arnold's separation to Caroline? Did their problems in any way precipitate Caroline's pregnancy?

8. What is it about Ellie that makes it difficult for Jane to confide in her? How might Jane's life have turned out differently if she had been an only child?

9. Given the complexities of Gwen's and Jane's relationships with their own mothers, do you think it's generally easier for them to be the mother of sons or daughters? Why?

10. Gwen's thoughts about Daniel are interwoven with memories of the other men in her life. Is it possible to have a relationship exclusively with one person, or are the ghosts of past lovers always present? Does this make romance—as a woman gets older—easier or more difficult?

11. Despite their external differences, are there ways in which Amanda and Gwen are actually more similar than different? What does the episode with the cayenne pepper reveal about their relationship?

12. Discuss Gwen's childhood friendships with Rowena and Hildy. How did they inform the woman that Gwen became?

13. Do you think Gwen and Daniel should have a child? Discuss whether you think their relationship will work out or whether Daniel will return to Sandra.

14. Consider the title of the novel, *Willing Spirits*, and how its meaning for Gwen and Jane evolves over the course of the novel.